It Happened in

THE HILL COUNTRY

3/5/21

Dear Katie —

I hope you'll enjoy this Texas tale!

Monica E. Simmons

Monica

ISBN 978-1-0980-1982-2 (paperback)
ISBN 978-1-0980-1984-6 (hardcover)
ISBN 978-1-0980-1983-9 (digital)

Christian Faith Publishing, Inc.
832 Park Avenue
Meadville, PA 16335
www.christianfaithpublishing.com

Cover Design By James Simmons

Printed in the United States of America

For Franny

ACKNOWLEDGEMENTS

A big T.O.E. thank you to the ever-extraordinary Janet Howe who helped bring this adventure to life. You are such an inspiration and the real Wonder Woman! I'm so blessed to have you as a friend.

To Brenda Small and Holly Probert—I'm forever in your debt! I'm so grateful for your time and your love of reading. Thanks for your input and support.

A special shout-out to Deb Schmitz—Thanks for sharing some of your "horse sense" with me!

CHAPTER 1

Jill Murray sat cross-legged on a large flat boulder high above the Blanco River. It was late October and the sweeping vistas below her rolled in waves of magnificent autumn hues. She never tired of admiring the vast beauty of the Texas Hill Country from her perch at the top of Rock Point Trail.

I love this time of year, she thought, uncrossing her legs and dangling them over the side of the rock as she continued surveying the colorful canvas. *The holidays are right around the corner, and there's already such a festive feel in the air!*

Her eyes moved further down onto the flatland in the valley, taking in her grandmother's sprawling, one-story home. Jill thought lovingly of Gran, the amazing woman who'd raised her and her older brother, Mike. As the family matriarch, Jenny Murray had always made the holidays special for them. The older woman approached this time of year in the same, full-throttle manner in which she lived life. Her motto was always, "Go big or go home!" Thanks to her grandmother, there were already extensive decorations up around their home, Wind River Ranch.

Jill studied the expansive property surrounding Gran's house and felt a rush of pride. Wind River Ranch was also home to Wind River Arabians, the largest private breeder of Arabian horses in North America. Under her brother's skillful management, the business had flourished, evolving into a multi-million dollar corporation and adding to the already substantial Murray family fortune. An accomplished equestrienne, Jill loved that Wind River Arabians had produced several championship horses. Over the years, their operation had become widely recognized for its dedication to furthering the legacy of many of the world's most important international bloodlines.

Jill started thinking about everything on her to-do list for the afternoon and knew she needed to head back down the trail. Allowing herself a few more minutes to enjoy the panoramic view, she found herself grimacing when her eyes roamed over Lone Star Springs, a relatively new residential community that shared an eastern property line with Wind River Ranch. The exclusive, gated development featured massive custom homes in a wide variety of architectural styles. Having grown up enjoying the wild, rugged terrain, she was not a fan of the huge structures, each situated on a one-acre lot. In her opinion, the houses seemed out of place, an unnatural blight on the previously unblemished countryside.

Before turning away, Jill followed the outline of the tall stone privacy wall running the length of the affluent subdivision. "I'm sure *that* cost them a pretty penny," Jill muttered. Feeling a soft nudge against her leg, she reached down to pet her dog.

"What is it, Simon?" she asked, shaking her head. "I know, I know … it's not very charitable of me to be so grumpy about all the new folks moving here. I suppose I should think more kindly of our neighbors." She sighed, scratching his soft, pointy ears, then continued, "But geez! These city folks coming here, building their McMansions! It truly drives me nuts!"

The German shepherd cocked his head and gave her his dog nod of approval.

"That's what I love most about you, Simon, you always agree with my point of view." She took one more appreciative glance around, then jumped down off the rock, landing gracefully next to him.

"All right, lazy bones, let's get a move on!" Jill said, grinning as she watched the dog who'd stretched out on the ground again, delighting in the warmth of the sun on his thick coat.

Always ready for an adventure, Simon lept up, wagging his tail happily. They'd barely begun their journey back down the trail when he stopped and cocked his head again, listening.

Jill stood frozen, channeling her dog's keen senses. She knew that the milder fall temperatures meant an increased likelihood of encountering a snake, something she hated with a passion. *Please, God*, she prayed. *Please don't let it be a snake Simon's hearing!*

Jill took her eyes off the shepherd for a moment, glancing down at her legs and feet. She'd deliberately worn tall hiking boots and heavy jeans, knowing they'd provide some measure of protection. *Let's just keep moving!* she thought. "Simon, come on, boy, let's go home," she pleaded with the dog who was still standing at attention.

Jill groaned in frustration. They were just a few yards away from the one place she was always careful to avoid—Snake Hollow. Unlike the many other spring-fed bodies of water scattered across the Murray property, the pond at Snake Hollow was always dark and murky. Surrounded by tall cypress trees, the spot was a haven for Western Cottonmouths.

Just the thought of the stout-bodied, venomous snakes made her shudder. She knew the water moccasins were especially active now in the cooler weather as they hunted for food to sustain them through the colder months. With its marshy banks, Snake Hollow was the perfect winter hideaway for the vipers. After a harrowing experience there as a child, she'd vowed never to step foot near the pond again.

"*What is it, boy?*" Jill asked Simon, growing impatient. "What do you hear?"

At this point, the dog did a complete about-face and headed back up the trail and across the top of the peak, barking for her to follow. In close pursuit, Jill had a sinking feeling about where he might be leading her.

Sure enough, she watched as Simon stopped just before entering a grove of low-hanging trees. Looking back at her with a questioning cock of his head, he seemed to be asking, "Are you coming?" Jill shivered. She still hadn't heard anything but the wind rustling the fallen leaves. "Simon!" she shouted. "Come back here! *Please*, let's go home, boy!"

It was then she heard it—a child's cry for help.

What in the world? she asked herself. *What is a child doing up here?*

"Hello!" she yelled, reluctantly moving toward her dog. "Where are you? We can help!" She stopped and waited, listening for a response. "Are you near the pond?"

"No!" came the frantic reply. "I'm *in* the pond! My foot is stuck in the mud and I can't get it out!"

I'm going to have to go back in there! Jill realized. It was her worst nightmare coming true.

As she bent to clear a branch, a rush of memories took her back to the day she and Mike found danger at Snake Hollow.

As kids, they'd fished here often. At that time the trees were smaller, allowing more sunlight into the grove. One fall morning they'd been fishing for crappie. After a couple of hours, the fish stopped biting, and the siblings decided to head home. They'd leaned their poles against a nearby tree while they packed up their gear. One of the rods had fallen over, landing in the tall grass. Reaching down for it, Jill had immediately felt a jolt of searing pain. She'd cried out in agony to Mike, who'd come rushing to her side.

Several loud barks brought her back to the present. She shook her head to clear it, took a deep breath, and moved in closer behind Simon who was working his way along the pond's slippery banks. The further in they went, the faster darkness fell.

The cypress trees had grown tall along the water's edge, their branches creating a gloomy dome of foreboding shadows. The air was still and stagnant. *It feels like I'm on another planet,* thought Jill. *It's so different from the sunny hilltop just a few yards away!*

But it wasn't the gloom and dankness of the place that terrified her. It was the strong, musky odor she'd hoped never to experience again—the stench of cottonmouths.

Jill had fixed her eyes on the ground, watching every step she took. She stole a quick glance up and saw that Simon, eager to reach the child in trouble, had gotten too far ahead of her. "Wait! I'm coming! Stay with me, boy, please stay close to me." The dog obediently stopped and waited while she caught up to him.

"It's okay, Simon. I'm all right." She was reassuring her dog as much as herself. "I'm right behind you, big guy. Let's just stay together, pal."

Simon began tracking again, while Jill worked her way carefully over the bulging tree roots, her eyes back on the muddy ground. "Hello!" she called out. "Please answer! We need to know where to find you!"

"Here! I'm here!" The voice was very close now, and Simon and Jill picked up their pace as they carefully maneuvered around the slick curve of the water's edge on the far side of the pond. Soon they were beside a young boy. He was lying on his back on the bank of the pond, one leg hidden in the muddy depths of the water and the other pulled up next to his small body.

Totally focused on rescuing him, Jill choked back her fear and, in a voice that belied her terror, she said, "Hey there. I'm Jill, and this is my dog, Simon. We're going to get you out of here. Are you ready?"

The boy nodded, but he was not looking at her. Instead, his eyes were locked on the tree limbs above them. "Snakes!" he gasped in a trembling voice, his hand pointing upward.

Jill couldn't stop herself from looking up. To her horror, she thought she could make out several water moccasins wrapped along the higher branches, enjoying the dappled sunshine. It was all she could do not to jump up and run away as fast as her feet would take her. Instead, she patted the boy reassuringly. "They seem to like hanging around this pond," Jill remarked, trying her best to sound nonchalant. "Don't worry; they're just sunning themselves. They're not interested in us."

"Are y-y-you s-s-sure about that?" the child stammered, unconvinced.

"Positively. How about this? Let's not look up. Let's just concentrate on what's going on down there with your foot," Jill suggested. She nodded her head toward the dark water where the boy's left leg disappeared just below his knee.

"What's your name?" she asked.

"My name is Ian Wilder, and I *really* want to get the heck out of here!" he replied.

"Well, Simon and I are totally on board with that plan!" she assured him. "Ian, we need to make sure your foot isn't broken. Can you wiggle your toes around?"

She could see the boy focusing on wiggling his toes. "Yes. Don't worry," he told her. "My foot's not broken. It's just *stuck!*"

"Okay, that's good news. That should make this pretty easy." She smiled at him, wondering just how deeply the boy's foot was buried in the thick mud. She figured the best plan of action would be to reach down below the surface of the water, grasp the boy's ankle with both hands, and pull with all her might.

This approach might have been the fastest way to free him, but Jill was reluctant to do it because she couldn't see the bottom of the murky pond. She couldn't bear the thought of submerging her hands into the dark water and risk getting bitten again by one of the slithering vipers. She knew that cottonmouths, when threatened, would bite—even underwater.

Jill quickly decided to go with Plan B. "Put your arms around my neck. I'm going to pull you up," she instructed. She wrapped her arms firmly around Ian's torso. "I'm going to give you a giant bear hug, then I'm going to stand up and pull you out of that pond! We'll need to do this together, Ian. You need to work your foot loose and pull your leg upward with me. We'll go on the count of three—one, two, three!"

She rose with him clinging tightly to her, the two of them pulling with every ounce of their strength. She could feel the child wiggling his leg, exerting all his effort into freeing his foot. All the while, Simon was pacing and whining his support.

"I think something's happening!" Ian exclaimed. "I can feel my foot getting looser!"

"Great! Keep on pulling it up, Ian! You can do it!" Jill shouted encouragingly.

Finally, there was a muffled popping sound as the boy was freed from the muddy pond. His foot emerged bare, but neither of them were concerned about leaving his tennis shoe buried in the muck. Ian wrapped both of his legs around Jill and was weeping quietly with relief. With the child glued to her body, she wasted no time heading out of the hollow, carefully watching her steps, with Simon close behind. The trio didn't stop until they arrived back at the boulder where Jill and Simon had rested earlier.

Exhausted, she sat Ian on the rock and looked him over carefully. *Well, this kid's covered in mud and has holes in both knees of his jeans, but other than that, he seems okay,* Jill thought. She slowly removed the wet sock from his formerly imprisoned foot and noticed his skin starting to bruise. "Wiggle your toes again for me, please," Jill requested.

Ian had stopped crying and calmed down considerably. He wiggled all five toes and also bent his small, bare foot up and down. "It's okay. I told you it's not broken, just a little sore." He looked at her shyly and added quietly, "Thank you for saving me."

"You're quite welcome. Simon and I are glad your foot isn't broken." The dog wagged his tail in agreement. Jill continued, "Well, okay Mr. Ian Wilder, aside from the fact that you've lost a shoe, and you're pretty dirty, let me be the first to congratulate you on surviving Snake Hollow."

"S-s-snake H-h-h-h-hollow?" Ian stuttered.

"Yes," Jill replied. "That's what my brother Mike named it. Not many have come out of there without getting a snakebite or two. You're one very lucky young man." She reached out to shake his mud-covered hand.

Ian returned the handshake with a smile, relieved to be out of the pond and happy to have made a new friend. Jill looked at the mop-headed child and thanked God that she and Simon had been in the right place at the right time. Now that the boy was safe, she crossed her arms over her chest and looked him squarely in the eyes, suddenly becoming very serious. "Now, you need to tell me *what* in heaven's name you're doing out here all alone and *why* you're trespassing on my property?"

CHAPTER 2

The boy's expression quickly changed from a smile to one of astonishment. "You *own* this whole mountain?" he asked in amazement.

Although she tried to keep a straight face, Jill couldn't help but laugh at his question, then quickly regained her composure. *This child could have been seriously harmed or worse*, she thought. *I need to find out what's going on with him.*

"First off, this is *not* a mountain. It's just a big hill. It's one of many hills on Wind River Ranch, which by the way, is where we are right now," she explained, keeping her voice firm. "This hill and pretty much all the hills around it have been in my family for generations. But let's get back to my questions for you, starting with *what* are you doing here?"

Ian's face flushed and Jill didn't appreciate that he offered no immediate answer. Unable to tolerate his hesitation, she spoke more sternly to him, "Look, there's no doubt your parents are very worried about you. Since you're not giving me much to go on, I'm guessing you live in Lone Star Springs?" she questioned, raising her eyebrows.

The boy nodded.

"You're going to tell me everything, but right now, I'm going to call your parents and tell them you're safe."

Jill was already pulling her cell phone out of her pocket as she spoke. "Your choice—Mom or Dad, just give me a number."

"I can't give you a number because I don't know their numbers," the boy replied miserably. "All my numbers are stored in my phone."

Jill blew out an exasperated sigh. "All right then, *where* is your phone?" she asked impatiently.

"It's back there," Ian answered, pointing back toward Snake Hollow. "That's part of how I got stuck in the pond." She thought he looked to be on the brink of tears again.

Jill rolled her eyes in exasperation and began punching numbers into her phone.

"Wait!" the boy pleaded. "Who are you calling? You're not calling the police are you?"

She paused and studied him carefully. "Yes, I'm calling a family friend named Roger. He's a policeman with the Dripping Springs Police Department. I'm sure there are people out looking for you and this is the fastest way to let them know you're not lost anymore."

Jill turned back to finish making the call when she heard his timid voice. "There's no one looking for me because no one knows that I'm gone."

Undeterred, she said, "We'll see about that. I know whenever my nieces or nephew have to miss their classes for something, my brother or his wife have to call and let the school know. If they don't, it's considered an unexcused absence and someone from the administrative office calls the parents to check on the student."

"I bet you didn't know that, did you?" she asked. Then, noting the grim look on Ian's face, she gave him a comforting smile.

Jill was relieved when Roger Dunn answered on the first ring. She wasted no time with formalities. "Roger, hey, it's me. I wanted to give you a heads-up that I found a young boy on our property earlier. His name is Ian Wilder. Apparently, he lives at Lone Star Springs. He's fine and we're on our way back to the house."

She heard Roger's breath of relief. "Jill, this is great news! As a matter of fact, we just got a call a few minutes ago from the boy's father. His name is David Wilder, and Ian lives with him. Mr. Wilder said he'd been in a meeting this morning and he'd missed the call from his son's school. The guy didn't check his messages until an hour or so ago. As soon as he did, he called us in a panic. He's driving back from Austin now. We'll contact him right away and let him know that his son is in good hands."

"Why don't you tell him to come directly to Wind River?" Jill suggested. "I'm going to call my brother and have him start heading up the trail to meet us. Ian's missing one of his shoes and his foot is a little banged up. He probably shouldn't be walking barefoot anymore than necessary. Mike can carry him down on his back."

"That sounds like a good plan," Roger agreed, his voice becoming soft and thick with sincerity. "Thanks for calling me, Jill. You know I'll always be here for you. I'll make the call, then head your way. I'll need to complete a report on this."

Jill ended the call, rolling her eyes at Roger's intimate tone. She quickly auto-dialed her brother, grateful that he, too, answered right away. "Mike, hey, I'm at the top of Rock Point Trail. I've got a young boy with me named Ian, who got lost up here. I could use some help getting him back down. I'll explain when we see you."

Jill's brother was in tune with her enough not to ask questions. He trusted her completely as she did him. "On my way, Sis. Do you need me to bring anything? First-aid kit, water?"

"No, but before you head up, please run over and let Gran know that Roger and the boy's father are both on their way to the ranch. I don't want her to be alarmed when they get there. Hopefully, we'll be home before they arrive." There was a slight hesitation before she added, "And also, please notify the front gate that Roger and Mr. Wilder will be arriving shortly."

"You've got it, Jill. I'm on my way!" With this, Mike ended the call.

She hadn't taken her eyes off Ian the entire time she'd been on the phone. She knew he'd been listening to her end of the conversations, but he made no comment and sat quietly stroking Simon's ears.

Jill broke the silence. "I know you heard me talking on the phone, Ian. The police are calling your dad now. Your school did contact him to report that you hadn't gone to class today and, needless to say, he's really worried about you."

The boy's shoulders drooped. "I promise I didn't know they would do that. I didn't mean to make everyone mad at me." He waited a moment then asked, "They don't send kids to jail, do they?"

She stifled a smile. "No, Ian, you won't go to jail. But Roger is coming over to ask you some questions. It's part of his job. He and your dad are going to meet us down at my house."

Ian was regarding Jill warily. "I heard you say your brother can carry me down. I'm ten. I don't need anyone to carry me around," he told her indignantly.

"Ian, I understand how you feel," she assured him compassionately. "But you need to trust me on this; it's the fastest way to get you back down the hill. I'm not sure which trail you took coming up here, but the one we'll be taking down has some steep, rocky spots." She nodded toward his foot and added, "Plus, we really need to get some ice on that as soon as possible."

Ian didn't argue with her. "All right," he said despairingly. "I'm going to have to face my dad, sooner or later. He's probably going to ground me for the rest of my life."

Jill had no answer for that.

She had a feeling the boy had some major problems at home and, though her heart went out to him, she felt it was important he understood the seriousness of his actions. She decided to share what she'd experienced as a child at Snake Hollow.

"Ian, I was just a little younger than you when I got bitten by a water moccasin right over there," she said, motioning toward the pond.

"Since then, we've always referred to that place as Snake Hollow. Mike was with me that day or I might have died from the bite. As for what happened to you earlier, if Simon hadn't heard your cries; I wouldn't have come to help you. You'd still be stuck in that pond and the outcome might have been tragic. When I said you were a lucky young man, I meant it. Now, tell me how you came to be up here. Start from the beginning," Jill ordered.

Ian's eyes were on the gated community far below them. "Okay, I'm sorry. Things just didn't go the way I thought they would. I already told you I'm staying down there," he said, pointing to the Lone Star Springs subdivision. "My dad brought me to Texas to live with him. It's just supposed to be for a little while. He knows I hate it here, and I want to go back to Arizona. That's where my mom lives."

Jill was confused. "Wait! Stop! Are you telling me you ran away from home and you ended up *here*? Where did you think you were going?" she asked incredulously.

The boy rolled his eyes at her. "No! I didn't run away from home! I just wanted to climb up this mountain." Catching his error, he corrected himself, "I mean, climb to the top of this *hill*. I've wanted to check it out ever since I got here, but my dad told me I wasn't allowed to because I would be trespassing." Ian looked at Jill guiltily. "I figured no one would find out if I did it while I was supposed to be at school."

Noting his unhappy frown, Jill gently encouraged him. "Go on," she said softly.

"I hate the school here," Ian moaned. "The kids are mean to me, and they call me names. I don't want to ever go back there. I just want to be with my mom."

"Ian, I understand it must be hard adjusting to a new place. I also know that kids can be cruel. Let's talk about how you managed to skip school today," she suggested.

He perked up a bit. "I left right after my dad went to work," he explained. "I figured I'd be back by the time he came home. I wasn't planning on getting stuck in the mud," the boy confessed, giving her a sheepish grin.

"What? Your dad went off to work and left you home alone?" *What kind of parent is this David Wilder?* she asked herself. Jill struggled to keep the concern out of her voice, casually asking, "Does he leave you alone often?"

"No! See, the bus comes through our neighborhood at 7:00 a.m.. Dad always takes me to the bus stop and usually waits until I get on. Except for today, he had a meeting in Austin. I told him that since I'm ten now, I would be okay to get on the bus by myself," Ian explained.

"So you didn't tell your father the truth?" Jill interrupted. "You'd already planned *not* to go to school." It wasn't a question but a statement. Ian could tell from Jill's tone that she was disappointed to learn that he'd lied to his dad. He was starting to feel pretty disappointed in himself as well.

Shamed, he tried to make her understand. "Yeah, I guess when you say it like that it sounds pretty bad. It's just that, like I said, I *hate* that school. I didn't think it would be a big deal to take *one* day to think about how to convince my mom to come get me."

"I'm going to stop you right there," Jill said. "You can continue the story while we're walking. I think it would be good for us to beat your dad and Officer Dunn to the house, so we really need to start heading that way." Jill handed him the sock she'd wrung out and lain flat against the warm surface of the boulder. "This is still pretty wet, but it's better than having you walking barefoot. Let me know if you have any trouble. I can always carry you on my back until we meet up with my brother."

She watched as Ian put his sock on, then reached up to help him down off the rock. In her haste to get them away from the pond earlier, she hadn't realized how light he was in her arms. Jill wondered if he might be teased at school because he was small for his age. Mike had a ten-year-old son who was considerably larger. *Of course, my brother's a pretty big guy*, she thought. *Maybe this boy's parents are more slightly built.*

Simon, sensing they were about to leave, was up and ready for action. An active dog, he loved being on the move. When Jill set the boy on the ground, the shepherd wagged his powerful tail and gave Ian a hearty lick across the face. Ian laughed and patted the dog lovingly. "Thank you, Simon, for saving me." Aware that the child was addressing him, Simon gave a couple of happy barks.

Jill laughed and said, "I'm pretty sure that's his way of saying you're welcome! Okay, Simon, lead the way home!" On her command, he turned, making his way down the path with Ian not far behind and Jill bringing up the rear. The dog glanced back frequently to make certain his two charges were following.

"That's so cool that he knows which way to go!" exclaimed Ian. "He's a really smart dog!"

"Yes, he is." Jill agreed. "Now, stop changing the subject and pick up the story from earlier today when you didn't get on the school bus."

Ian seemed more relaxed now, and his words came easier. "Well, it was really no big deal. After my dad left, I just walked to the back of the subdivision. There's a hole in the wall I like to squeeze through.

I love to explore things. Did you know there's a cool stream back there?"

"Actually, I did know that," Jill answered. "The land your dad's house is built on used to belong to my family many years ago. The reason the subdivision is called Lone Star Springs is because of that very stream."

"Cool!" Ian shouted back to her. "So anyway, I'm kind of an artist. I take pictures of things with my phone and then sketch and paint them later. I have all kinds of neat photos of butterflies, dragonflies, turtles, and stuff like that. You should see them! My mom is an artist. She used to do oil paintings. I'm into watercolors. I think they're the best."

Jill was smiling as she walked behind Ian. *He's really opening up to me*, she thought. *What an interesting child.*

"I think that watercolor would be a great medium to capture all of the fantastic colors and beauty around here," she said. "It sounds to me like you're a very talented young man."

Jill hadn't liked hearing that Ian had been dishonest with his father, but she understood the lure of nature. She'd been drawn to it all her life, so much so that she'd moved back to Wind River Ranch after living in Dallas for three years after college. The Hill Country was in her blood. It was home.

How ironic is it that now this child is confiding in me about his desperation to leave this beautiful place because he's so unhappy here? she wondered. Jill needed to know more about his circumstances. "Ian, I get why you wanted to explore behind the wall. I even understand why you'd want to climb to the top of a big hill. There's nothing that compares to the view up here! But I still don't know what would possess you to enter into Snake Hollow. It's too far off the path to just stumble upon it. How did you happen into the grove?"

Slowly continuing his downward climb, Ian responded without missing a beat. "Oh, I would never have gone in there if it hadn't been for some deer," he said. "There was a whole bunch of them. When I got to the top of the hill, I saw them, and they started walking away. I was pretty tired, but I followed them. They disappeared when they went over the top and, by the time I caught up to them again, they were down by the entrance to Snake Hollow."

He took a breath and continued, "I wanted to take their pictures so I could draw them. I got some good shots, but then I guess I scared them and they took off. A couple of them went behind the trees and I wanted to stay with them. They were so pretty!"

Ian abruptly stopped talking, and Jill wondered if he were reliving what had happened to him after he'd entered the hollow.

"And then?" she prodded.

"And then, I went through the trees, and it was kind of dark in there, and there was a yucky smell. But I could see the two deer standing on the other side of the pond. They were drinking water and they looked up and saw me. But they didn't seem afraid of me anymore."

"There was this big flat rock just barely below the surface of the water. I figured I could stand on it, and get some closer pictures of the deer. When I tried to jump to it my foot slipped on the edge of the pond and, well, I didn't make it."

Ian was unhappily recalling what Jill knew was a very traumatic experience. He sounded miserable, yet he continued his story, "I dropped my phone in the pond. I couldn't even see it because it sunk all the way to the bottom before I could grab it." The boy paused for a moment. "Probably the stupid snakes ate it."

"Ha! That's pretty funny!" Jill replied with a chuckle. "Trust me, water moccasins are much more interested in eating frogs, fish and small turtles then feasting on cell phones. They'll even eat other snakes, but they won't normally bite a human unless they feel threatened."

"I guess the one that bit you felt like you were going to hurt it," Ian mused.

"Huh-uh, mister. I'm not going to let you try and change the subject again," Jill reprimanded. "By the way, you're really good at that! We're not talking about me now. This is all about *you,*" she clarified, wanting her words to sink in. "So, now I'm learning that you lost a shoe *and* your cell phone. Anything else?"

"Nope! That about sums it up. That's when you and Simon came to help me," Ian said with a sigh. "I know I'm in big trouble when I get home," he fretted. "My dad has been really cool since my mom said she didn't want me to live with her and her new husband. She said they needed to have some time alone together, and she'd send for me soon." He hesitated and then added softly, "I hope she's ready for me now."

Jill's heart went out to the young boy when she heard that his own mother didn't want him to live with her. *There's got to be more to the story*, she hoped.

She thought about how to respond. "You want to go back to her because you hate it here," Jill said, repeating what he'd told her earlier. "You know, it's not such a bad place. It's where I grew up, and I turned out all right, don't you think?"

Ian stopped walking and turned to her. "You're more than all right. You saved my life and we'll always be friends." She noticed his cheeks reddening as he added, "Plus, I think you're really pretty."

"Now, that's the best thing I've heard all day!" she exclaimed with a grin. "A gal could get used to those kinds of compliments. Thank you!"

They'd only been walking for about ten minutes when Simon started barking. "I bet that's my brother," Jill told him. "He must have run all the way up here."

Sure enough, the German shepherd moved a little further down the hill ahead of them and through a small break in the trees, Jill could make out the large form of her brother moving swiftly up the trail toward them. She was touched that Mike had responded to her so quickly. *I can always count on him*, she thought fondly.

Jill was aware that the sheer size of her brother could be an imposing sight to those who didn't know him. She decided to prepare Ian for their introduction. "Okay, Ian, you're about to meet a real Texas cowboy," she said. "Mike's big, and he's loud, but he's a pretty great guy and he's going to help us."

She noted that the boy didn't respond. He'd stopped dead in his tracks and was staring in awe at the tall, muscular man who had suddenly emerged from the bend in the trail in front of him. Mike

Murray paused long enough to look the muddy boy over from top to bottom before quickly moving past him and pulling Jill into a big hug. "Are you all right?" he asked, concern in his voice.

"I'm fine. I'm fine! Please let me go!" she begged him, laughing. "Mike! Stop! You're squeezing my guts out!"

Mike immediately released her. "Sorry, Jill. I was so freaked out when I got your call." He was still scrutinizing her closely, convincing himself she wasn't hurt.

Jill reached out and touched his arm, saying, "Michael, I promise I'm fine. I was just hoping that maybe you could give Ian here a lift down to the house on your back."

The big man took a couple of short steps back to where Ian stood. He noticed Simon sat next to the boy protectively. *Well, it looks like these two have bonded*, he thought.

"I don't know, Sis, he looks like a pretty heavy colt to me. Guess I can give it a try though," Mike said as he turned and winked at his sister. "We might have to take turns carrying him." With that, he squatted down and instructed Ian to climb on his back and hold onto his neck. Shyly, Ian complied, looking quite small and fragile on the man's broad frame.

"I want to try to be back home before Ian's dad arrives," Jill told her brother. "He's probably speeding like crazy from Austin to get here."

"Don't worry, we've got this," Mike shouted back to her. He was already half-trotting down the hillside trail, following Simon at a steady clip.

As Jill worked to keep up with his pace, she heard her brother's thundering voice saying to Ian, "Kid, I don't know who you are or how you ended up here today, but I bet it's a doozy of a tale and I for one, can't wait to hear it!"

CHAPTER 3

As they neared the bottom of the hill, the trail widened, and Jill was able to walk alongside her brother and Ian. She was glad they'd have a little time to talk before reaching the house.

"Hey, slowpoke," Mike said as she fell into step with him. "Your pal Ian was just telling me about how you rescued him from Snake Hollow. Good goin'!"

"All in a day's work for this superhero," Jill said with a grin, noticing that while she was a bit winded from their brisk descent, Mike was breathing normally and in his usual cheerful mood.

Realizing she was tiring, he let out a deep belly laugh and said, "Ian, it's a good thing my sister called me to help you down, or you'd still be stuck up there on that hill!"

Ian laughed along with Mike. "Trust me," the boy assured them, "I'm happy to be away from Snake Hollow, but I'm *really* not looking forward to hearing what my dad's going to say when he finds out I skipped school." With that, he added somberly, "He's been through a lot lately, and this just makes things worse."

Touched by the child's sensitivity toward his father, Mike reached around and patted Ian on the back. "You know, our grand-dad used to tell me, 'If you wanna dance, you have to pay the fiddler.' I used to hate it when he'd say that, but it makes sense. You see, son, in life you're going to make mistakes, so you pay for them and then move on. I'm sure it's all going to be okay."

Jill appreciated her brother's kindness toward Ian. He'd always been great with kids and was an exceptional father to his own brood.

"Mike's right, Ian," Jill agreed. "The most important thing is that you're not hurt. I'm sure that's the main thing your dad cares about!"

The wooded part of the trail had ended, and they'd entered into an expansive meadow. Simon, thrilled at being so close to home, dashed ahead of them, running at full speed toward the back gate.

"That silly dog!" exclaimed Mike. "What if we'd wanted to make a grand surprise entrance? He's gone and blown that now hasn't he, Ian?"

Ian gave no reply. His eyes were on the police vehicle parked in front of the large house ahead.

Jill, too, had spotted the squad car and glanced over at Ian, who was riding high on Mike's back. "Don't worry," she assured him. "We're going to be right there with you. Mike and I have known Roger Dunn since we were all kids. He's a nice man, and is also very good at his job."

"I might also add that our buddy Roger has been in love with my sister since we were all in grade school!" Mike exclaimed playfully. "But Ms. High and Mighty here keeps givin' him the cold shoulder!"

Feigning disgust, the brawny man gave a dramatic, full-body shudder that nearly threw Ian off his back. Then he complained loudly, "Girls! Geez! Can't live with 'em, can't live without 'em!"

"Very funny! Now, give it a rest, Michael!" Jill demanded firmly.

She knew her brother took great joy in pestering her about Roger. She'd tried to explain to him more than once that she considered the man a friend—nothing more.

Jill didn't want anyone meddling in her personal life. She'd suffered a serious heartbreak in Dallas when she'd split with her long-time fiancé, Stephen. *Living at Gran's with Mike and his family has brought me even closer to them*, she thought. *And my schedule is always full. I can be happy without a man in my life.*

The trio approached the gate as Jill noted with a chuckle that Simon had left the latch open, leaving them access to the house. "Thanks!" she shouted to the German shepherd, who was on the wrap-around porch, busily lapping water from his large silver bowl.

Upon hearing his name, the dog paused and regarded her briefly before quickly resuming his drinking.

"Simon can open gates?" Ian asked.

Jill was relieved that the subject had changed from her love life to her pet.

"Oh yes," she answered. "As you saw earlier, Simon is one smart dog. You'd be amazed at all the things he does around here. Someday he'll probably be running the place!"

"That sounds like a great idea to me," piped Mike. "Maybe then you and I can just kick back and let this place go to the dogs!"

He'd barely spoken the words before a pack of dogs appeared, charging toward them at full speed. They were barking like crazy, obviously pleased to see Mike and Jill returning home.

"Our welcoming committee," Mike told Ian.

He gave a deep barrel-laugh, then stooped to let the boy slide off his back. "Don't worry, they're a friendly bunch. Well, they might lick you to death but, other than that, you're in no danger."

Jill had already relatched the gate behind them and was squatting down, trying not to get knocked over by the excited dogs, all vying for her undivided attention.

"Get in here, Ian!' she yelled, inviting him into the mayhem. "These guys and gals need all the sugars they can get! They miss us when we're gone—even if it's just for a short time."

Ian knelt beside her, joining in the welcome home celebration.

"Now, this one is Brie," Jill said, rubbing the sides of a blonde Labrador. "Her husband is Joe." She held out her other hand to a lab whose coat was a shade darker. "The German shepherds are Nellie and Cody—brother and sister from Simon and his wife Trixie's first litter. And last, but certainly not least, is Little Quigley."

A small, mixed-breed dog had somehow jockeyed his way through the pack and worked his body into Jill's arms. "Quigley Wiggly showed up one day and decided he wanted to be part of the family," she explained, scratching the multi-colored dog's ears. Jill leaned over and said in a low voice to Ian, "He thinks he's a German shepherd, so please don't let on that he's kind of a mutt!"

Ian was thrilled with all the dogs. He couldn't imagine how awesome it would be to have just *one* dog, much less five, six, or however many Jill and her family had at Wind River Ranch.

"Okay troops, let's keep moving!" Mike ordered. He'd picked Ian up and swung him easily across his back again. Jill followed once more with their small herd of dogs close at her heels. They worked their way past various stables and corrals before finally arriving at Gran's house.

Jill could hear Ian's squeal of excitement as the boy marveled at all the fall decorations. There were hundreds of colorful pumpkins in every shape and size adorning walkways and lining the main drive. A scattering of hay bales and scarecrows added to the festive scene. "Wow, I love all the great decorations! You guys really go all out for fall, don't you?" he asked.

Mike was quick to reply, "I guess you could say that. In addition to many other crops, our grandparents mastered growing pumpkins here. We use tons of 'em around the ranch to doll the place up this time of year, but most of the harvest goes to local churches and charities."

"Wait! Don't forget the pies, Mike!" Jill shouted. "We bake lots and lots of yummy pumpkin pies!"

"It's true, there's never a shortage of pumpkin pie or, honestly, pumpkin *anything*! And if you're impressed with what our grandmother does for fall, you should see how she decorates for Christmas. It's pretty incredible!" Mike told the boy.

Once he reached the house, Mike carefully slid Ian down off his back, setting his feet on the wide wooden porch. The two waited while Jill skipped up the front steps as she'd done a thousand times before.

She hadn't been far behind them, but Mike never missed an opportunity to razz her. He nudged Ian softly before saying, "Here comes the slowpoke!"

"You know, that slowpoke stuff is getting pretty old, Bro!" Jill retorted.

She reached over to Ian and whispered conspiratorially, yet intentionally loud enough for Mike to hear, "He's still jealous because I beat him in a big endurance horse race last year."

Ian giggled and pointed at Mike. "You let a *girl* beat you?"

"Aw, she just got lucky and chose a better horse," he mock-complained, "I'm sure it had nothing to do with who was in the saddle!"

Jill caught the note of pride in her older sibling's voice. She knew that although she and Mike had always been competitive, when it came to anything involving their Arabian horses, they shared every victory.

She was about to return Mike's barb when the massive front door opened and an attractive older woman stepped out. Jill quickly moved toward her grandmother and they shared a tender embrace.

Jenny Murray slowly pulled away and was surveying her granddaughter closely as she said, "I'm glad you're back in one piece, sweetie. Now, why don't you introduce me to this young man?"

The women turned their attention to Ian. The boy, standing very close to Mike, wore a worried expression.

"I'd be happy to do that," Jill replied. "Ian, this is our grandmother, Mrs. Murray."

Ian looked shyly up at the woman and said quietly, "Hello." Then, before he could stop himself, he blurted out, "Wow! Everyone around here is so tall!"

As if on cue, the three Murrays burst into laughter. Their shared joy in the small boy's unexpected remark helped to lighten the mood. Soon, Ian was smiling with them.

Moving over to Ian with grace that belied her nearly eighty years, the older woman held out her hand. "Mrs. Murray sounds very formal. Why don't you call me Gran Jen?"

Ian seemed thrilled with the suggestion and extended his own hand into her firm handshake. "Okay!" he replied.

"Great! I'm glad we have that settled. Let's go inside and get you cleaned up a little, maybe put some ice on your foot," she said kindly, noticing his limp. "Our friend Roger is here and he would like to meet you, but I told him that we were going to wait until your father got here to talk about what happened today."

She took his hand and led him into the house. Mike and Jill could hear their grandmother asking the boy if he was hungry because she had a peanut butter and jelly sandwich and some milk ready for him.

Looking at Jill, Mike asked, "What would we do without our sweet Gran Jen? She always takes care of everyone."

"She is pretty awesome," Jill agreed, shooting Mike a mischievous grin. "But I bet ol' Roger didn't like Gran telling him that he'd have to wait for Ian's dad to get here before she'd let him talk with the boy. It was pretty scary for him up there today."

I bet it was frightening for you, too, Mike thought, remembering the day when they were young and he'd run, Jill in his arms, down the hill after she'd been bitten by the snake. He decided to keep things light. "Roger may not like having to wait for Ian's father, but everyone knows who rules the roost around here. I'm sure Gran put him in his place."

The siblings chuckled together. They were used to their grandmother's take-charge approach—especially when it came to matters involving Wind River.

"After you, superhero," Mike said with a deep, regal bow, allowing Jill to enter ahead of him.

"Such manners!" she exclaimed playfully. "And that's *Ms.* Superhero to you!"

The two were still teasing each other as they stepped into the spacious foyer, stopping short when they spotted Roger walking toward them.

The tall police officer strode quickly toward Jill, pulling her into a hug. "I'm so proud of you," he said. "What you did for that kid today was really great!"

Jill waited long enough so she didn't appear rude, then moved away from him. "Thanks, Roger, but honestly if it weren't for Simon, I wouldn't have known Ian was in trouble."

"Ah, always the modest one!" Mike chimed in. "How about a hug for me big guy?" he teased.

Roger shook his head.

"No hug for you, but I will shake your hand, my friend."

Watching as the two long-time buddies shook hands and clapped each other on the back, Jill declared, "So macho!" She then said to Roger, "Gran told us she put the brakes on your talking with Ian until his father got here. I think that was a good idea. He's had a rough morning." Not waiting for his reply, she turned and headed toward the kitchen. "I'm going to see if Gran's got a PBJ with my name on it, too!"

Mike didn't miss the fact that Roger's eyes followed his sister as she left the two alone in the foyer.

"Man!" he remarked. "You've still got it bad for her even after all these years, don't you?"

Roger sighed heavily and replied, "I just keep thinking that maybe one of these days, Jill will care about me the way I do for her."

Mike felt for his friend, but he knew his sister seldom changed her mind about anything once she'd made a decision. Jill simply didn't feel an attraction to Roger. *Still*, he thought, *you never know what could happen between two people who've shared such a long history.*

"Hey, let's you and I hang out in the great room until this guy shows up," Mike suggested. The two were walking that way when they heard a chorus of barking outside and the sound of a vehicle roaring up to the front of the house.

They'd barely made it back to the foyer before their ears were assaulted by loud banging on the front door. From the other side, a male voice was shouting, "Hello! I'm David Wilder! I'm here for my son, Ian!"

He was still pounding on the heavy door when Mike swung it wide open, causing the stranger to stumble forward from the momentum. Fortunately, Mike reacted quickly and broke the man's fall before he hit the ground.

Mike was grinning as he pulled him back up to his feet, noting they were about the same height. But unlike the rancher's strong, bulky build, Ian's father had a leaner, more athletic physique.

"Hello, David. I'm Mike Murray," he said. "And over there"— he gestured to his right—"is Roger Dunn. Roger's with the Dripping Springs Police Department. He and I go way back. I believe you two spoke on the phone earlier."

The distraught father quickly recovered from his near spill and shook hands with the other men. "Great to meet you both," he said, anxiously looking around. "Now, where is my son? Where is Ian?"

CHAPTER 4

Jill had just bitten into the second half of her sandwich when her brother barreled through the kitchen door. She, Ian and Gran turned as one as Mike told them that Ian's father had arrived and everyone was going to meet in the great room.

"Showtime," Jill mumbled to Ian, her mouth full of sticky peanut butter. She reached over to give Gran a hand down from the high counter stool.

Ian had already jumped off his chair. Jill knew the boy was nervous about what was about to happen, yet she liked that he was excited to see his dad, taking it as a sign they had a good relationship.

Mike led the way to where the other men were waiting, grinning as David moved quickly toward his son the instant he saw him. In the blink of an eye, Ian was in his father's arms.

He pulled the boy up with him into a tight hug. Jill noticed that the man had tears of relief in his eyes. It was a tender, sweet moment, and she looked away from their reunion, feeling she was intruding on what should have been a private exchange between father and son.

"I'm sorry, Dad! I'm so sorry!" Ian cried. "I never meant for any of this to happen!" The child buried his face into his father's shoulder.

He rubbed Ian's back, comforting his child. "Ian, it's all right. You're not hurt, are you?"

The boy looked up and assured his dad that he was fine. "My friend Ms. Jill saved me. I mean, she has this great big dog named Simon, and he heard me yelling for help, and then..."

"Whoa, hold on a minute, Son! I want to hear everything you have to say, but I'm at a disadvantage here." He turned and walked over to introduce himself to the women in the room, starting with the elder one. "Hello, I'm David Wilder, but my friends call me Dave."

Gran smiled and said, "Welcome Dave, I'm Jennifer Murray, and it's a pleasure to meet you." Wrapping her arm around Jill's waist, she added, "and this is my granddaughter, Jill. She's the one who helped Ian today. Well, she and her sidekick, Simon, that is!"

Dave offered his hand to Jill, who returned the handshake with a firm grip of her own. He hesitated for a moment, struck by her magnificent eyes. "Hi, Jill, it's nice to meet you. Thank you for what you did today," he said softly.

She gave him a bright smile. "You're welcome, and it's nice to meet you, too," she replied.

Dave had to pry his eyes away from her. *Let's stay focused here*, he told himself. He was still trying to collect his thoughts when he heard Roger loudly clearing his throat.

The police officer shot Dave a hostile scowl before turning and smiling at Gran. "Why don't we all take a seat and get started?" he suggested authoritatively. "That is, if it's all right with Mrs. Murray."

"Of course!" she replied. "Let's give Ian a chance to tell his story." Gran motioned to the oversized leather sofas and chairs around the room. "Would anyone care for something to drink?"

"I'm on it!" Mike told her as he moved over to the bar at the far end of the room, and opened the fridge. "How about I get everyone a bottle of water?" He'd already loaded up six bottles in his large hands and was passing them around as they each found a seat.

Roger pulled out a small notebook and pen and prepared to write. "Okay, Ian, just like your father said, tell us what happened today and start with this morning at the bus stop."

The boy slowly told them about his day, stopping periodically to answer questions. Jill sat quietly next to her grandmother and listened to his story, watching Dave closely as Ian spoke.

She was impressed with the child's attention to detail, admiring his way with words as he described the beauty of the things he'd seen, and even the horrible scent of the water moccasins at the pond. *It must be the artist in him*, she thought. *He has a way with words far beyond a ten-year-old's level.*

From time to time, as he was talking, Ian would glance over at Jill. When he did, she would give him an encouraging nod and a smile. She thought he was doing a great job and found herself feeling a sense of pride in the boy.

It was then it hit her that the morning's events would forever bind them together. In rescuing him from Snake Hollow, they would always share something very memorable.

When she knew Ian was nearing the end of his story, Jill leaned over to her brother and whispered something in his ear.

Mike rose and excused himself from the room. "I think I know everything from this point on. I'll be right back," he said.

A few moments later, Ian concluded his story by saying, "And that's pretty much it! That's what happened." There was a collective silence as everyone digested the information the boy had shared.

Suddenly, Mike's booming voice could be heard as he returned with Simon. "I think it's time for everyone to congratulate the dog of the day!" he announced as the shepherd trotted happily into the great room.

"Simon!" Ian shouted with delight from the sofa, running over to him. The dog was equally thrilled to see his new friend again, greeting the child with several licks across his face.

"Dad, this is Simon! He's the dog I was telling you about. Simon heard me calling out for help! He got Ms. Jill to come to Snake Hollow and save me."

Dave joined Ian, kneeling down beside the large dog. "Well, I guess I'm forever in your debt," he said, reaching out to pet the shepherd. "I bet those big ears help you hear lots of things! I'm so glad you heard Ian today."

"Dave, I think he'd like to shake your hand," Mike said.

"Oh, well, that's a great idea," Dave replied, holding out his hand. Simon immediately responded in turn, offering up a furry paw.

Ian was still fixated on Simon. "He's really brilliant, Dad," the boy gushed. "He can open gates and a lot of other stuff. He's the best dog ever!"

"Yes, I can certainly see why you're so impressed with him," Dave agreed. "He is quite a dog!" Dave rose and turned to speak to everyone. He noted they'd all gotten up from their seats and now circled around him, Ian and Simon.

"Ian loves dogs," Dave explained, somewhat awkwardly. "He's been begging his mother and me to get one for him for the past couple of years. It just hasn't been the right time."

He paused for a moment and watched his boy pet the dog tenderly. He knew there was more he needed to say, especially to the pretty blonde, standing next to her brother. He'd been aware that the statuesque beauty had been evaluating him since they'd all gathered in the great room.

Dave looked at Jill and said, "There's no doubt that Simon played an important role in saving Ian today," he began, giving a nod of acknowledgment to the dog. "But if you hadn't been nearby and gone to my son's aid..." He paused, getting choked up again, but forced himself to finish what he wanted to tell her. "I just can't even bear to think about what might have happened. There are not enough words to express my gratitude to you. Ian means everything to me. Thank you for what you did today. Thank you from the bottom of my heart."

Jill had always been an emotional, compassionate person. She was so moved by his heartfelt gratitude; she walked over and hugged him. "You're so welcome, Dave. I'm glad I was there to help," she said.

Jill found herself immediately comfortable in Dave's warm embrace. It was as if all her senses came alive as she breathed in his cologne and felt the strength of his taunt body next to hers. She had no idea how long she'd been in his arms until she heard Roger clearing his throat again and felt his touch on her arm. Jill caught herself blushing slightly as the police officer said, "As they say, all's well that ends well. I guess everyone can get back to their own business now." Roger used one hand to close his notebook with a loud snap.

She'd taken a couple of steps backward when Jill realized Roger's hand remained possessively on her arm. She moved closer to Gran, distancing herself from him. It was a clear sign that his touch was unwelcome. Aware of her obvious move away from him, Roger awkwardly shuffled his feet and put his hand in his pocket.

Dave had been affected by Jill's impulsive hug. He was trying to catch her eye again as he noticed her deliberate maneuver away from

Roger. He wondered what was going on between the two of them, but turned his attention back to his son and said, "Ian, you and I are going to have a serious talk when we get home. But before we go, I believe there's something you need to say to Mrs. Murray and her family."

The boy stopped stroking Simon and looked up at Gran, Mike, and Jill. "I'm sorry I went on your property today. I promise I won't do it again." He waited a moment while they accepted his apology.

Ian turned his head and included Roger in his next statement. "And I'm also sorry I wasted everyone's time." He looked over at his father to make sure he'd covered everything.

"Oh! And thank you, Gran Jen, for the PBJ and milk. I was really hungry!" he concluded.

"*Gran Jen?*" Roger asked Jill quietly, eyebrows raised. "Seems a little overfamiliar for someone you guys have known for just a few hours, don't you think?"

Gran overheard Roger's remark. "Calm down, Roger," she reprimanded. "I told Ian he could call me Gran Jen. As I recall, that's what you used to call me when you were a boy."

Before Roger could respond, there was a loud commotion coming from the front of the house. Simon, barking wildly, bolted out of the room toward all the excitement.

The sound of children laughing and talking noisily could be heard echoing down the hallway. Suddenly over all the noise, they heard a female voice calling out, "Mike? Jill? Where is everyone? Is that Roger's car out front?"

"Gina, we're all in the great room!" Mike shouted back to his wife. He was already walking to meet his family. Before leaving the room, he instructed everyone to stay put. "I want Dave and Ian to meet the rest of the Murray family."

Roger moved to the door, calling after Mike, "Hey, bud, I've gotta take off." He stopped and offered Dave his hand. "Nice to meet you, *David*. I hope you can keep your little guy out of trouble in the future."

Dave noted how Roger had intentionally used his given name. He thought about Jill's slight flinch when the cop had put his hand on her. Neither of these things bugged him as much as Roger refer-ring to Ian as "a little guy."

What an idiot, Dave thought, but he smiled and assured Roger that his son was not going to be a problem moving forward. "Ian's already apologized for his actions today," he reminded him. "He feels bad about what happened, and he'll be disciplined when we get home." With that, he turned to Ian and said, "We're going to leave, too, as soon as we meet the rest of the family."

Roger approached Jill and leaned close to her. "Hey, will you walk out with me?" he asked. "I want to talk to you about something."

Jill shook her head no. She hadn't cared for the way Roger had spoken to Dave and had no intention of leaving the room, wanting to be present when Ian met the other kids.

"I'm sorry, Roger, but Ian and my nephew are the same age. I want to wait and see if they know each other from school," she told him.

Unhappy with her refusal, Roger frowned. "Wow, you've taken quite a liking to this kid, haven't you, Jill?" He didn't wait for her to answer, but looked at his watch and muttered, "I've got to get back. I'll stop by another time. Maybe we can talk then."

She barely responded, giving Roger a half-hearted nod of her head. He walked through the double doors, narrowly missing Mike who was coming back into the great room, his family gathered around him.

"See ya, Roger!" Mike called after him.

The family of five walked in together. Twins Kate and Kelli headed straight for Gran who'd resumed her spot on one of the sofas. The eight-year-old lookalikes adored their great-grandmother and the older woman delighted in their affection, snuggling up with a girl on each side.

Mike laughed and said to Dave, "Well, there go our twins Kate and Kellie. That's my lovely wife, Gina, talking with Jill. And *this*, this is Jeremy, our fourth grader named after my granddad, Jeremy Murray. As usual, it's hard to keep everyone together!"

"Hi, nice to meet you!" Gina gave a polite wave to Dave. She was eager to talk with her sister-in-law. "What in the world is going on around here?" she asked Jill.

"It's kind of a long story, Gina," she told the pretty redhead. "But I promise I'll fill you in on all the details later. Suffice it to say it's been a heck of a day!"

"Okaaaaay," Gina responded, looking across the room. "Mostly I want to know all about that hunky guy who's talking with Mike and Jeremy."

Jill was also observing the guys who were engaged in conversation near the huge stone fireplace.

"That's not a hunky guy, that's Ian's father," Jill explained. "Ian is ten like Jeremy. He told me he's been having some problems with the kids at school and I've been wondering if the boys were in the same class."

"Ah," replied Gina. "Well, that explains *everything*," she said sarcastically. "And by the way, 'that guy' may be Ian's father, but he's *still* a major hunk."

Jill loved Gina as if she were her own sister, but like Mike, she sometimes crossed the line when it came to meddling in her personal life. When Jill said nothing, she heard Gina mutter, "Hmmm, a girl might wonder if hunky guy in living room has anything to do with Roger's grumpy goodbye to the kids and me?"

Jill had tuned Gina out. Her focus was on the two young boys across the room. Their voices were raised, and they appeared to be arguing. *Oh no!* she thought, remembering that Ian had told her the kids at school picked on him. *Could my sweet nephew be a bully?* Jill excused herself from Gina and moved toward the fireplace.

"Jeremy," she interrupted, "what's going on? Do you know Ian?"

As the two stood facing each other, Jill noted Jeremy was at least six inches taller than Ian. He was respectful to his aunt, but stood firm, not taking his glare off the other boy.

"Yes, Aunt Jill," Jeremy answered. "I know him from school, but we're *not* friends."

Jill felt her stomach sink. The Murrays were a loving family by nature and she was surprised and disappointed to hear her nephew's words. *They're just young boys*, she thought. *What could possibly have happened to make them dislike one another so much?*

Mike made it clear he was not going to tolerate his son's rudeness. "Jeremy," he said sternly, "that does not sound like the young man I know. What on earth did Ian do that made you not want to be his friend?"

Everyone was quiet as they waited for Jeremy's response. At last, he blew out an angry breath and said, "He disrespected you, Dad. This loser called you a *dirty farmer!*"

CHAPTER 5

Stealing a quick glance at Mike and seeing his dumbstruck expression, Jill nearly lost it. *I wish I could take a picture of his face!* she thought. *It's not often he's at a complete loss for words.* She was certain he was having a hard time not howling with laughter at being called a "dirty farmer." Jill knew they'd be chuckling about Ian's comment for years, but for now, the conversation had taken a serious turn.

To his credit, Mike didn't crack a smile, instead; he rubbed his chin as if thoughtfully considering the insult and how he'd respond to it.

Gina was the first to break the silence. She gathered her daughters, then reached to help Gran up, announcing, "Jill, the rest of us gals are going to start working on some homework."

Kate and Kelli had been fascinated with the drama unfolding by the fireplace. They were protesting loudly, but obediently followed their mother out of the room.

Before taking her leave, Gran paused at the door. "Mike, you need to hear both sides of the story," she advised. "I'm sure Ian has something he'd like to say." She smiled over to the boy for support and then she was gone, leaving Jill and the guys to work the situation out.

Dave put both hands on his son's shoulders and squared him off, so they were facing each other. "Ian, you called Mr. Murray, a *dirty farmer?*" he asked.

Ian didn't deny it. "I did. But like Gran Jen said, there's more to the story."

Dave sighed patiently and shook his head. "Well, let's hear it," he said.

Ian stared at the floor, remorsefully. He couldn't believe he was back in the hot seat. Carefully choosing his words, he explained, "Well, a couple of days ago, I was in the school lunchroom. There were these guys at one of the tables, and I went over to join them. I guess they didn't want me to sit with them. They kept talking about me like I wasn't even there. They called me a shrimp and said I was a dweeb and some other stuff like that."

Jeremy sighed heavily and interjected, "I got my lunch and went to hang out with my friends and they were talking trash to him." He nodded toward Ian. "I told everyone to just shut-up and eat their lunch."

"I *don't* like being told to shut up," Ian said stiffly. "You guys were being jerks."

Jeremy squared his shoulders and said indignantly, "*I* was not being a jerk! I wasn't even talking to you. I was talking to the other guys."

"What happened next, Ian?" Dave prompted.

"I told them to stop talking about me," Ian replied. "I was getting embarrassed and I didn't know what else to say, so I told them that *my* dad was a famous major league baseball pitcher."

Jeremy broke into the conversation again. "Yeah, dude! That just made things worse," he told Ian. "You can't just go around making stuff up about your dad being some kind of superstar!"

"And that's when *he* called me a liar," Ian declared, pointing his finger at Jeremy. "That made me even madder. So I said, 'At least my dad isn't a dirty farmer like yours.'" He looked apologetically at Mike. "I'm really sorry, Mr. Murray. I know you're not a dirty farmer."

Mike gave Ian a reassuring pat on the back. "Don't worry about it, kid. I've been called worse." He then turned to Jeremy and said firmly, "Son, calling someone a liar is a very serious accusation. I think you need to apologize to Ian."

"*But, Dad!*" Jeremy cried. "He shouldn't be saying things that aren't true. That's why I called him a liar!"

Suddenly, they were all talking at once until Dave shouted for silence, holding up both hands for impact. "Enough!" he demanded. "This is getting way out of control!"

The room grew quiet, and all eyes were on Dave. "What Ian said is true, Jeremy," he said. "I used to play professional baseball." He paused a moment, then humbly added, "I don't know about the being famous part, but I had a few good years on the mound."

Dumbfounded, Jeremy regarded Dave with newfound respect. "For real?" he asked.

"For real," Dave replied simply.

"Wow! A real, live professional baseball player in our house! And a pitcher at that! Can you believe it, Dad?" Jeremy asked, turning to Mike.

Mike was grinning from ear to ear. "That's pretty cool!" he said, inspecting Dave more closely. "You pitched for the Arizona Bears, right?"

"That's right. I'm surprised you know that since I didn't play much the last couple of seasons. My elbow was jacked up pretty bad after all those years of pitching. Had some ligament reconstruction done and was able to finish my contract out after that as a relief pitcher. Played some outfield positions, too. I was one of the lucky ones," Dave said.

"My father was a big baseball fan. That's how I caught the bug," Mike said. "I remember going to Arlington and seeing some games with him." He looked over at Jeremy. "My son never knew his Grandpa Matthew, but I gave him my dad's baseball card collection. It's been a way to keep his legacy alive."

Totally impressed with Dave, Jeremy looked at Ian and said, "Your dad's really awesome! I'm sorry I called you a liar."

Dave smiled at Jeremy then spoke to his son. "Ian, the way I heard it, Jeremy tried to help you out by telling those other guys to stop hassling you in the lunchroom."

Ian's pleasure in being vindicated for Jeremy's insult quickly dissolved when he realized that his father was right. "I'm sorry for what I said about you, too," he told the other boy.

"Forget it, man," Jeremy said, then an idea came to him. "Hey, do you want to go to my room and check out my sweet baseball card collection?"

"Sure!" Ian replied, enthusiastically. "And maybe sometime you can come to my house and I'll show you mine!"

The boys were about to leave the room when they heard Dave say, "Hold on, Ian. We need to head home. You and I still have a lot to talk about. Plus, we need to get out of these nice people's hair."

Mike took the opportunity to pull Dave aside, appealing to him quietly, "You're really not keeping us from anything. How about we give these two a few minutes to get to know one another a little better? I think it would be good for both of them."

As much he needed to have a serious discussion with Ian, Dave knew that his son could use a friend. "All right, Ian," he said, looking down at his watch, "you've got fifteen minutes, then we've really got to go."

Ian and Jeremy hastily made for the door. "Thanks, Dad!" Ian shouted over his shoulder.

Mike, Dave, and Jill were chuckling together. "Ah, to have that much energy again!" Jill exclaimed as the ten-year-olds ran out. "I think, all things considered, that went very well!"

She offered her hand to shake Dave's. "You've got a great kid, Dave. It was a pleasure meeting you," she said, somewhat formally. "Now, if you'll pardon me, I'm off to serve Mr. Simon his dinner."

Mike observed as the two shook hands. He'd been aware of the way Jill had been eying Dave ever since the former pitcher had entered the room. *She's intrigued with this guy*, he thought. *Maybe my little sister needs some help here.* He cleared his throat and asked, "Hey, Sis, why don't you let me take care of Simon? I've gotta feed all the other hounds anyway."

Mike didn't wait for her reply. He whistled for the dog as he headed for the door. Simon looked up to Jill for confirmation that it was all right for him to go with her brother.

"Simon, you go on with Uncle Mike," Jill instructed. "And tell him you expect a T-bone for supper tonight. After all, you deserve one!" She knelt and gave her dog an affectionate hug before they left the room. When Simon's wagging tail had disappeared down the hall, Jill turned and looked at Dave.

The man's dazzling smile nearly disarmed her. "Are things always this exciting around here?" he asked.

CHAPTER 6

Jill knew Mike had deliberately made himself scarce so that she could be alone with Dave. *Always meddling*, she thought. Yet for the first time, she was glad he had. Much to her surprise, she'd felt an instant liking for the former pitcher. It was an attraction that had quickly grown stronger as she watched him with his son. She could see the two shared a strong, loving bond.

Completely caught up in Dave's mega-watt smile; Jill realized she hadn't answered his question about life at Wind River. There was an awkward silence between them as he awaited her reply.

Ordinarily confident and outspoken, Jill was suddenly shy. "To tell you the truth, Dave, we're always busy here, but the events of today were certainly unprecedented." *Ugh! What kind of an answer was that?* She was mentally kicking herself for sounding so uptight.

At her stiff response, Dave's smile faded. *Wow! She must really be ready for us to leave*, he thought. He took a moment to evaluate the situation. *This woman not only comes from a very wealthy family, she's also incredibly beautiful. Jill probably wouldn't give me the time of day if she hadn't happened across Ian.* He studied her for a moment longer, mesmerized. *There's something about her...*

Dave realized he was staring and quickly apologized again for the trouble his son had caused yet felt he needed to say more. He wanted to talk to her. "I'm glad the kids made peace. Ian could really use a friend here. All he talks about is going back to Arizona to live with my ex-wife." Dave shook his head disappointedly. "I was hoping over time, Ian would change his mind and want to stay with me."

Jill watched as he casually crossed his arms across his broad chest and leaned comfortably against the wall. She was pleased to see that his smile returned as he continued, "You see, I was gone a lot when Ian was younger, and now I'm hoping to make up for some of the time we lost. Of course, more than anything, I just want Ian to be happy."

"Isn't that what every parent wants for their child?" Jill asked. "I have a hunch that he and Jeremy will be pals. My nephew is a baseball fanatic, so they have that in common. The boys may have gotten off to a rocky start, but they seem to be on the right track now."

"I hope so," Dave replied. He'd noticed that while she spoke, her long fingers idly toyed with the top of a pumpkin resting on a nearby sofa table. "Your family must really love fall," he remarked, smoothly changing the subject.

"What? Oh, yes!" Jill flushed, pulling her hand away from the centerpiece. "Well, we love *all* of the holidays but tend to go a little over the top from Halloween through Christmas. For our family it's one long celebration." She looked around the room at the many decorations and laughed happily. "I'd like to tell you we do it for the kids, but the fact is, the holidays bring out the kid in all of us."

"I've never seen so many pumpkins!" Dave exclaimed with a chuckle. He was relieved to see that she was visibly relaxing and becoming more comfortable around him. "I like the way they were lined up along the driveway to the house. Very creative!" He grinned, then, suddenly looked guilty. "I might have taken a couple of them out with my car. I was in a pretty big rush to get here!" he confessed.

Jill stiffened and held out a hand with her palm upward. "Listen, mister, in these parts pumpkin smashing is a serious offense," she informed Dave with mock-authority. "That will be ten bucks a gourd. Pay up!"

He gave a boyish grin, enjoying her sense of humor, then slapped her hand lightly. "You'll have to prove it before I'll pay it!"

She blushed and drew back her hand. "Oh, I suppose we'll let it slide this *one* time," she told him. Still smiling, she went on to tell him about some of the special traditions they shared at the ranch.

As she spoke, Dave admired her striking features. He was utterly enchanted with the breathtaking woman whose bright blue eyes lit up as she pointed to the tallest window in the great room. "Over there is where the Christmas tree goes," she explained. Then, adding with a giggle, "Well, *one* of the trees anyway! As you've probably suspected, we have lots of Christmas trees—not as many trees as we have pumpkins, but definitely lots of trees!"

Realizing she was rambling, Jill stopped talking. "I'm so sorry, Dave," she said. "I got a little carried away. As I said, it's not just the kids who get excited about the holidays!"

"No. Please don't apologize," Dave told her sincerely. "It all sounds really amazing."

They looked at one another, and Jill felt the connection. *Oh, my gosh, does he feel this, too? What the heck is happening?* she wondered. *I don't even know this guy, yet it's so easy to talk with him!*

Dave was about to ask her to tell him more about the holidays at Wind River Ranch, but before he could, he heard the unmistakable rumble of Ian and Jeremy running down the hall toward the great room.

"I'm back, Dad!" Ian announced as he came through the double doors. He knew his father had been kind in allowing him to see Jeremy's baseball cards. "Fifteen minutes on the nose!" he declared proudly.

Dave stood up straight and placed his hand on Ian's shoulder. "Great job, buddy. Thank you for keeping an eye on the time."

He then looked at Jill, reluctant to say goodbye. "Well, I guess we'll be going. We need to get home, get this one cleaned up and discuss some things," Dave said. "Thank you again for everything."

With that, he put his arm around Ian, and Jill stepped aside to allow them to pass.

"Wait!" Jeremy shouted. "You didn't ask your dad about Halloween in the Loft!"

Dave looked over at Jeremy. "What in the world is that?" he asked, a bemused look on his face.

Mike came striding into the room. "What? Who hasn't heard of Halloween in the Loft?" he asked. Then, in a creepy, menacing voice, he said, "'Tis a night for the bravest of the brave! 'Tis a night on Hallow's Eve when the goblins come out and the ghosts—"

"All right, Mike! Stop it already!" Jill interrupted, scolding him. "You're scaring the kids!"

Dave looked from Mike to Jill for more information.

"Every year we have a big Halloween party in one of the barns," she explained. "Everyone goes up into the loft, where there's storytelling and cider and that kind of stuff." She shot an accusatory glance at her brother. "None of it is too scary of course, because they're just kids." She repeated the last part with emphasis, "*Just kids, Michael!*"

Dave laughed out loud and feigned a shudder. "Halloween in the Loft sounds terrifyingly terrific!" he remarked.

"It's really *not* scary. My dad is just being silly!" Jeremy explained earnestly. "Please, Mr. Wilder, can Ian come?"

Both boys were looking up at Dave with pleading eyes.

"Tell you what guys, let me think about it," Dave said. "As you both know, Ian and I have some things to work out." He turned to Mike and Jill. "May I get back with you on this?" he asked. Dave thought Halloween in the Loft sounded like a lot of fun, but he didn't want to give his permission to let Ian attend until they'd talked about what had happened that morning. He also needed to determine Ian's punishment.

Jill understood Dave's position. "Hey, guys, I think that sounds fair," she told the boys diplomatically. She then said to Dave, "Think about it and let us know. We'd love to have you both back. It's next Saturday evening at six. The kids all wear their costumes. It really is a blast!"

"Why don't you give Dave your number so he can call you when he decides?" Mike suggested, helpfully.

While Dave was preoccupied locating his cell phone, Jill rolled her eyes at her brother and mouthed, "Really?"

Mike smiled sweetly at his sister and shrugged innocently.

After he'd secured Jill's number, Dave gave a nod to Ian and said, "We need to head home, kiddo. It's been a long day."

They walked as a group to the front door where Gran was waiting to say goodbye.

"I hope to see you again soon, Ian," she said, smiling as she stooped down to embrace the boy. "You're always welcome here at Wind River Ranch—except next time you visit, please, just come to our front door!"

Gran's humor wasn't lost on Ian, who laughed and accepted her invitation. "Thanks, Gran Jen. I want to come back. Jeremy invited me for Halloween in the Loft, but I'm not sure my dad will let me come because I'm in trouble and all," he told her.

"Well, whatever your father thinks is best," Gran replied. Then she looked at Dave and took his hand. "It was my pleasure to meet you today, Dave. Please don't be a stranger."

"Thank you, Mrs. Murray," Dave responded, then he added, "for everything." His eyes connected with Jill's for a moment before they each looked away.

After everyone had said their goodbyes, the Murrays watched from the porch as Dave pulled away and started down the long drive toward the front gate.

Mike poked Jill in the ribs playfully before going back into the house. "I kind of like that guy," he said.

CHAPTER 7

Jill was working with Macey Jean, a black mare she favored for competitive dressage events. Standing at nearly sixteen hands, the horse was a tall Arabian. They made an impressive pair, moving as one around the arena. Totally immersed in perfecting every maneuver, Jill was happy for the distraction. It had been days since she'd given her number to Dave and, as much as she hated to admit it, she was disappointed not to have heard from him.

It's just as well, she thought. *He seemed like a nice guy, but with his good looks and minor celebrity status, he probably has women falling all over themselves to get his attention.*

"Well, not this gal," she whispered down to Macey Jean. "I've got more important things to think about than that man." Jill shifted her left leg behind the animal's girth, and the magnificent Arabian responded smoothly by cantering gracefully to the right.

Jill finished their exercise and released Macey Jean to one of the groomers. Ordinarily, she enjoyed the work of a post-ride and believed it further bonded her with the horse, but there was no time for it today. She'd promised Gran she would help her run errands.

An hour later, as they were driving into Dripping Springs, Gran asked Jill if she'd heard from Dave. "Not a peep," she said, keeping her eyes on the road, and giving a carefree shrug. "I guess he decided not to let Ian come to the party."

"Well, that's too bad," Gran said. "I thought it would be good for the boy."

"I thought so, too," Jill replied.

"I was also looking forward to getting to know Dave better," the older woman said, looking out the window. "He seemed like an interesting man."

Jill looked over at her grandmother. "Yes, he did," she agreed. "But I'm sure he has his reasons for not allowing his son to come over." She swiftly changed the topic of their conversation. "Now, where would you like to go first?"

Gran chuckled. "I know what you're doing, Jill Murray. You don't want to talk about Dave. I won't bring him up again." Then she added gently, "It's been nearly two years since you broke up with Stephen. I'm so happy to have you back at the ranch, but I worry about you being lonely."

"*Lonely?*" Jill asked, dubiously. "Oh, Gran, I promise you, I'm not lonely. I have you, Mike and Gina—plus my nieces and nephew. I have Simon and the horses, and…"

Gran placed her hand on Jill's leg and patted it lovingly. "Stop. You know what I'm talking about. But I understand. You don't want to talk about it, and that's fine."

Later that evening, after the family finished dinner, the Wilders came up in conversation again when Mike asked Jeremy how things were going with Ian.

"Great," Jeremy assured him. "Turns out he's really funny and likes to make people laugh—like you, Dad!" He thought for a moment, then added, "In fact, he might even be funnier than you because he can do impressions of people!"

Mike's eyes filled with merriment as he leaned back in his chair and replied, "Is that so? Well, maybe we'll have a joke-off competition the next time he's over. We'll see who the mostest funnier guy is!"

"Funniest," Gran corrected him from across the table. "We'll see who's funniest."

Mike held up his hands in playful surrender. "Gran, I can't be expected to be good-looking, funny, *and* smart!"

The family had a good laugh, and Jill saw her opportunity. "Is Ian's dad going to allow him to come to Halloween in the Loft?" she asked, trying to keep her tone casual.

Jeremy beamed. "Ian told me at lunch today that he thinks his dad will say yes." He turned to his aunt, and said, "Mr. Wilder is gonna call you and talk about it."

Jill had a difficult time masking her pleasure at this news. "That's great, Jeremy," she replied with a smile. "It's going to be a really fun night!"

At that moment, Jill felt buzzing in her vest pocket. Observing Gran's no-phones-at-the-table rule, she quickly excused herself, pulling the phone out as she rose. While clearing her dinner plate with her other hand, Jill checked to confirm who the caller was and smiled happily. She headed toward the kitchen, ignoring Mike's snicker.

"Tell Mr. Baseball we said hello," he teased.

Jill placed her plate on the kitchen counter as she accepted the call. "Hey, Dave, you have great timing! We were just talking about you and Ian. Jeremy told us you might be calling about the party." She was walking to her bedroom as she spoke.

"Hi, Jill. Sorry it took me so long to get back with you. I felt it was important not to reward Ian by allowing him to go to a party right after he'd been in trouble over at your place. I hope you understand," Dave explained.

"Totally," Jill assured him. "But I guess I'm still confused. Is he coming or not?" She was smiling when she asked. He could hear it in her voice.

"No, *he's* not coming," Dave said in mock-indignation. "*We're both* coming. I was under the impression the invitation was for both of us."

She chuckled at his affronted tone. Feeling like a silly teenager, she corrected her error. "Of course the invitation was for both of you. Don't worry; there will be plenty of other adults here."

"That's great! I was starting to feel insecure for a moment there. I'd hate to think you guys liked me just because of my kid!" Dave exclaimed laughingly.

Jill had plopped herself sideways across an overstuffed chair, hanging her long legs over one of the arms. "Somehow, Dave, I don't believe there's an insecure bone in your body!" she teased.

"You're probably right about that—except when it comes to this single-parenting thing. I'm feeling way out of my depth," he confided. "I even searched online for tips on acceptable punishments for what Ian pulled last Friday."

"And what did the all-knowing Internet recommend you do?" she asked.

Dave chuckled and said with a weary-sounding sigh, "Well, it seems that children lying to their parents is a pretty common occurrence. However, running away from home and trespassing onto snake-infested private property is somewhat...what's the word I'm looking for?" He paused briefly as if he really had to think about it. "Oh yeah, *unprecedented!*"

She laughed, recalling how awkward the word had sounded when she'd said it to him a few days before. "My apologies for forcing you to use a dictionary!" Jill bantered. Then she added seriously, "I'm sure whatever discipline you decided on was the right choice."

Dave appreciated her confidence in him. "I gave Ian a few more chores around the house, and he's grounded from video games for a while, but I felt like it was important he come to your Halloween party. He and Jeremy are getting along great, and your nephew is helping him make friends with some of the other kids at school."

She sensed the relief in his words. "That's great news, Dave. I'm really glad to hear it."

"Thanks," Dave said, hearing Ian calling to him from the kitchen. "Hey, I need to let you go. Ian needs a hand with his homework. Oh, is there anything we can bring for the party?"

"Nope!" Jill replied. "We've got everything covered. We'll see you two on Saturday at six."

Smiling, Jill ended the call, lazily working off her boots, while thinking about Dave. She couldn't deny her attraction to the man and was anxious to see him again. *Saturday can't come soon enough!* she thought.

⇒◈⇐

On the morning of the party, Jill was enjoying a cup of coffee on the front porch. She'd risen early to watch the sunrise with Simon, scooting her favorite rocker forward so she could rest her boots on the railing. On her lap was a final checklist of things to be done before their guests arrived.

In the days leading up to the event, Gran had been using her own list, assigning tasks to family and staff. The big barn had been cleaned and readied, decorated from top to bottom with fall flora, scarecrows, and dozens of pumpkins.

This year, Gran had assigned the loft preparations to her grand-daughter. Thrilled to be in charge of such an important part of the party, Jill worked with a crew, removing cobwebs from the ceilings and walls, then scrubbing the knotted wooden floors.

She was grateful for the wide, sturdy staircase leading up to the sizable space. They'd brought in folding chairs and round tables, setting them up next to the half wall overlooking the lower part of the barn where the adults would gather.

On the far side of the loft were several hay bales arranged in a semicircle around a small raised stage. *The kids are going to love hanging out here, listening to stories and playing games,* she thought happily.

Jill was engrossed in her list when Mike stepped out onto the porch to join her. When he saw she was working on the party, he chuckled.

"Halloween in the Loft is getting more involved every year. Gina and Gran are in the kitchen, going over all the food and drinks for tonight." He grabbed a rocker, pulling it forward so he could sit down beside Jill. "I don't know why everyone's always worried we're going to run out of food," he said, shaking his head. "We always have way too much of everything. I'm sure this year won't be any different."

Jill looked pointedly at her brother. "Running out of food is a hostess's worst nightmare!" she told him. "I'm glad I'm not in charge of refreshments this year. That's a really tough job-even when you're working with caterers."

He shook his head and grinned amiably at her. "Gran should just put me in charge of food. It's super easy—hot dogs and sodas—done and done!" He'd finished his coffee and stood to leave. "I'll catch you later, Sis. I've got some work to do." Mike placed his empty cup on the rail next to her boots. "Would you take this inside when you go?" Without waiting for an answer, he headed for the steps, then turned around and said, "Oh, and I meant to tell you that I told Dave to come over a little early. He asked if there was anything he could do to help, and I took him up on the offer. He and Ian will be here around three."

She let him get a few feet away before responding. "I'm going to start calling you Meddling Mike!" she shouted with laughter in her voice.

Jill was amazed at how quickly the day passed. She'd finished the main items on her to-do list and hurried into the house to shower before Dave and Ian arrived. Pulling on a silver silk blouse and pairing it with dark designer jeans, she finished the look with black, rhinestone-studded boots. She seldom wore makeup since she'd been back at the ranch, but decided that mascara and definitely some lip gloss were in order for the evening. *After all*, she reasoned, *it is a party! Would I have bothered with makeup if Dave weren't going to be here?* she asked herself.

When she'd finished getting ready, she gave a nod to Simon who'd been snoozing in the corner of the warm bathroom. "Ready to party, my friend?" Jill asked. The big dog immediately rose to his feet and followed his mistress down one of the long corridors toward the front entrance of the house.

"We're going to make a quick detour, buddy," she told him. The two sauntered into the kitchen where several people were scurrying around preparing food for the party. Her sister-in-law was seated at the counter reviewing her list.

"It smells divine in here!" Jill exclaimed, giving Gina a quick hug.

"Thanks. I'm just about ready to turn things over to these guys," Gina said, nodding toward the catering team. "I've got to get the girls into the fairy princess costumes Gran made for them. They're going to be adorable!"

"My nieces are always adorable," enthused Jill. "Let me know if you need some help. I don't get to do enough girly-stuff around here!"

She grabbed a couple of eggrolls from a nearby chafing dish, then crossed the kitchen and exited into the formal dining room.

Making sure it wasn't too hot; she tossed a bit of the roll to Simon who snatched it out of the air. "You know, you should try chewing your food!" she scolded. "You might enjoy it more."

Glancing at her watch, Jill saw it was well after three o'clock. *That was good. Keep it cool,* she thought. *Don't go looking for Dave and appear too anxious. He might think you're desperate.*

Not seeing his car parked near the house, she walked in the direction of the big barn. It wasn't there either. Her heart sank as it became clear that Dave hadn't shown up early as he'd told Mike he would. Jill was disappointed. It wasn't that they needed extra help. They had the party covered. The fact was, she'd been looking forward to spending some time with him before the rest of the guests arrived. She knew that had been Mike's intention when he'd accepted Dave's offer for him and Ian to come over early.

Well, Mr. Wilder. This does not bode well for you. Around here, your word is your bond. I've had it with flakey men in my life!

"I don't know why I thought Dave would be different from any of the other men out there," Jill told Simon. "Let's check and see if Gina needs any help; then we'll go for a quick walk through the stables. I want to say hello to Macey Jean; then we'll finish up in the loft."

Jill was murmuring sweetly to Macey Jean, stroking the mare's smooth, arched neck, when she heard Dave calling her name.

"Jill? Are you in here?" he asked again.

"Better late than never," she said softly to Simon, checking her watch once more. *Five-thirty!* she thought, shaking her head in dismay. "Come on, pal, let's see what the guy has to say for himself."

"Yes," she called back. "I'm heading that way." Walking back to the entryway, she could see Dave's body impressively silhouetted against the late-day sun. She plastered a smile on her face, determined not to let the man see how disappointed she was with him.

"Wow!" he said, smiling as she approached him. "This is really something! I didn't realize you had so many horses here." It chafed her even further that Dave offered no explanation or apology for his tardiness. She wished he didn't look so good in his burnt orange polo and faded jeans that hugged his lean body in all the right places.

Don't let him get to you, Jill, she told herself. She kept the fake smile intact. "Yes, Dave, we have a lot of horses." Despite her resolve not to show she was peeved at him, Jill couldn't seem to help herself. She continued dryly, "Wind River Ranch *is* a horse ranch, after all, so *of course* we have horses."

Dave was no fool. He'd caught her condescending tone and wondered why she'd responded so coldly to him. The smile on his face disappeared. In retrospect, he wished he'd replied differently, but caught off guard, he quickly said, "Of course you have horses here."

Suddenly, Jill was visibly angry, glaring at him. She asked, "Dave, are you mocking me?" She was fixing him with steely-blue eyes. *"Again?"*

"What are you talking about?" he asked, perplexed by her behavior. "I get the impression you're mad at me. Did I say something wrong?"

Jill stood in front of him with her arms crossed, and her brow furrowed in frustration. She looked him squarely in the eyes and said reproachfully, "When you tell someone you're going to arrive at three, you should arrive at three. A person should always keep their word."

She turned to go, flipping her long, blonde hair over one shoulder. "Come on, Simon!" Jill commanded loudly. "We've got some lamps to light in the loft." With that, the two marched out, leaving a bewildered Dave standing alone in the half-dark entryway.

CHAPTER 8

It didn't take long for Dave to realize there'd been a serious communication breakdown. *Jill obviously hasn't checked her phone in the past couple of hours,* he thought. *She doesn't know I called and left a voicemail letting her know we'd be late. She must think I'm a real louse!*

Dave hated that Jill thought he'd been so inconsiderate. He prided himself on being punctual and respectful of others. What had happened to delay him was something totally out of his control. He'd planned on explaining this to her when he arrived, but she hadn't given him a chance. *I've got to make this right,* he thought, moving quickly to catch up with her.

Soon he was walking beside Jill. This time, he thought before speaking, wanting to choose the right words. *Remember, this woman saved your son's life,* he reminded himself. *She's going to feel bad when she finds her phone and sees the missed call then listens to your message.*

"Jill, please don't walk away from me! May I just please talk with you for a moment?" Dave pleaded.

"Listen, *Mr. Baseball*, I've still got some things I need to take care of now for the party. Why don't *you* go find Mike and talk to him?" Jill replied curtly, dismissing him.

"And why don't *you* go find your cell phone?" Dave countered in a wounded tone. *Her pride is going to force me to embarrass her,* he thought. "When you do, you'll see that I called you the moment I realized Ian and I weren't going to be able to be here at three." Hoping to soften his words, he added, "After that, you might want to listen to the message I left. I wanted you to know how disappointed I was not to get to spend some time with you."

Jill abruptly stopped walking and turned to look at him. For a couple of minutes, she said nothing, just studied his face to see if he was telling the truth. Jill realized that because she'd been so excited to see Dave again, she'd left her phone on her dresser, not giving it a second thought.

Suddenly, Jill was hit with the absurdity of the situation. *I'm looking at a man I don't know, trying to decide if he's lying to me. I've been acting like such a nut!* she thought. *Here's this nice, incredibly handsome guy who has done nothing more than arrive a little late for a children's Halloween party, and I was so mean to him!* She burst into hearty laughter that ended with a snort.

Seeing his mistress enjoying herself, Simon, standing beside Jill, gave a couple of happy barks to add to the merriment.

Jill quickly regained her composure when she saw Dave's baffled expression. "I am so sorry!" she said. And a tumble of words followed: "I truly don't know what's gotten into me. I don't even know you, yet I placed an unreasonable expectation on you because of a bad past experience. It was wrong for me to do that. I shouldn't have spoken to you the way I did. Please accept my apology!" Jill was nearly out of breath when she'd finished asking for his forgiveness.

Dave was both captivated and confused by her. *One minute she's angry, the next she's laughing and apologizing*, he thought. He wondered if he should be upset that she'd talked down to him, then dismissed him so rudely, but he didn't feel angry. In fact, he was surprised that what he *did* feel was the desire to pull her into his arms and ask her if they could just start the evening over again.

It's time to dial everything back a notch, he told himself. *As Jill said, she doesn't know you and you don't know her. You may be attracted to her, but you've already been through the wringer with your ex-wife. Let's keep a level head here.*

He took a couple of steps back, moving away from her. "Hey, it's okay, it's no big deal," he assured Jill. "Don't worry about it."

"No, I feel bad about what I said to you. I was out of line," she insisted.

"Jill, I promise you, I'm over it. It's really fine," he repeated. "Now, you said you had some things left to do for the party. Let's go get them done!" he suggested, grinning to prove he was ready to move on.

She could see that Dave wanted to drop the matter. *Maybe it's for the best*, she thought, still feeling bad about how she'd treated him. "Sure, that sounds great! Follow me," she said with a smile.

She was able to temporarily forget about the incident as Dave helped her with the final touches. He stood beside her as they surveyed the room. Jill couldn't have been more pleased with the appearance of the loft. The lamps she and Dave had lit cast an eerie light across the space, playing off the walls, ceiling, and floors. The caterers were bringing up pan after pan of hot food, transferring it into the readied chafing dishes. The air was filled with an intoxicating blend of delicious aromas.

Dave saw Jill's look of satisfaction. "This place looks and smells incredible. The kids are going to be thrilled," he said.

"Well, it's a team effort, but thanks. I appreciate that, especially after I was such a jerk to you," she forced herself to look up at him, still embarrassed by the episode.

"Jill, let's just enjoy the evening, all right? It's in the past." Dave looked at his watch. "When does everyone usually start arriving?" he asked as they descended the stairs.

She didn't need to respond. His question was answered by the happy shouts and squeals of several children streaming into the barn. There was an assortment of characters, and Jill delighted in greeting every guest and admiring each child's costume. Soon, Dave stepped into the action, assisting the smaller ones up the stairs and helping everyone get settled on hay bales.

Jeremy and Ian came running in together to join the party. They'd both decided to dress-up as pirates. Jill met them at the bottom of the stairs with a hearty, "Ahoy, mates! Ye scoundrels make sure ye behave yerselfs ta-night, or I shall make ye walk de plank!" The boys laughed at her terrible pirate impression and bounded up to the loft.

When Mike and Gina arrived with their girls, Jill got down on one knee and allowed each fairy princess to tap her on the head with their wand. "You two beauties always make my wishes come true!" she told them lovingly. "I won't hug you because I don't want to crush your fairy wings, but you know Aunt Jill loves you." Kate and Kelli worked their way slowly up the steps, holding onto the rail. "Gina, you and Gran did a marvelous job on their costumes," Jill exclaimed. "They're adorable!"

After Gina and the twins left, Jill gave Mike her full attention, eyeing his costume with a grin. "Now, what do we have here?" she asked with a chuckle.

The big man removed his black top hat with one hand and theatrically swooped into a low bow. "*I* am the Master of Ceremonies," her brother explained. "I decided it was time I dressed the part."

Jill rolled her eyes at his flamboyant attire. "Mike, you've got flames shooting up your sleeves. Did you even *look at* yourself in the mirror before you left the house?" she asked in amusement.

"Oh, Sis, check out the back! It's even cooler than the front! It's got a dragon on it!" He turned around, and sure enough, there was a huge red dragon embroidered across the back of his jacket.

Jill was bent over in laughter. She could barely get the words out, "That's *got* to be the most outrageous thing I've ever seen in my life!"

Thrilled with her reaction, Mike replied, "Thanks! I'm so glad you love it as much as I do!" With that, he moved quickly up the stairs, taking them two at a time. She could hear his booming voice greeting the kids and welcoming everyone to Halloween in the Loft. *He's in his element*, Jill thought.

Jill was looking up and listening to the fun in the loft when Gran came in with a group of several more children and their parents. They stood and talked for a few moments before joining the others upstairs. The older woman lingered a moment longer to tell her granddaughter what a wonderful job she'd done.

"Thanks," Jill said, giving her a hug. "This is always so much fun for everyone. Thank you for opening up the ranch for the party." Gran smiled and gave her a quick wink before carefully working her way up the stairs.

Jill had been doing a mental headcount, checking off the guests as she greeted them. She walked toward the barn entry to see if the last of the stragglers were coming up the drive.

She found herself outside, staring up at the sky when she heard footsteps behind her. "Hey, Jill." It was Dave. "I hope I didn't startle you. Your grandmother sent me down to help you get more ice."

Jill chuckled to herself. She knew there was plenty of ice for the party. She'd seen to that herself, but was happy to spend a few minutes alone with him. "Great! Let's say hello to these last few guests first." She nodded her head at the approaching cars and said, "According to my list, this should be the last of them."

They walked together back to the foot of the stairs and waited while two more families arrived. Jill and Dave greeted them and directed them to the loft.

"This is awesome!" Dave told her. "Listen to the kids up there! They're having a blast! Oh, and before I forget, that was a great pirate impersonation I heard you doing earlier—NOT!" he said with a smirk.

"*What?*" Jill demanded in mock-indignation. "I'll have you know I do a great pirate imitation!"

Dave gave it a shot of his own, "Blimey! Nay, it t'was arrrrrful!"

They looked at each other and broke into laughter. Totally engrossed in their own conversation, they hadn't noticed Roger walking in with a young boy dressed as a cowboy.

Seeing Dave sharing such a heartfelt laugh with Jill did not sit well with Roger. *Well, it sure didn't take this guy long to make his move,* he thought, making no secret of his displeasure. Ignoring Dave, he strode over to Jill and pulled her into a hug. "Thanks for inviting me over again this year," he said. "Your family always throws the best parties." Releasing her, he picked up the cowboy and placed the child on his hip. "You remember my nephew, Ryan, right?"

"Of course," Jill replied. "Those are great boots," she told the child. "You look like a real cowpoke." Ryan giggled and blushed at her compliment.

Jill looked sharply at Roger, then asked, "And you remember Dave Wilder, right?" Dave had been quietly watching the exchange between Roger and Jill. He was still trying to figure out the dynamic between the two.

"Sure," Roger replied, finally acknowledging the other man with a quick nod of his head. "Are you heading upstairs now, Jill?"

"No, you go on with Ryan. I think everyone is here now. I know Mike is eager to begin his official role as Master of Ceremonies. You'll recognize him—big guy in an obnoxious tux!" She laughed and turned to Dave, motioning for him to follow her. Over her shoulder she called to Roger, "We're going to fetch more ice, and then we'll be up."

Jill could feel Roger's eyes on her back as she and Dave left the barn together.

"Man! That guy *really* doesn't like me," commented Dave as they headed to the Morton building that housed the ice machines. "I'm sure it has *nothing* to do with the fact that he's in love with you."

"Roger *thinks* he's in love with me. He and I have known one another all our lives. I've made it clear I don't consider him anything more than a friend," Jill explained. "It's been really challenging ever since I moved back to the ranch. He's over here a lot and, well, it's just annoying," she huffed.

They'd reached the ice machines, and Dave filled two buckets while Jill watched. "I think that's enough ice," she said. "Do you need me to carry one of those buckets?"

He regarded her with one eyebrow raised high. "Seriously?" he asked. "You think I can't handle carrying a couple of buckets of ice?" He gripped a handle in each hand and easily lifted the buckets up, then feigned they were too heavy. "Why'd you let me fill them so full?" he groaned.

Jill laughed at his charade. "I was hoping you'd refuse my offer to help. I was just trying to be polite. Trust me; I tote enough heavy buckets around here as it is!"

They walked slowly back to the barn, enjoying each other's company. Jill gave Dave a walking tour as they passed several barns, stables, and other buildings. The evening was clear and cool. It was growing dark, and soon, the sky would be peppered with shining stars. Jill stopped to admire the view. "Don't you just love how you can really see all the stars here?" she asked Dave. "I missed seeing them when I lived in Dallas."

Dave had stopped beside her; his head tilted to the darkening sky. To Jill's surprise, he broke into song, his voice clear and resonant: "The stars at night are big and bright! Deep in the heart of Texas!"

"Awesome! You have a great voice!" Jill told him. "Keep singing—I've always loved that song!"

"I'll do no such thing!" declared Dave dramatically. He thought for a moment then confessed with a grin, "Mostly because those are the only words of that song I know!"

Jill giggled and helped him out, singing, "The prairie sky is wide and high!" She stopped and clapped her hands together four times. Then they both sang, "deep in the heart of Texas!"

They were still plugging their way through the song as they approached the barn, hearing the party in full swing above them. As they took in the laughter and shrieks of delight from the loft, Jill smiled over to Dave. "This is always so much fun!" she exclaimed.

Unexpectedly, Dave set the ice buckets down.

Surprised he'd stopped, Jill looked at him questioningly. "What? You need me to lug those buckets up the stairs for you?"

"No, Jill. I told you, I'm taking care of the ice." His tone had become serious. Under the bright security light of the barn, she could see concern reflected in Dave's eyes.

He waited until he had her full attention before he spoke again. "You said earlier you'd set an unreasonable expectation on me based on something bad that happened to you in the past," he said in a gentle voice. "I want to know what made a strong, beautiful woman nearly take my head off because she thought I hadn't called." He paused for a couple of beats, letting his words sink in. "Most of all, I want to know—who hurt you, Jill Murray?"

CHAPTER 9

Until then, Jill had been enjoying her time with Dave. *Does he think I'm going to pour my heart out to him right now?* she wondered in dismay.

Bristling, she squared her shoulders and replied, "I know I owe you an explanation about why I overreacted." She crossed her arms over her chest. "And frankly, you still owe me one about why you were late." She was eyeing him warily as he mirrored her stance, crossing his own arms and holding her gaze. "The ice is melting. We should take it upstairs," she said.

"We should," Dave agreed. "But we won't. Not yet." He stood firm and tall, looking at her defiantly.

Jill was not used to anyone telling her what to do. She made a move to gather the ice buckets, then quickly set them back down, surrendering under their weight. "*I* would not have filled these to the top," she said, glaring at Dave. "They're too full and heavy for me."

"Jill," he said patiently, "I've got the ice. Talk to me."

She was reluctant to share such personal information with Dave, but she had felt a connection with him from the moment they'd met. *Am I ready to be vulnerable again?* Jill asked herself.

"Okay, Mr. Baseball," she said with a drop of sarcasm, using her brother's moniker for Dave again. "I dated a guy named Stephen Conrad all through college. He was, well, *is* an attorney at a large firm in Dallas. He asked me to marry him shortly after I graduated from Southern Methodist University. I had a degree in broadcast journalism and planned on pursuing a career in television. I'd interned at a local station in Dallas. Once I graduated, I landed an anchor job, hosting a weekly show called *Texans Helping Texans*." She stopped talking and gazed up again at the sky, lost in telling the story. "It was an amazing opportunity that had me traveling around the state. It was so rewarding interviewing people who work at shelters, food banks and outreach centers. A lot of these folks are volunteers, and their stories are so moving. The show helped draw awareness to these awesome places and support came pouring in from around Texas. It was an exciting time."

Jill smiled sadly and looked away for a moment. "Stephen had a hard time with my being gone so often. He also had a hard time keeping his word, and I caught him in several lies. The man was so busy trying to make partner in his father's firm, he was constantly canceling on me at the last minute. There were even a couple of times when he flat out stood me up." She stopped to collect her thoughts. "I tried to be understanding about his unreliability and tolerated it for much longer than I should have. Everyone told me we made the perfect couple." Jill took a moment to consider what she'd just said and let out a snort of laughter. Embarrassed, she gave Dave a sheepish smile. "I'm sorry about that! I tend to snort whenever I find something extremely funny. I know it's very unattractive."

Dave had a hard time not cracking a smile. It endeared her to him that such a lovely woman could make a sound so unladylike.

"Tell me more," he encouraged. "I want to hear it."

Jill continued, "I felt strongly about the charities *Texans Helping Texans* supported. My heart was closest to the battered women's shelters. The last Christmas I was in Dallas, the news station I worked for had organized a huge ball benefitting three of these organizations. Stephen knew how important they were to me, and he stepped up to the plate." She shot Dave an impish grin. "Sorry, no baseball pun intended!"

At this, Dave gave her a small smile. "Go on," he said.

"Well, Stephen promised me that his father's firm would underwrite the entire cost of the benefit and we'd have enough funds left to buy Christmas gifts for the children. Needless to say, I was ecstatic! It was a dream come true," she told him, her face suddenly becoming troubled.

Dave watched as Jill looked down and kicked the dirt with the toe of one sparkly boot. "Let me guess," he suggested dryly, "your fiancé didn't come through with his promise."

Ex-fiancé!" she stressed, and Dave could hear the pain in her voice. "After weeks of assuring me we'd have the money, he called two days before the gala and told me that he'd misspoken and the firm was unable to underwrite the event. Two days before!"

Dave could see that telling the story brought back painful memories for Jill. Reaching over to gently touch her arm, he said, "I'm so sorry. That must have been devastating for you."

He was taken aback as Jill straightened and stood even taller. "It might have been devastating for any other person," she told him matter-of-factly, "but not for a Murray. I know I can always count on my family. I called Mike. He and Gran dropped what they were doing and came to Dallas to help. We worked together, pretty much around the clock, and were able to pull the gala off without a hitch! The event was a huge success, and most importantly, there were Christmas gifts for every child and all the moms."

"That's really awesome that your family stepped in to help," Dave said.

Jill smiled at him, but there were tears in her eyes as she finished the story. "I wanted to do something on my own. Something independent of all of this," she said motioning around the ranch. "But it wasn't meant to be, and maybe it was for the best. I gave Stephen his ring back, quit my job and moved back to Wind River where I belong."

She'd no more than finished the last sentence when she felt Dave's strong arms around her. "Thank you for sharing all of that with me, Jill," he said, tenderly into her ear.

For a moment, Dave thought she might be sobbing into his chest as he felt her firm body quaking against his own. Dave wasn't sure he wanted to hear the answer, but felt he needed to know. He asked softly, "So, are you still in love with him, Jill? Is that why you're crying?"

She pulled away and looked up at him. "I didn't realize I was crying, but if I was, it's because I get emotional when I think of my love for my family. I'm also very grateful that I broke it off with Stephen. We really didn't belong together. You probably just felt me laughing with relief!"

Dave felt a wave of relief of his own that she wasn't hung up on her ex. He studied her face. *She is breathtakingly beautiful,* he thought. "I'd like to get to know you better, Jill," he said.

She was silent for a moment, regarding him thoughtfully, then smiled and said, "Wow, well, all right. I know I've been all over the place emotionally tonight, Dave, but I'm not a hard person to figure out. As I've told you, my family means everything to me. I'm stubborn and outspoken, but I'm honest and always strive to do my best. I love horses and dogs. I work hard, and I play hard." She stopped to take a quick breath, and added, "Oh, and I love to laugh and have fun! That about sums me up!"

Dave had been listening intently, loving that Jill hadn't moved away from him. Seeing that she was waiting for his response, he cocked his head and raised one quizzical brow.

"What?" she asked with a giggle. "Too dramatic for you?"

"No, you're not too dramatic at all," he replied, reaching over to stroke her hair. "It's just that you left out one of your best qualities."

"Oh? And what might that be, Mr. Wilder?"

"You snort when you laugh!" Dave deadpanned. His remark had them both laughing. "I love the way you laugh, Jill, especially your little giggle. It's adorable."

Jill smiled then suddenly thought about how long they'd been gone. "We'd better get back, or my big, bad brother will come looking for us," she said with a roll of her eyes. "Mike is very protective of his family."

Dave quickly gathered the ice buckets. "Well, I wouldn't want the Dragon Master of Ceremonies after me," he replied with a grin.

Jill agreed. "Ah, so you noticed his new tuxedo?" she asked, giggling again. "For sure, I wouldn't put anything past a guy who has flames on his sleeves!"

Dave could hear the affection for her brother in Jill's voice. "I think it's great that your family is so close," he said.

"Yes, we're very blessed," she said.

Wanting her to keep talking, he continued, "Ian told me that Mike saved your life after you were bitten by a water moccasin."

"Yes, but that's another story for another day. Suffice it to say that Mike and I are beyond close. Ever since our parents died, we've been each other's rock."

"You don't need to explain it to me, Jill. It must be great to know you have someone who always has your back. I envy you that," Dave said. He added reflectively, "I had someone like that once, but it turned out that he didn't have my back ... he had a knife in it."

They'd reached the stairs to the loft, and Jill knew they should head up with the ice, but she really wanted Dave to elaborate on his comment. "Tell me more," she prodded. "I'd like to get to know *you* better!"

For a moment, Dave looked uncomfortable. Then, with a grin, he started up the stairs with the heavy buckets. He glanced casually back over his shoulder and said, "*That, Jill* is another story for another day. Come on! We're missing out on all the fun!"

She followed Dave and showed him where the caterers were storing ice. He shot her a bemused look when he took stock of the abundant amount of ice already in the bin. He'd had a hunch that Gran had sent Jill and him on an unnecessary errand, but he was grateful for it. He was also thankful the older woman seemed to be encouraging her granddaughter to spend time with him.

Jill touched his arm lightly. "Let's grab some food and then sneak over to the kids' side of the loft," she said. "I see a couple of empty hay bales at the back of the room."

"That's a great idea," Dave agreed. "The kids look like they're having way more fun than the grown-ups!"

The two filled their plates from the buffet. "This all looks and smells delicious," Dave said. "What a spread! How about you take our plates and I'll get us something to drink," he suggested, his eyes surveying the beverage options. "Would you like tea or punch?"

"I'll have iced tea," she replied with a giggle. "Looks like we have plenty of ice." Jill gave him a playful wink as she took his plate and headed toward the children.

Juggling both plates, Jill chose a hay bale furthest from the stage. She didn't want to be a distraction for the kids who were intently listening to Mike sharing one of his tall tales. It was one of her favorites about a cowboy who got lost on the range after he'd gone after a stray calf. She remembered her grandfather telling them the story when she and her brother were young.

Mike has granddad's gift for storytelling, she thought, listening to her brother's deep voice rise and fall in intensity. He was animated, using his entire body for an even more dramatic delivery. She could hear the steady hum of adult conversation across the loft, but the children were quiet, totally immersed in the tale.

Jill had barely sat down on a hay bale when Roger moved in beside her. He leaned in closely so as not to interrupt the story, and said, "Now, *that's* a man with a gift! Anyone who can keep a room full of rowdy kids quiet for this long deserves an award!"

Jill nodded. "Mike's like our grandfather. He could always spin a yarn," she said quietly, then added, "Roger, Dave's on his way over. I've got his plate here." She looked down at the plates in her hands and back at him and smiled. She was trying to be polite, hoping to avoid an awkward situation.

Roger frowned and rose slowly to his feet. "I just wanted to come over and visit with you for a minute, Jill. You know I've been wanting to talk with you for days, and you keep putting me off," he accused.

He'd raised his voice a degree and Jill held up her hand, shushing him with a stern look. "Roger, I'm not putting you off," she whispered. "I just don't think you and I have anything we need to talk about."

"Everything okay here?" Jill heard Dave's voice behind Roger.

"Oh, *everything's* just great, *David,*" Roger said before angrily walking off.

Dave sat down on the hay bale in the spot Roger had vacated. Without a word, he placed their drinks on the wooden floor and took his plate from Jill. They ate in silence, listening to Mike wrap up the story. When her brother was finished, he took a bow and the children went wild, clapping and jumping up and down, asking him to tell them another one.

"I want to hear another one, too!" Dave said to Jill. "Your brother is great at this. Where does he get his material?"

"These tall tales have been passed down from one generation to the next, and they're an important part of American folklore," Jill answered. "Some date back to when early frontiersmen swapped stories; others are actually based on real events. They've just been embellished with unbelievable feats. That's what makes them so much fun!"

"He really brings the tale to life and makes it's easy to picture it in your head."

"The mark of an exceptional orator," she noted with pride. "There are even tall tale competitions. Mike's never entered one. He just enjoys performing them for the kids."

They watched as her brother continued the show. "I know you guys want to hear another story," he said, "and I had a special one that I wanted to tell you..." He let his voice trail off as if he were too sad to continue. Shaking his head, he explained, "I can't tell it. I mean I know it's Halloween, but the tale is just too scary."

What a drama king! Jill thought, thoroughly amused. She knew Mike was going to tell the story and that he was just building suspense. *He is so good. I've heard these tales a hundred times and I want to hear them again!*

The children cried out their assurances they could handle a scary story and begged him to begin. "All right, okay, I'll tell it to ya, but you guys are probably gonna have to sleep with the lights on tonight. It's pretty intense," he told the crowd. Mike grabbed the stool from behind him and took a seat. His eyes roamed across the children, watching as they settled down to listen. He nearly went out of character and smiled when he saw his two fairy princess daughters huddled tightly together in anticipation.

He waited until the room was completely silent. Then he began in his melodic baritone voice, "You see, many years ago when early settlers came to Texas, there was a large population of bears roaming these very hills." Mike paused and motioned with his arms, indicating the environment around him. He continued, "Now these bears were a threat to the settlers who were trying to raise cattle."

"This isn't a scary story!" interrupted one of Jeremy's friends. "It's just a story about bears." Some of the older boys nodded in agreement.

Mike let out a sinister chuckle. "Ah, you boys need to be patient. This is *not* a regular bear story. In fact, I didn't want to spook anyone right off the bat. But I'm going to tell you the name of this story is... The Ghost Bear. And it happened to my great-great-great-grandfather, so I know it's true."

He held up his hand, demanding silence. "Now, if I may continue?" Mike looked sternly at the boys and when they immediately grew quiet, he began again, "It was a dark, windy night..."

Jill listened intently as her brother shared the tale of a ghostly grizzly that stood twice as tall as their historic relative. The giant beast would appear only at night. Mike described in detail the bear's eerie glow, its long, yellow fangs, and gleaming eyes. At one point, when her brother imitated the bear's mighty roar, she nearly jumped off the hay bale.

Jill looked over at Dave who was totally enthralled with the tale, and noticed that he, too, had been startled by Mike's unexpected roar. She snickered, and Dave reached over and patted her leg. "*That* was a little intense!" he whispered.

Jill nodded in agreement, disappointed when he removed his hand. *I tingle at his touch*, she thought.

Some of the adults had come over to listen to the story and oohed and ahhed along with the kids. Mike was standing now, creating quite a stir as he masterfully brought the tale to its powerful conclusion. This was where his great-great-great grandfather galloped up on his horse behind the Ghost Bear, swiftly lassoing it around the neck, dropping the huge beast over a cliff.

"After that, the Ghost Bear was never seen around these parts again," he said. "Except there are some nights when the moon is full, and there's just a bit of chill in the air, you can hear his mighty roar echoing through these canyons." And with that, the storyteller gave one last bear roar, so loud it bounced off the rafters and throughout the loft.

Children and adults all went nuts, clapping, and shouting their appreciation. Jill noticed that her brother almost looked a little bashful at all the attention and applause. Their eyes met across the room, and she beamed at him proudly. "Bravo!" she shouted. "Bravo!"

When order had been restored once more, Mike suggested that everyone return to their seats and invited the adults to grab their chairs and join in the fun. It took a few moments to get everyone settled again.

"What's next?" Dave asked Jill. He'd gone to dispose of their plates, returning with more drinks and a couple of brownies from the dessert table.

"I have no idea what he's up to," she replied. "My brother is nothing if not spontaneous."

They returned their attention to the Master of Ceremonies. "I have it on good authority that we have a new talent tonight for Halloween in the Loft. I spoke with this young man earlier and he told me that he would be pleased to share a couple of jokes and do some of his impersonations with you. And so, without further *adieu*, please join me in welcoming Mr. Ian Wilder!"

Dave and Jill looked at each other in surprise. "You didn't know about this?" he asked.

Jill shook her head. "Jeremy told us that Ian was great with impressions. He's been doing them at school for the other kids. I can't wait to see them!"

"Well, that makes two of us!" Dave exclaimed, pulling out his cell phone to record Ian's performance.

Mike reached out a hand and pulled Ian up onto the stage. He lowered the microphone then backed away to let the boy do his thing. Ian appeared completely at ease in the spotlight. He told a few jokes and already had the crowd in the palm of his hand when he asked if they'd like to hear a few impressions. The audience clapped and cheered.

Ian performed several impersonations of well-known singers and actors. He also mimicked someone trying to get on a horse for the first time and a football jock waiting to see if he'd passed his math test so he could play in the Friday night game. His body language and voice inflections were spot-on.

Dave had moved to the front of the stage for a better vantage point. *I bet he's so proud of Ian*, Jill thought. *I know I am!*

"And last, but certainly not least, I would like to do one more for you," Ian told the crowd, then he looked over at Mike. "With your permission, Mr. Murray, I'd like to do my impersonation of you."

Blown away by the boy's skill, Mike had moved to sit with the rest of the audience. "What? *Me?*" he asked, pointing to his chest and laughing good-naturedly. "Well, all right, kid! Let's see what you've got!"

Ian smiled back at Mike and said, "Thank you for being a good sport! Oh, and I'll need your top hat, please."

The tall black hat was passed to Ian, who quickly stuck it on his small head. It was far too large and he had to push it back so it wouldn't cover his eyes.

Although his voice wasn't nearly as deep as Mike's, Ian copied the man's mannerisms and vocabulary perfectly. He mimicked the same grand, sweeping motions the Master of Ceremonies had used earlier. He also mentioned Wind River Ranch, including the dogs and horses.

Jill was moved by Ian's impression of her brother. He'd captured Mike's big personality to the letter, poking fun at him without a hint of disrespect. If anything, the performance had been a tribute to the man who'd carried him down the hill the day when fate had brought them all together.

When Ian finished, he removed Mike's top hat and took a bow. The crowd was on their feet applauding and shouting for more.

Mike returned to the stage and gave Ian a bow of his own. "Ladies and gentlemen! The amazing Ian Wilder!" he shouted.

"Wow! You're a fantastic showman!" Mike exclaimed, smiling down at the boy.

"Thanks, everyone for coming out tonight! Thanks to my lovely wife Gina and my awesome sister Jill. Most of all, I'd like to thank my incredible grandmother, Mrs. Jennifer Murray, for everything. Now, ya'll grab some more food if you're still hungry and there are gift bags for everyone on your way out. Happy Halloween in the Loft from the entire Murray family to yours! We bid you goodnight!"

CHAPTER 10

The last of the guests slowly trickled out of the barn, thanking the Murrays and saying goodnight. Several people remarked about the awesome food and decorations, but overall, everyone was wowed by Ian's performance.

Dave, standing next to Jill and Mike at the door, accepted their praise on his son's behalf.

"Ian should have hung around and said goodnight to these folks," Mike said. "He would be eating this up!"

"Well, we wouldn't want all this attention going to his head!" Dave replied, laughing. "Plus, I know Ian was more interested in hanging out with Jeremy and the other kids in the house." He paused for a moment, then continued, "You know, Ian's always been great at telling jokes and mimicking people, but I had no idea how talented he's become! I was amazed by what he did tonight."

"He's a natural entertainer," Mike agreed.

"He sure had *you* nailed, Bro!" Jill teased, then she went into her own impersonation of Mike, speaking in her deepest voice, "I've gotta get them there horses out to the back pasture and clean them barns. Eew, what is this? I got horse hockey on my boot!"

Watching the two cracking up, Mike feigned offense, then joined in the laughter.

"Jill, that was almost as bad as your pirate impersonation!" Dave remarked.

"Oh, gosh!" Mike exclaimed, acting very alarmed. "*Not her pirate impression!* I'm so sorry, Dave. No one should be subjected to that kind of torture!" He turned to his sister. "You should leave the performing to the *true* professionals," he told her with an arrogant air.

"Seriously, Mike, thanks for having Ian come up on stage with you tonight. I know it will do wonders for his confidence and he really needs that right now," Dave said appreciatively.

"Well, you're welcome, Dave," Mike replied. "When Jeremy told us how funny Ian is, I thought it would be a good idea. Jeremy asked Ian if he would be comfortable doing it and your son jumped at the offer. He only had a couple of days to prepare his material. I couldn't believe how good he is! You may have a future celebrity on your hands."

"If I know Ian, he's already thinking about what he'll do for next year's Halloween in the Loft!" Dave predicted.

"I'm definitely going to suggest that he includes an impression of Jill next time. Now, *that* would be hilarious!" With that, Mike began doing an impression of his sister, tossing imaginary long hair over his shoulder and saying in a high voice, "I have no idea which pair of boots I want to wear today! Hmm, what do you think, Simon? Should I go sporty cowgirl or sparkly cowgirl?" He tapped his forefinger against his chin as if considering his options.

Jill punched him in the shoulder playfully. "I *do not* rely on my dog to help me choose my footwear," she said defensively. Then she continued with a sly smile, "I *do*, however, trust Simon implicitly when it comes to selecting the right horse for me to race against my brother. You remember, Mike, who won the Travis Cup, right?"

Mike shook his head in chagrin but had the grace to admit she'd bested him in the race. "I didn't know it was Simon who'd tipped you off!" he said, scratching his head thoughtfully. "Next year I'm going to have that dog advise *me*. No way you're winning two years in a row!"

"Ian mentioned something about a race between you two," Dave remarked. "He thought that was pretty cool." He looked admiringly at Jill and added, "He was really impressed that you'd beaten your big brother. What *is* the Travis Cup anyway?"

"A one-hundred-mile-long endurance competition. It's a grueling race for both horse and rider," Mike replied for her. "Ian's right to be impressed by Jill. She's an exceptional equestrienne who's won many competitions," he boasted proudly. "She totally dominated The Travis Cup this year."

Embarrassed by the sudden attention, Jill decided to change the subject. "I think everyone's gone now, shall we head over to the house?"

"Let's do it," Mike agreed. "I see a cold beer in my future, plus I'm ready to get out of this tux!"

"Aw, is it time to put the Dragon Suit away for another year?" Jill chided. "I sure hate to think that such a unique piece of art will be stowed away until next October."

"Well, if you're nice to me I'll wear it for you on your birthday, Sis," Mike assured her. "If you love it *that* much, I'd hate to deprive you of its awesomeness!"

They were all laughing again as they left the barn and walked toward the house. "Where did you even find that tux?" Dave asked Mike. "It's pretty radical!"

"I know, *right*? I had it made and picked it up last time I was in Austin," he answered, adding, "You can't find a garment of this quality off the rack, you know."

Jill rolled her eyes and shook her head. "And you accused Gran and me of going over the top for Halloween in the Loft! Face it, Mike, you're still just a big kid at heart!"

Mike continued to chuckle and replied, "You're probably right about that!"

When they got to the house, Mike went to change clothes and check on his family and Jill led Dave to the great room. "I know Mike said he was going to have a beer, but I'm going to have a glass of wine. We also have soda and water. Which would you prefer?" she asked, moving to the large bar.

"I'll have whatever you're having, please," Dave replied.

He was admiring a large sculpture of a galloping horse. The bronze was cool to his touch as he lightly stroked its flowing mane. "This is a really incredible piece of art," he said.

"I adore that sculpture. My father commissioned a local artist to create it. You can tell it's an Arabian by its wedge-shaped head and small muzzle," Jill explained, coming to stand beside Dave. She looked at him and smiled. Seeing he was interested in hearing more, she continued, "Arabians are actually the oldest breed of horses, dating back to over four thousand years ago. Ancient Egyptians used them in battle to pull their chariots."

She'd set their wine glasses down and ran her hand along the piece, lost in thought as she spoke. "His big eyes, broad forehead, and large nostrils also help to identify him as an Arabian." Dave noticed her long, elegant fingers lovingly tracing the horse's facial features. "See this slight bulge on his forehead?" she asked.

Seeing him nod, she went on, "It adds sinus capacity, which served these horses well in their native desert climate." Jill noted the horse's arched neck and flowing mane. "Arabians often run with their heads raised high so they can breathe deeply through their wide, open nostrils." She lightly touched the horse's nose. "It was for this reason they were called 'Drinkers of the Wind.' It's said that Arabian horses draw their speed, strength, and courage from the wind from which they were created."

Ending her explanation, Jill looked up at Dave apologetically. "I'm rambling. Sorry about that, but I'm very passionate about horses. I could go on and on," she said dreamily. "Arabians have always been a huge part of our lives."

"Please don't apologize," he said. "I'm fascinated by what you told me. I'd love to learn more."

His words thrilled her. "Well, if you hang around here long enough you'll learn a lot about horses," she assured him, handing him the wine.

"I look forward to that," Dave told her with a smile. He held up his glass. "Cheers!" he toasted.

"Cheers!" Jill repeated as they clinked their glasses softly together, and each took a sip.

"What do you think? It's a red blend, one I really enjoy," she said, watching his reaction.

"It's very good," replied Dave. "Of course, I don't know a lot about wine."

Jill smiled. "The grapes were actually grown here," she explained. "We have a small winery on the property. It's down the road a ways.

There are many wineries in the Hill Country now. They've become quite a tourist attraction for this area."

"I guess you and your family will have to give me an education in horses *and* wine!" Dave then added laughingly, "And to think I was worried about being bored after baseball!"

"Trust me; there's never time to be bored around here!" Jill said, warmly.

Dave looked around the room. "There's no television in here," he observed.

"Oh, Gran doesn't believe in watching television except on special occasions. She says when people are together, they should be totally engaged with one another," Jill told him.

She hesitated, then said, "We do have a television in the den. Is there something you want to watch?"

Just you. I could watch you all day. The thought popped into his head unexpectedly. *This is crazy! The longer I'm around this woman, the more attracted to her I become!*

"No, actually I seldom watch TV myself," he shared. He took a sip of wine and gave her a boyish grin. "Except for sports, that is!"

"Shall we sit?" Jill invited.

"Lead the way," he replied, motioning for her to choose a spot.

Despite the mild temperature outside, a fire had been lit, adding to the coziness of the room. Jill eased comfortably into one of the oversized leather chairs in front of the fire and put her feet up on the ottoman. Dave did the same in the chair next to her. "Should I take my boots off?" he asked politely. "My mom would kill me if she saw me with my boots on the furniture! But then again, I don't think my mother's ever even seen me wear boots…" His voice trailed off as he tried to remember if she had.

Jill laughed and said, "No, Gran wants people to relax and be comfortable here. You can keep them on."

Dave looked down at her sparkly feet. "Those are some pretty spiffy boots you're wearing," he observed. "Party boots?"

"Definitely party boots." Jill confessed, "I have a sizable boot collection. Collecting them is sort of a hobby of mine."

He grinned at her. "Ah, you have another hobby! Define "*sizable collection*," Dave demanded, one eyebrow raised.

Jill looked a little guilty. "About two hundred," she admitted.

"*What?* Do you mean two hundred boots total or two hundred *pairs* of boots?" he asked in disbelief.

She gave him a smirk and said, "Two hundred pairs. Now, don't start in on me. I've been collecting them for years. Some of the boots even belonged to my mother. I'm lucky we share the same shoe size, a perfect ten."

Dave whistled softly through his teeth. "A perfect ten," he repeated, meeting her eyes.

She mistakenly thought he was making fun of the size of her feet.

"Hey you," she said, whacking him with her hand. "I'm a tall girl. We tall girls can't have tiny little feet. They wouldn't hold us up very well!"

"Ow!" Dave winced playfully. "That hurt! I wasn't making fun of you. I like that you're tall and I like your big feet! Oh, sorry, I meant your *proportionately-sized* feet." He smiled at her sweetly. "I was trying to give you a compliment. I concur that you are a perfect ten. It's easy to see why Roger has been chasing you all these years."

Jill blushed and turned away. She'd only had a couple of sips of wine, yet she felt giddy.

"Hey, hey, hey," Mike bellowed as he, Gina and Gran entered the room. "Would you two like some company or would you prefer to be aloooooone?" He emphasized the last word, giving it a spooky effect.

Dave stood. "I should probably collect Ian and get going," he said, looking at his watch. "It's getting late."

"Nonsense, Dave," Gran assured him. "Sit and relax. The boys are playing video games in Jeremy's room. They're having a good time, and there's no school tomorrow. We were hoping that maybe Ian could spend the night? You can fetch him in the morning after you join us for breakfast. How does that sound?"

"I bet Ian would love that. Thank you, Mrs. Murray," Dave replied, then frowned. "But I didn't bring any of his things over. Maybe we should do it another time?"

Mike intervened, saying, "We've got everything he needs here, Dave. Your boy will be fine."

"And, Dave, please call me Gran Jen," Gran requested with a smile.

Dave beamed at the older woman. "All right, thank you, I will."

He returned to his seat next to Jill while the others prepared their drinks, but politely rose to his feet again as Gran and Gina chose their spots.

"You have lovely manners, dear," Gran told him. "Your mother taught you well."

Dave waited until the ladies had settled then explained, "My mother is an incredible woman, but it was my father who set the example for me. He taught me to always put God first, family second and myself third. He said if I did that, my life would be happy."

"And has it been happy?" Gran asked. Dave noticed that the woman's eyes were the same-steel blue as Jill's. They seemed to see right through him, piercing in to find the truth.

"It's been...well, it's had ups and downs," Dave replied. "But for the most part, it's been incredible. I had a successful career playing a sport I love. I've traveled the world, and I've met many interesting people. Of course, being with Ian is what makes me the happiest. All of that other stuff takes a backseat to spending time with my son."

Mike raised his beer high. "Here's to family!" he toasted.

"To family!" everyone echoed in response, lifting their glasses.

Dave felt as if he should share a little more about himself. "Like everyone else, I've had some rough times. Most of my downs have been due to bad decisions I've made along the way."

"We all make bad choices from time to time," Gran assured him. "If we learn from them, it helps build our character." She chuckled softly in an effort to keep the mood light. "Mike, do you remember when you were courting Gina, and you rode over to her family's place on that black horse?"

"Yes, Gran, and for your information, nobody calls it 'courting' anymore," he said, reaching over to give his grandmother a loving pat on the arm. "And it wasn't just a *horse*. Lightning was a *stallion!*" Mike insisted with a grin. "I was a daring knight on a midnight mission to woo my love into saying yes to my marriage proposal!"

"And daddy almost shot you!" Gina said, picking up the story and turning to Dave. "You see, my father didn't know that it was Mike who came galloping up to our house in the middle of the night. All of our dogs were barking like crazy, sounding the alarm that we had an intruder. By the time I got downstairs, my father was on the front porch with his shotgun aimed at my would-be knight in shining armor!"

"Okay, all right, now, let's back up the story a bit," Mike interjected. "In my defense, I'd been at their house earlier that day and asked her father's permission to marry Gina. Fortunately, he said yes." Mike looked lovingly at his wife. "Next, I knew I had to make my proposal really special so she would say yes, too. My plan was to ride in and toss a couple of pebbles up on her window. Gina was supposed to throw open the window and see me on bended knee, professing my undying love for her, then asking for her hand in marriage. It *could* have been very romantic."

Gina jumped in again to finish the story. "It was still very romantic! Granted, it might have been a little more so if Mike had remembered to let my father in on his plan," she said with a grin. "Daddy finally realized who our midnight caller was and put the shotgun down." She looked at Mike. "I still got the proposal on bended knee. It was still very sweet and I still said yes." She leaned over and gave him a quick kiss on the cheek. "You know I love you and loved that you rode in on a horse to sweep me off my feet!"

"Thanks, babe," Mike cooed back. "But again, it wasn't a horse; Lightning was a *stallion.*"

This brought more laughter from the room, but Gran wasn't finished yet. "Jill, do you remember when you thought it would be a good idea to rescue one hundred dogs in one hundred days?"

"Ugh, Gran! Please don't tell that one!" Jill begged.

"Oh yes, Gran. I think Dave would like to hear *that* one!" Mike said, happy to have the attention focused on someone else. He'd scooted even closer to Gina, nestling in for the story.

Gran delighted in telling about the time young Jill had gone on a mission to rescue one hundred homeless dogs in as many days. "You see, this was before the Internet, so it was much harder for her to get the word out," Gran explained. "She worked for hours making posters. I drove her around the county, putting them up for the cause."

"I just felt sorry for all the homeless dogs!" Jill cried. "I wanted them to have a voice. Dogs should have a voice," she said firmly.

Dave smiled at her encouragingly. "It sounds like a great campaign," he said.

Gran continued, "Well, we'd put the ranch's phone number on the posters, and before we knew it; we started getting calls about dogs."

"*Correction*, my dear grandmother," Mike interjected. "Jill put the address to the ranch on the posters and we started getting donations delivered here. And when I say donations, I mean *dog* donations. We had a steady stream of vehicles coming up the drive. People were dropping off their unwanted pooches by the truckload," he said. "I've never seen so many dogs in all my life!"

"They were all so cute!" Jill exclaimed. "One Hundred Dogs in One Hundred Days was about finding them all loving homes. I had no idea it was going to blow up like it did!" She looked at her grandmother with love. "Thanks, Gran, for not turning any of them away."

Her grandmother laughed. "I had no choice, Jill! Those people dumped their dogs on us and scooted out of here in the bat of an eye! It was *your* compassion and kindness that made me see how important it was to help them." Gran paused and looked over at Dave. "Because of Jill's One Hundred Dogs in One Hundred Days campaign, we built a shelter in Dripping Springs. It's a no-kill facility with state-of-the-art equipment. We have a team of trained employees and a full-time vet on staff. There are also volunteer opportunities for people who want to help."

"It's a very special place," Jill agreed. "I spend a lot of time over there."

"I'd like to take Ian sometime," Dave said. "I think I mentioned to you all that he's been begging for a dog for a long time." His voice faltered, as he continued, "Of course, before he gets a pet, I need to make sure he wants to stay here in Texas with me. If he still wants to go back to his mother in Arizona, I may end up moving back there, too. I've decided I'll do whatever I need to do to be a part of my son's life. I've missed enough of it already."

CHAPTER 11

That night, Jill had a hard time falling to sleep. She couldn't stop thinking about how much she'd enjoyed being around Dave. *I love his great sense of humor*, she thought. *He obviously adores his son, and he challenges me to open up about my past.* She knew there was a lot more to learn about the man, feeling that he now knew a lot more about her than she did about him. *I'm definitely going to remedy that the next time we're together.*

Jill thought about how the evening had ended. It had been around ten when Dave noticed Gran stifling frequent yawns and had taken that as his cue to leave. He'd asked Mike to show him to Jeremy's room so he could tell Ian goodnight. After he and Mike left the room, Gran bid her goodnights and headed off to bed, leaving Gina and Jill alone.

"Oh my gosh! *That man!*" gushed Gina. "He's the perfect package! Great-looking, awesome manners, and he's probably loaded from his baseball days. You're a lucky girl, Jill! What are the odds you'd meet someone like Dave out here in the sticks?"

"Gina, get a grip already! And please don't forget that you're married to my brother, so it makes me uncomfortable to have you carrying on about how hot some other man is!" Jill reprimanded. "Also, I'm not interested in his money. Nor do I *need his money*. You know that."

Gina looked repentant. "I'm sorry, Jill. Of course you're not pursuing the guy for his money! I don't know why I said that."

"*Pursuing him?*" Jill took great offense at Gina's words. "I've never *pursued* a man in my life. I've never had to." Because she'd felt insulted, she spoke more arrogantly than she meant to and silently regretted it. *Have I been pursuing Dave?*" she asked herself.

Realizing she'd hit a nerve, Gina quickly apologized again. "I'm not saying the right things at all tonight!" she said, contritely. "I'm really sorry! I know you've never had to pursue a man. All our lives the guys have been gaga over you. Look at you, you're beautiful inside and out! What I *meant* was, if something works out between you and Dave, it won't be for your money." She gave Jill a pleading look. "Do you forgive me?"

"Come and give me a hug, you hopeless romantic! Geez, I just met the man," said Jill. She'd already stood up, waiting for Gina to come over to her. "I love you, too. Maybe we're both just a little punchy tonight. It's been a long day. I'm gonna call it a night."

Not willing to let the conversation end on a negative note, Gina insisted on making her admit one thing. "All right, Jill, but before you go, can we at least agree that Dave Wilder is one fine specimen of a man?"

Jill looked the determined redhead up and down. Gina had her hands on her hips and was tapping the floor with one foot, impatiently awaiting an answer.

Jill shook her head, defeated. "Yes, Gina, we can agree that Dave Wilder is one fine specimen of a man!"

She was exiting the room when she heard her sister-in-law give a whoop of joy and clap her hands together. "I knew it!" Jill heard her exclaim.

Sunday morning arrived, and Mike joined Jill and Simon for coffee on the porch. "That was a blast last night," he said. "Not sure we can top it next year."

Jill rocked slowly back and forth. There was a slight chill in the air, and she was glad she'd worn a soft fleece pullover. "It was a lot of fun. I guess we'll see about next year when we get there," she replied distractedly.

They both sat quietly for a few moments before Mike said, "Penny for your thoughts."

Jill regarded him with a sad smile. "That was one of granddad's favorite sayings. He always wanted to know what we were thinking. I sure miss him," she said, her eyes on the sun peeking out over the horizon. "Remember how the three of us would meet out here in the summertime to watch the sunrise?"

Mike nodded. "We've shared many a sunrise together, Sis. He nodded his head to the east and said, "This one looks like it's going to be spectacular."

They watched as the sun made its slow ascent over the hillside, a magnificent splay of colors shot out from around the scattered clouds. The sky turned amazing shades of pink and lavender before gradually evolving to a brilliant orange-red.

Neither of them spoke for the time it took for dawn to transition into the day. No words were necessary as the siblings' chairs rocked in unison.

Finally, Jill broke the silence. "I don't think there's anything more beautiful than a Hill Country sunrise." Mike noticed she had a tear in one eye and knew it was because his sister was so moved by the beauty of what she saw.

"I'm with you on that, Jill," he agreed.

"I'm thinking about getting a good workout in before breakfast," she said, glancing at her watch. "Care to join me? We've got a lot of time before Dave comes to pick up Ian."

Mike leaned over to set his empty cup on the railing. "Yeah, that sounds like a good idea. I know neither of us had time to hit the gym yesterday with everything we had going on. But let's sit here for another few moments and just chillax," he suggested.

Simon, who'd been sleeping beside Jill's chair, grew suddenly alert. His big ears pointed straight up as he stood, then quickly bounded off the porch. He raced across the deck and soared over the lawn.

Jill and Mike looked at each other and laughed. "Squirrel!" they said in unison.

"I'm so glad that he rarely catches the poor creatures," she said, shaking her head.

Mike shrugged. "I don't know; maybe we could have some fried squirrel with our pancakes this morning! What do you think Dave would say about that?"

"I know what *I'd* think about it, eeeew!" Jill eyed him suspiciously and asked, "How should *I* know what Dave would think?"

"Come on, Sis," Mike replied. "We all see the way you look at him. Admit it, you're smitten with him." He gave Jill's leg a playful shove and shot her a devilish grin. "I know Gina and Gran are, too. Dave seems like a pretty special guy." He added gently, "Maybe he's the one for you."

"Mike!" she exclaimed. "I'm sure Gina told you that she got me to agree that I thought Dave was, um ..." She hesitated, unable to tell her brother that his wife had referred to another guy as 'one hot specimen of a man.' Instead, she said, "Gina got me to admit that he was good-looking."

Mike shot Jill a sideways smirk, and she knew Gina must have shared the details of their conversation.

Jill gave an exasperated sigh. "Let's just remember what he told us last night. If Ian decides to live with his mom; Dave will be moving back to Arizona. I don't want to get too close to him, then have him leave. He made it very clear that his priority is his son and I'm not going to muddy the waters by getting involved with the guy."

Mike didn't respond for a moment, then said kindly, "Now I understand why you've been so pensive this morning. I get it, and you're right. I don't want to see you get your heart broken. I'll back off on the matchmaking," he promised, air-drawing an X over his heart with his forefinger. "I promise." He stood, and they watched as Simon came trotting back to the porch.

"Well, I guess no fried squirrel for breakfast today!" Mike said, noting that the shepherd had returned without his prey.

"That's just as well," Jill replied. "I'll see you in the gym in twenty minutes."

The siblings worked out regularly in the family's home gym. The room was a large addition their grandparents had built to help their grandchildren train for the various disciplines in which they competed. The space was designed and furnished by a prominent fitness firm and had the look and feel of a high-end sports club.

In addition to several large pieces of fitness equipment and free weights, the well-appointed gym also featured a steam room and dry sauna. Three of the walls were mirrored, making the room appear even larger than it actually was. One wall was floor-to-ceiling windows with a view of the family's stunning pool and outdoor living area.

Mike was warming up on one of the treadmills when Jill walked into the room. She filled her water bottle from the dispenser in the corner and climbed on an elliptical trainer not far from him.

The two said little to one another as they worked out. Each wore headphones and enjoyed listening to music while they went about their routines. It wasn't until they were spotting for each other with the barbells that Mike finally spoke. "You know, if we gave Ian one of Simon's new pups, he'd have a great dog and another reason to stay with his dad."

Jill had been about to lift the weighted bar when she quickly sat up and pointed an accusing finger at her brother. "Mike Murray, now you listen! I won't have you meddling in this situation. I know your heart is in the right place, but you just promised me you'd butt out," she huffed. "Now, butt out!"

"All right, all right," Mike sighed, resuming his spotting position. "Sorry. It was just a thought."

———— ••◦•• ————

After she'd showered, Jill went to Gran's sitting room to have her hair done. The elderly woman had offered to pull her granddaughter's blonde locks into a French braid. Jill knew Gran's fingers had grown stiff with arthritis, but she hadn't wanted to miss the opportunity to spend some quiet time with her grandmother.

Seated on the edge of a blue, velvet chaise lounge chair, Jill looked back and gave Gran an affectionate smile. "Thanks, Gran, for doing my hair. You always do such an amazing job with the braiding. I can never get it to look the same way you do!"

"Braiding your hair is still one of my favorite things to do. It takes me back to when you were a little girl. It was always so hard to get you to sit still long enough for me to finish it!" Gran said, chuckling softly at the memory.

"I bet!" Jill agreed with a giggle. "It always felt like it took an eternity to get it done, and I felt like I was missing out on something Mike was doing without me!" She grinned and confessed, "As much as I love having you do my hair, I still have a hard time sitting still!"

They laughed together, then Gran said, "Don't think I haven't noticed you squirming in that chair. I wonder if it's because you're excited to see Dave again?"

Jill sighed as she toyed with an elastic band. "Oh, Gran," she said. "I really like him, but as I told Mike this morning, I'm not going to get to close to Dave in case he decides to move away. That wouldn't be fair to anyone!"

"Sweetie, that is very mature of you." She'd finished Jill's hair and was admiring her handiwork. "I suppose we'll have to wait and see how it all works out. In the meantime, though, there's nothing wrong with having another friend." She rubbed her granddaughter's shoulders lightly and added, "You're done, and you look beautiful, if I do say so myself! Now, let's go see if Marcie needs some help with breakfast."

The kitchen was teeming with activity in preparation for Sunday's breakfast. Marcie Burns, the Murray's longtime chef, was overseeing the meal, instructing one of her assistants who was working at the griddle.

"Good morning, Mrs. Murray, Ms. Jill," Marcie greeted the women as they entered the busy kitchen. "We'll be ready to serve at ten-thirty per your request. "Would either of you care for coffee or juice?"

Gran accepted a glass of orange juice, but Jill declined and asked, "Is there anything we can do to help?"

Marcie shook her head. "No, thank you. Ms. Gina was in here earlier, and she set the table. Looks like we've got a couple of guests joining us this morning." The large woman thoroughly enjoyed cooking for people and subscribed to the more-the-merrier approach.

Nothing made her happier than hearing praise about the meals she prepared.

"Marcie, you are a gift from above! Thank you for everything you do for our family," Gran told the woman warmly. She knew that Marcie had her hands full. In addition to her responsibilities at the main house, she also managed The Cantina, Wind River's dining hall for the staff who lived and worked on the ranch.

"It's my pleasure, Mrs. Murray," Marcie assured her employer.

Gran looked over at Jill said, "Mike already let the front gate know that Dave would be back so he'll be able to come right up. Why don't you and I wait for him on the front porch?"

"That would be nice," Jill replied. "Shall we?" she asked, offering her hand to Gran.

They had just taken their seats in the rockers when they saw Dave's car coming up the long drive. Gran checked her watch. "Right on time," she observed with satisfaction.

"And here comes the welcoming committee!" Jill laughed, watching the dogs running up to the front of the house. Gran noticed that her granddaughter's dog was not among the eager pack. "Where's Simon?" she asked, surprised that the shepherd wasn't at Jill's side.

"Oh, I took him over to spend some time with Trixie in the barn," she replied. "I have a hunch he's close to being a father again. I'm going to call Ned and see if he'll swing by tomorrow and check on Trixie."

"That's a great idea," Gran said, knowing the shelter was closed on Mondays and the vet would be free to come to the ranch. "Ned is the best."

They were eyeing Dave who'd stopped to lavish affection on the dogs. When he saw the women on the porch, he gave a friendly wave and shouted over, "I'll be right there! I've got to say hi to these guys and gals first!"

"Seems Dave is a fellow dog lover," remarked Gran. Then, smiling innocently over at Jill, she added softly, "just an observation."

Before Jill could respond, Dave was on the porch with them.

"Beautiful morning, isn't it?" he asked cheerfully. He was wearing a casual forest green, button-up polo opened at the collar. Jill had a hard time pulling her eyes away from him. The fitted shirt accentuated Dave's deep emerald eyes. *Oh my gosh*, she thought, *I think he just caught me checking him out. Dang! And why does he have to smell so great on top of everything else?*

"Thank you for inviting me over for breakfast," he said. "I'm really looking forward to a home-cooked meal!"

Jill loved his boyish enthusiasm. "You're going to love Marcie's cooking. She makes the most amazing omelets and the kids go bananas for her pancakes!" she exclaimed. "I'm starving, too."

Gran rose to her feet. "Well then, let's eat!" She took the arm Dave offered and the three of them went into the house.

Mike and Gina met them in the foyer with the twins, and the boys could be heard running up the hallway. When Ian saw his father, he shot past everyone and rushed over to Dave. "Dad! I had the best time! Jeremy and I played video games, and we watched a movie and we had popcorn and…"

"Slow down there, Son!" Dave told Ian laughingly. "I'm glad you had so much fun and I can't wait to hear all about it." He turned the boy around to face the Murray clan who had gathered around them. "But I think right now everyone's ready for breakfast!"

Ian giggled. "I'll tell you the rest later. I'm ready, too!"

"All righty then, let's do it!" Mike's bellow echoed down the hall.

Gran led the way to the dining room. The long oak table comfortably accommodated the family and their guests with ample room for more. As Mike pulled out a chair for Gran at the head of the table, Jill disappeared into the kitchen to let Marcie know they were ready. When she returned and was seated next to Dave; Gran led the blessing.

Dave watched as platter after platter was delivered to the table. He was more than a little impressed with the way the Murrays lived. He knew the family was extremely well-off, he just hadn't thought about them having such a large staff. *Of course, they have help. There's no way they could run this huge ranch by themselves. Yet, even with all their money, they're such kind-hearted people*, he thought.

Jill looked at him, questioningly. "Is everything okay, Dave?" She'd been trying to hand him a bread basket and had been unable to get his attention.

"I'm sorry, what did you say?" he asked.

"I wanted to know if you cared for a biscuit. Marcie makes them from scratch on the weekends. They're delicious—especially with butter and honey," Jill told him with a smile.

"Sure! I'd love one," Dave replied, accepting the basket with a grin. He could hardly keep up with the vast amount of food being passed to him. He leaned over and forked up a couple of fluffy buttermilk pancakes for Ian who promptly drenched them in warm maple syrup. He shook his head lovingly at his young son, giving him a wry smile and motioning for him to use a napkin to wipe off his milk mustache.

There was a happy hum of laughter and conversation as everyone dug into their breakfast. Gran was telling Mike that Jill was going to ask the vet to come by to check on Trixie.

Thinking he might be forgetting someone Jill had introduced him to, Dave leaned over to her and asked, "Please remind me, who is Trixie?"

Hearing his father's question, Ian quickly jumped into the conversation. "Dad! Trixie is Simon's *wife*," he rolled his eyes as if this information was common knowledge. "They're gonna have puppies!" the boy added gleefully.

"German shepherd pups are the cutest!" Jeremy exclaimed.

"*All* puppies are cute," Jill added dreamily. "Plus, there's all that awesome puppy breath to look forward to!" She looked happily around the table. "It won't be long now, and I'll be a grandmother again!"

"I must say, you look great for a grandmother, sweetie!" Gran remarked.

"Right back at you, Gran," Jill said, beaming at the woman at the end of the table.

Mike was about to add his two cents when the doorbell rang. "I'll get it," he said.

Marcie, who was in the dining room, clearing some plates, held up her hand. "I'm happy to answer the door, Mr. Murray. You keep enjoying breakfast with your family."

Mike smiled at her. "Thank you, Marcie."

Marcie had already set down the dishes she'd cleared on the side table and gone to see who was at the door.

A few moments later, Roger walked into the dining room. "I hope you don't mind," Marcie said to Gran as she scurried in behind him. "Mr. Dunn said he hadn't had breakfast and I thought he could join you."

Gran smiled and politely said, "Of course, you know Roger is always welcome." She motioned to an empty chair at the far end of the table. "Roger, why don't you have a seat over there across from Dave? Marcie, would you please bring in another place setting?"

Mike greeted his friend, "Hey, buddy! It's great to see you again. What brings you out on this fine Sunday morning?"

Roger had taken his seat and was eyeing Jill closely as he moved to allow Marcie to bring in a table setting and a steaming cup of coffee.

"I had some business at the station earlier," Roger replied. "Then I thought I'd swing by here and see if Jill and I could spend a little time together." He dished up some eggs and a couple strips of bacon from a nearby platter.

Jill shook her head in annoyance. *How many times do I have to tell him that we don't need to talk alone?* she wondered. "I've got a pretty busy day planned, Roger," she said tersely.

Roger frowned, thinking, *She's putting me off again.* He looked over at Dave. *And what is this guy doing here? Doesn't he ever go home?* He didn't like the way the newcomer was moving in on Jill. *She's mine,* he thought, *and I'll fight for what's mine!*

Jeremy piped up, "Gran, may Ian and I be excused from the table, please?"

"Me, too," Kate and Kelli said in unison.

Gran looked over at Mike and Dave to see if they approved. Seeing no objection, she asked the kids to take their plates into the kitchen as they left. Gina moved to help the girls with their dishes.

Roger was eyeing Dave resentfully. It was killing him to see Jill sitting so close to him. When she leaned over to say something into the other man's ear, Roger balled his fists under the table. *Let's just see how much Jill and her family like this guy after I drop my news on them,* he thought. He took a deep breath and waited for the right moment.

With the young ones gone, there was suddenly an awkward silence in the room. Mike didn't like the way Roger was staring at Jill and Dave. He also noted that his sister's jaw was set and there was a flash of defiance in her eyes. He knew he needed to do something to diffuse the tension in the room. Speaking loudly to get Roger's attention, he suggested, "Hey, let's you and I go do some fishin'. I hear they're really biting at the lower, western pond."

Roger broke his stare at Jill for a moment and said, "Mike, I didn't come here to fish. I came to talk with your sister."

Wanting to come to Jill's defense, it was all Dave could do to stay silent. He didn't feel it was his place to get involved, yet he knew Roger was out of line, and she was clearly irritated. He wasn't surprised when Jill spoke up and set the man straight.

"Roger, I've tried to tell you politely several times that we don't need to talk. But since you've come all the way over here, please, whatever it is you have to say, just say it now!" she insisted.

"Well, I'm sorry you feel that way, Jill. I really am," he said. They could all hear the tinge of sarcasm in his voice. "Because the last thing I'd ever want to do is embarrass you in front of your dear family."

Gran abruptly stood and demanded sharply, "Roger Dunn, I don't know what you're hinting at, but you need to get to the point and stop playing games!"

"Oh, I assure you, I'm not playing games, Gran Jen," Roger said, turning his gaze to the matriarch of the family. He paused for dramatic effect, then continued, "I guess I was just wondering if Mr. Wilder here has told you about his wife calling the Phoenix police about a domestic disturbance he was involved in at their home?"

Roger leaned back in his chair, taking a moment to enjoy the surprised expressions around the table. Then he turned and stared directly at Dave. "You remember, don't you, David? When you became violent and scared your poor wife and young son half to death?"

CHAPTER 12

Roger was thoroughly enjoying the moment after he'd shared the information about Dave, but his satisfaction was short-lived. Much to his dismay, Gran shook her head and stiffly asked him to leave. He was dumbfounded. He couldn't understand why she was asking *him* to go.

Offended, he rose to his feet, making a production of scooting the heavy chair across the floor noisily. "Of course, I'll leave, Gran Jen," he said sourly. "I'm sure Mr. Wilder would like the opportunity to tell you all about his past. I imagine you'll find it very interesting."

"Goodbye, Roger," Gran said crisply. "Please see yourself out."

Gran waited until he'd left the room, then looked over at Dave. "Dave," she began, "I've always prided myself on being an excellent judge of character. You've made an impression on this family and we've brought you into our fold. It is my hope that we have not done so in error. Perhaps, you'd care to explain what Roger just told us."

Dave had been sitting quietly, watching things play out. He wasn't surprised Roger had shown up and tried to disgrace him in front of the Murrays. *He must have really dug deep to get what he'd been so eager to share with Jill and her family,* he thought. *The guy must have used his cop connections to obtain information. What a total jerk!*

Dave kept his eyes on Gran as he quickly stood. "What Roger said is only partially correct. Years ago, my ex-wife did call the cops on me. That's as far as it went and no charges were filed against me. I'm sure he deliberately left that information out."

He continued in earnest, "Your family has shown nothing but kindness to my son and I and your respect means the world to me." He stole a quick glance at Jill and was disappointed to see that she was looking down. *She doesn't even want to look at me!* he thought. *I need to tell them everything.*

"Of course, I owe all of you an explanation. I'd like to start at the beginning," Dave said.

Ever protective of his family, Mike said loudly, "Dave, we want to hear all of it, and frankly, if something you say doesn't ring true, you and I are going to have a talk of our own outside." Mike had turned his chair toward him, and Dave noticed he was angrily working his strong jaw.

Gran intervened, "Michael, let's give him a chance to talk. Go ahead," she said, nodding to Dave.

Dave took a deep breath and began by saying, "Well, I had a friend named Parker. We met in grade school. Like me, he loved baseball. We were inseparable, spending all our free time playing ball. Not only were we very close, our families became good friends. Parker was a talented catcher and he was offered a full ride to play in college. I had been recruited by Arizona State, so we were both on our way to living our dreams of playing in the big leagues." Dave paused for a moment, remembering. "Unfortunately for Parker, he was plagued with injuries. He did graduate eventually, but sat on the bench for most of his last two years. It was really a rotten break for him."

Dave took a sip of water. "Parker and I continued to stay in touch over the years, and although things were not going as he'd planned for his own career, he seemed genuinely happy for my success. While still in college, I was drafted by the Arizona Bears. It was a heady experience. I was only twenty-one and it was a lot of money and a lot of excitement at one time. You see, I grew up in a middle-class home. My parents are modest, down-to-earth people."

He smiled slightly, thinking about his folks. "My dad worked overtime so we could afford the many baseball camps and clinics I attended. I might have been physically prepared for the big league, but I was nowhere close to being ready for all that came with it."

"One weekend, some of my teammates were taking a trip to Vegas and invited me to come along. That's where I met Ian's mother, Missy, who was there with a couple of friends. The women came over to our table and asked if they could join us. One of my teammates was a real idiot. When I started to introduce myself, the guy blurts out something like, 'Wait! You mean you don't know who this is? This ladies, is the soon-to-be famous pitching phenom Dave Wilder. This dude just signed a multimillion-dollar contract with the Bears!' He was obviously trying to impress the women. But to me, it was mortifying. I really didn't appreciate him making a big deal out of it in front of everyone."

Dave shook his head. "Looking back, I wonder if that's why Missy latched onto me. We all hung around for a while together, then; when everyone else said goodnight, she pulled me aside and asked if I'd like to grab some coffee with her. We found ourselves in the casino coffee shop talking until two the next morning.

"Missy told me she was an actress and had appeared in a couple of films in minor roles. She was between jobs and had been crashing at a friend's house while auditioning for parts. I won't deny that I was taken by her good looks and outgoing personality. She seemed to be very interested in me. She said she had family in Arizona and asked if we could get together the next time she was in town.

"I gave her my number, and a few days later, Missy called telling me she was in the area. We ended up going out a few times, and she decided to extend her visit. Things were going great between us. Parker had come for a visit, and he instantly liked her, as did all my teammates. The media loved us—the actress and the baseball player," Dave said, a touch of bitterness in his voice.

"Everything between Missy and me went way too fast. I was focused on my career, but she really wanted to get married before I started spring training. We tied the knot in Vegas at a chapel not far from where we first met."

Dave went on to tell the Murrays about the huge home Missy had chosen for them and her lavish spending habits. "I didn't care about the money, honestly," he told them. I just wanted to play ball. When you've grown up without a lot of money, you learn it's not what makes you happy.

"One of the things that *did* make me happy was being able to buy my folks a new house. It was the least I could do for them after all the sacrifices they'd made for me over the years." Dave smiled, remembering how awesome he'd felt handing his dad the keys to the front door.

"Anyway, after a while, Missy grew tired of being left alone so often. When I was home, things were strained, and there was a lot of tension between us. She seemed to resent me for doing the very thing that put a roof over our heads and allowed her to buy the things she wanted. Missy told me she was unhappy in our marriage. It was the first time either of us had admitted we'd made a mistake. When I suggested she start auditioning for some roles to fill her time, she got very defensive, telling me that she'd sacrificed her career for me and her acting days were over. I was shocked, but not nearly as much as I was the next day when she told me she was pregnant."

Dave noticed that Jill had scooted her chair away from the table. She'd crossed her long, slender legs and was shaking her foot in an agitated manner. He knew it was a lot of information to take in, but he needed them to know why things happened the way they had.

"I had hoped having Ian would bring Missy and me closer together. But as you might have guessed, well…things just got worse. A couple of years after he was born, I moved out of the house. It was just better for all of us. Missy was good about letting me spend time with Ian whenever I could. I found out later that she left him with sitters pretty often so she could go out with her friends. I know she loves our son, but my ex-wife is not exactly stay-at-home mom material, at least not in the traditional sense.

"One afternoon, I came home early from a trip and decided to swing by and pick up Ian. I normally would let Missy know when I was on my way over, but in my rush to see my son, I didn't call. I was surprised to see Parker's car in the driveway when I pulled up to the house."

Dave looked down at the floor and shook his head. "Missy had changed the locks after I'd moved out, so I knocked, and Parker answered the door. The look on my best friend's face said it all. He tried to tell me that he and Missy were just friends, but I wasn't buying it. I knew Parker too well and I knew he was lying to me. I heard Missy calling from inside, asking him who was at the door. When she saw me standing on the porch, she came over and pretended like

Parker had just dropped by to see if I were home. Finally, Parker told her to stop with the charade. He said they owed me the truth, which was they had been seeing each other for years. The betrayal cut me to my very core. I'd never experienced anything like it."

Taking a deep breath, Dave went on, "Parker invited me into *my* house, to sit on the furniture that *I* bought and talk it out. I refused his offer and told them both I just wanted my son. That's when things got ugly."

At this point, the Murrays could see Dave was getting worked up. His words came faster as he picked up the pace of the story.

"Missy looked at me and told me I couldn't take Ian. It wasn't a good time, she'd said. I reminded her that I had every right to spend time with our child. This is when Parker interrupted and told me that he and Missy had plans to take Ian over to his parents' house that evening.

"He also let me know he and Missy were going to get married." Dave raked his fingers through his hair anxiously. "Then Parker got in my face and told me that he was going to be the husband Missy deserved and the father figure that young Ian needed in his life.

"I remember just standing there like a total fool. When I started to speak, Parker held up his hand and went on to tell me that he and Missy would appreciate it if I would call before I came to the house. 'You need to respect our privacy,' he'd said."

Dave looked at the people sitting around the table and sighed. "I've never been a violent person, but in that moment, I saw red. It was like the rug had been completely pulled out from under me. Before I knew it, I had punched Parker smack in the nose." He stared up at the ceiling, recollecting his thoughts. "I'd love to tell you that if I had it to do over again, I might handle it differently. But I honestly don't know that I would.

"I guess while Parker and I were going at it, Missy called the police. By the time they arrived, Parker had found some ice for his nose, and we were both cooling off. Seeing that we were going to be able to work out our differences; my ex-wife had a change of heart and charmed the cops into believing she'd made a mistake in calling them."

"As I've said, no charges were filed, but they both resented me for punching Parker and threatened to go to the press. I agreed to see someone for anger-management, and they backed off on that." Dave was thoughtful for a moment, then said, "I'm not sure how Roger came across this information, unless he knows someone on the Phoenix force. None of it was ever in the press." He stuck his hands in his pockets and attempted to get Jill's attention again. "Roger must have really wanted to dig up some dirt on me."

He gave a feeble smile. "I'm not angry anymore, by the way. It's like Mrs. Murray said, learning from your bad decisions builds character. I know I made a bad decision in marrying Missy, yet I'm happy that I've got a wonderful son. And as I've told all of you before, I will do whatever it takes to be a good father to him."

Dave concluded by saying, "If you all would like for me to leave now, I'll understand. I never meant to be anything less than honest with you. I was actually planning to tell Jill all of this as soon as we had the chance to talk."

The room was silent for a couple of moments while they waited for Gran to reply. For Dave, it seemed like an eternity until she finally said, "Dave, that is truly a heartbreaking story. I'm so sorry Roger painted you in such a bad light. I'm sure you're aware that he has a thing for our Jill." She smiled and looked at her grandchildren, saying, "I still think Dave's a good egg." She nodded toward him before rising and excusing herself from the room.

Mike stood and shook Dave's hand. "Thanks for telling us all that, man. I'm sure some of that stuff doesn't come easy for you. I'm going to go find Gina. Catch ya'll later," he said, casting a concerned look at his sister before he left the room.

Jill was sitting alone at the big table. She'd yet to comment or make eye contact with Dave.

"What about you, Jill?" he asked her softly. "Would you like me to leave?"

She shoved her chair back and was immediately in his arms. "Parker sounds like a horrible person who deserved more than just a busted nose!" she exclaimed. "What happened to him? Did he end up marrying Missy? Is he Ian's new stepfather?"

Hearing that Jill wasn't going to hold his past against him, Dave felt as if a ton of bricks had been lifted off his shoulders. He was relieved that she understood the truth about what had happened, yet he was caught a little off guard by her questions.

"No, after all of that, the two of them didn't end up getting married. They stayed together long enough for Parker to see how selfish Missy is, and for her to realize that he wasn't going to be able to keep her in the lifestyle she'd grown accustomed to," Dave explained. "Of course, she received a nice chunk of change in our divorce settlement, but that woman spends money like there's no tomorrow!" He smiled at Jill. "Her new husband is an attorney for an oil company. According to Ian, he's fat and bald."

Jill found herself smiling with him. "What about Parker, do you ever talk to him?"

He gave her a humble smile and said, "Parker called about a month later and begged my forgiveness. He admitted that he'd always been envious of how my baseball career had taken off and his had ended. I don't know if that's what motivated him to move in on Missy, but I thought it was big of him to come clean with me about it."

"So you forgave him?" Jill asked.

"Of course! I had to forgive him! I told you, he was like a brother to me," Dave replied. He waited a couple of beats before adding with a smirk, "but full disclosure—after all that, I only trust him as far as I can throw him!"

Jill looked him up and down. "I'm with Gran; I think you're a good egg, too, Dave Wilder." She shot him an impish grin and teased, "Although, I will say that it did take you forever to get to the point!"

He held her at arms length and said, "I'm sorry if I bored you with my story!"

She was still smiling at him. "Really, you could have just cut to the chase and told us that your best friend tried to steal your wife and kid and then got in your face about it, so you punched the guy."

"*Ex-wife*, let's be clear on that, and frankly, there was no way to cut to the chase and have you all understand how big a deal it was for me," Dave said seriously. "It was a really dark time. And, as much as it would be easy to place all the blame on Missy and Parker, I was at fault as well. I know that now."

Jill was ready for a change of subject and scenery. "I have an idea. What are your plans for this afternoon?" she asked.

"I need to check with Ian and see if he has any homework to do before school tomorrow. Other than that, I'm open," he replied. "What do you have in mind?"

"I have a couple of ideas. But homework definitely takes priority. Let's go find Ian and see what he says." With that, Jill grabbed Dave's hand and led him out of the dining room.

They found the boys in Jeremy's bedroom playing video games. Her nephew had an impressive setup, with a big screen television mounted to the wall and an elaborate game system beneath it. Sprawled out in matching swivel chairs, the kids were totally immersed in their game.

Jill waited until there was a break in the action. "All right, Jeremy, Mr. Wilder needs to talk with Ian. Please pause the game for a minute."

Jeremy reluctantly obeyed his aunt.

Dave smiled at Ian. "Have you done your homework, Son?" he asked.

Ian gave his father a guilty look. "No, Dad. I've got a stupid science project due tomorrow, " he admitted.

Dave turned to Jill with an apologetic sigh. "I'm really sorry, but I'll have to take a rain check this time."

"Hey, it's no big deal. School's more important," she assured him.

"Ian, go ahead and finish your game, then meet me on the front porch, okay?" Dave asked. Seeing that his son was focused on playing again, he gave a quick laugh and spoke to Jill. "Please let Gina know I'll wash Jeremy's clothes and get them back to you guys."

Jeremy laughed at his remark. "Ian can totally keep those clothes, Mr. Wilder. I'm way too big for them now." Then, knowing Ian was sensitive about his size, he turned to his friend and said, "I'm sure you'll grow into them soon."

This brought a smile to Ian's face. "Thanks, buddy," he said, giving Jeremy a high-five before they resumed their game.

Jill and Dave walked slowly toward the front door. They were both disappointed he had to go.

"It's been another interesting time with you today, Dave," Jill told him as they walked out onto the porch and sat in the rockers. "As much as I hated what Roger did to you, I'm glad everything's out in the open." She paused for a moment then asked, "This is *everything*, right? The last thing we need is Roger over here again with more dirt on you!" She'd tried to keep her tone light, but he caught the note of seriousness in her voice and Dave knew he needed to reassure her.

"Yes, Jill," he replied, then added, "Like I said, it was a dark time in my life, but it's over now." Dave regarded her thoughtfully, hoping she could hear the sincerity in his voice. "You told me that you weren't a hard person to figure out. Well, neither am I. Please know, I will always be honest with you."

He smiled when she cocked her head and said, "And I, with you."

They rocked together for a few minutes, an easy silence between them as they enjoyed the afternoon sun and waited for Ian. "Are you going to tell me what you thought we might do this afternoon or are you going to keep me wondering?" he asked playfully, pleased that she wanted to spend time with him. *Whatever it was, it's too bad I couldn't have said yes*, he thought.

"You're so funny," she said with a giggle. "As I told you, it was no big deal. I just thought maybe you'd like to go on a hike together. You know, and work off some of that huge breakfast!"

"Next time I come over, I'll bring some appropriate footwear," Dave said, looking down at his boots. "I'd love to go hiking with you."

He paused for a moment; then an idea came to him. "How about you come over to our place tonight for dinner?" he suggested. "I can throw a couple of steaks on the grill."

Before accepting, Jill took a moment to think about the concern she'd shared with her family earlier in the day. *What if Dave relocates to Arizona?* But her resolve to protect her heart was lost when she saw the hopefulness in his deep green eyes.

"I'd love to," she replied with a grin. "What time should I be there?"

CHAPTER 13

When they'd returned home, Ian pulled out his homework assignment. There was a list of project options, and together they chose one that could be completed with materials they had on hand.

Ian named their project "The Mini Tornado." They sat side by side at the long kitchen bar, intent on their work. Dave read the instructions while Ian cut a circle of tissue paper into a spiral. He listened closely as his father instructed him to then tie a string to the outer edge of the spiral and hold the circular paper high over a light bulb. As the heat rose from the bulb, the spiral began to spin. Ian shrieked with joy, "It works! It works! See it spinning, Dad? We made a tornado!"

Dave nodded his head, grinning at Ian's reaction. "You did a great job, Son! It's really cool. Look at it go!" he exclaimed as they watched the paper spin.

Dave reviewed the assignment again. "Now, your teacher wants you to outline what you did and include your observations about the project. It says you should list all trials and errors you had during the experiment."

Ian laughed. "Does that mean the first three tornados that I destroyed trying to cut them out?" he asked.

"Good thing we had plenty of tissue paper," Dave said, ruffling Ian's hair. "Now, maybe that wasn't such a stupid project after all, eh?"

"No, you made it fun, Dad. Thanks for helping me," Ian replied.

"You're welcome, that's what dads are for, right?" he asked, looking affectionately at his son.

Ian gave his father a devilish grin. "I guess that's why I can also count on you to type up the analysis while I go watch TV," he said slyly.

Dave faked a big belly laugh. "Hahaha, all right, Mr. Funny Guy, I'm going to start pulling dinner together and *you're* going to start typing."

While the boy concentrated on finishing his assignment, Dave turned on some soft music and took stock of the refrigerator. *Steak, salad, and potatoes,* he thought, then remembered he also had some fresh corn on the cob. *I'll throw that on the grill with the steaks. And of course, I can't forget the peas, Ian's favorite vegetable!*

He was rummaging through the produce drawer when he heard Ian ask, "Dad, do you like Ms. Jill?"

"Of course I like her, Son. She saved your life, and she's also a really nice lady," he answered. As he turned around, he saw that Ian was leaning forward with both elbows on the bar, his face resting in his hands, in full interrogation mode.

"What? Why are you looking at me like that?" Dave asked.

Ian rolled his eyes dramatically. "I don't mean, 'do you like her', Dad! I mean, you know, do you, *like-like* her? Because if you *like-like* her, you should totally just kiss her."

Dave shook his head. *I've got a ten-year-old who's going on thirty!* he thought. Not wanting to discuss his feelings for Jill, he quickly changed the subject. "I have an idea, buddy. Why don't you stay focused on finishing your homework, and I'll stay focused on our dinner?"

Ian was looking down at the keyboard as he typed. "Well, let me know if you want to talk about it. We guys have to stick together."

"Thanks, bud, I'll remember that," Dave assured him, thankful that Ian had dropped the subject.

Jill was in her room, trying to decide what to wear to Dave's. Her hair was still tied in the French braid Gran had done earlier, so she thought it wouldn't take long to get ready. Now, glancing at her watch, Jill realized she was running short on time.

"I'm making this way harder than it should be. It's just a casual dinner at a friend's house," Jill said, looking at Simon, who was dozing in the corner. The shepherd cocked his head to one side as if he were going to say something, then immediately rested his chin back on his front paws.

"You're no help at all, my friend," she sighed, considering the many options in her large, walk-in closet. "I can see I'm on my own here."

After much deliberation, she chose a simple burgundy cashmere sweater, pairing it with some dark jeans.

"Now, which boots should I wear?" Simon stirred for a moment, then gave her a huge yawn. "What's the matter, boy?" she asked. "Are you all tuckered out from our hike?" Jill chuckled as she surveyed her massive boot collection. "I'm going with these," she announced, pulling a well-worn brown pair down off one of the long shelves. She stroked the soft leather lovingly. "They belonged to mom," she said more to herself than to Simon. She was lost in thought for a moment, trying hard to remember her mother. It made her sad that she was unable to recollect anything about her.

Sitting on the vanity, Jill pulled on the boots and decided to apply some makeup. She swiped on some mascara then brushed a rosy blush across her high cheekbones. Last, she added some rose-colored lipstick. Satisfied with her reflection, she grabbed a light leather jacket and headed out with Simon at her heels.

She stopped in the great room where Mike, Gina, and Gran were gathered in front of the fireplace. She walked over and gave her grandmother a kiss on the cheek. "I'll see ya'll later," Jill told them. "I'm heading over to have dinner with Dave and Ian."

"You look beautiful, darling," Gran said with a smile. "And you smell nice, too."

Jill felt the color rising in her cheeks. "Thanks, Gran. I love you."

Her brother rose to his feet. "I'll walk out with you, Sis," he said.

The siblings walked down the hall together, and Mike opened the front door. "Hey, Jill," he said when they got to the porch. "Give me Dave's address." He already had his cell phone out and was ready to enter the information.

"Really, Mike?" she asked him, dismayed. "I'm a big girl, and Dave lives right over there," she said, waving her hand toward the Lone Star Springs community.

"Really," he said, crossing his arms across his broad chest. "Look, I'm not messin' around. You can either give me the guy's address or you can park yourself in my truck and *I'll* take you over there myself. Your choice."

She knew it was no use arguing with him, so she pulled out her phone and gave Mike the information. "Okay, *dad*! What time is my curfew tonight?" she asked sarcastically.

Ignoring her comment, Mike gave her a grave look and said firmly, "Dave seems like a good guy, but there's still a lot we don't know about him, so let's just be smart about this."

Jill was going to make a snide remark, but she could see Mike was sincere in his concern for her well-being.

She gave him a hug and said, "You're right, Mike. You know I love you, and I'm really sorry I gave you a hard time."

He hugged her back. "I think nine-thirty is plenty late enough, young lady," he said, pointing his index finger at her sternly. "Tonight's a school night."

Jill laughed as she turned to go, yet wondered if he'd been serious with his last remark.

Heading down the driveway, Jill smiled when she looked in her rearview mirror and saw Mike and Simon standing in the circular drive, watching as she drove away.

When Jill reached Wind River's front gate, she pressed a button on her visor to open the automatic gate. While waiting, she entered Dave's address into her car's navigation system. *Interesting, it's only fourteen minutes from my house to his*, she thought looking at the information on the screen.

Arriving at the entrance to Lone Star Springs, she used the access code Dave had given her to open the elaborate front gates. She followed the route along the wide, winding residential streets, passing massive homes on large manicured lots. Dave's house was a two-story stucco located in a cul-de-sac. Jill pulled her car into the circular drive and checked her face once more in the mirror. *Good grief!* she thought. *You've just been gone a few minutes. It's not like your makeup has had a chance to get messed up!* Jill realized she was nervous. *Just go in there and have a nice time with your friends*, she told herself.

Jill reached over and grabbed her purse and a bottle of wine off the passenger's seat and headed to Dave's front door.

As soon as she'd rung the doorbell, Jill heard Ian shouting from the other side of the door, "I'll get it! I'll get it!" She smiled, happy to know the boy was excited about her visit.

Ian was all smiles as he opened the tall door. "Hi, Ms. Jill! Dad and I made a Mini Tornado for my science project. You wanna see it?" he asked before she'd barely stepped inside.

Jill leaned down and gave him a swift hug. "You bet I do, Ian. Science was always one of my favorite subjects!" When she looked up, she saw Dave coming toward her. *He moves so fluidly, almost cat-like*, she thought as he moved closer to her. She noticed that he'd changed his clothes and now sported a soft yellow pullover and faded relaxed jeans that hung loosely just below his waist. He wore a stunning smile as he pulled her into his arms, giving her a warm, welcoming embrace. "We're so glad you decided to join us for dinner tonight. Come on in! Ian, you've got to show Ms. Jill your Mini Tornado," he said, giving their guest a friendly wink. "He may have to explain the science behind it to you. It was a very involved project."

Ian erupted into giggles. "Oh, Dad! The only reason it was involved was because it took us so long to find the string!" He turned to Jill and said, "Well, *that* and also, I accidentally cut the first three tornadoes in half trying to make spirals."

"It sounds *very* involved, indeed!" she agreed. They laughed as they continued walking together to the kitchen. Ian took his usual place at the counter while Jill followed Dave and stood next to him at the center island.

"I want to know all the details," Jill said. "It sounds awesome!" She handed Dave the wine. "I thought we could have this with dinner." Then, looking over at Ian who was busy typing up his report, she added, "Or you can save it for another time if you think that'd be better."

Dave appreciated Jill being mindful of drinking in front of his son. He thanked her for the wine and placed it in the fridge. "That was very thoughtful of you."

He watched as she walked over to the counter and began looking over Ian's homework, enjoying the way she interacted so easily with him. *This woman genuinely cares about what he's telling her*, he thought, impressed with her questions and the way she made the boy think about aspects of the project he hadn't considered.

Mesmerized by her every move, Dave was having a hard time taking his eyes off the tall, blonde Texan. *It just feels so right having her here with us*, he thought contently. *It's the first time since I bought this place that it's really felt like home.*

At that moment, Jill noticed Dave staring at her and he made a quick act of checking the potatoes. "These are going to need a few more minutes," he said, poking them with a fork. "I'm going to set the table. You guys keep talking."

Jill blushed and laughed self-consciously. "Let me give you a hand, Dave. I'm a terrible cook, but I set a mean table! Want to help?" she asked, looking at Ian.

"Sure!" Ian said. "And I know where everything is. Come on, let me show you where we keep all the forks and stuff."

She followed Ian around the bar, holding out her hands as he pulled out silverware and napkins. "We usually put everything else on the counter and fix our plates there," the boy told Jill. "Dad calls it family-style, but it's usually just me and him."

Jill responded quickly, "Well, you two *are* a family. Families come in all sizes."

Ian considered what she'd said. "True, but I wish I had a big family like Jeremy. It would be really cool to have sisters or a brother."

"I understand," Jill told him warmly. "I always thought it would be fun to have a sister, but I got a big stinky brother instead!" This got an appreciative laugh from both the Wilders.

Jill had noticed a door from the kitchen leading into another room. "Is this the way to the formal dining room?" she asked.

Dave exchanged a quick glance with Ian before answering, "Yep, that's our formal dining room!"

Jill was moving through the doorway when she suddenly sensed Dave close beside her. "Here, let me get the light for you." He reached across her to turn on the light. As he did, his arm brushed lightly across her own, and she felt a surge of heat run through her at their contact. *There's such energy between the two of us*, she thought.

With a flip of the switch, the room was illuminated, and she blinked in surprise to see there was no table. The room was completely empty. Jill turned to see the guys roaring with laughter. It was then she realized she'd been set up.

"Very funny, you two!" she exclaimed, laughing with them. "Why did you send me in here to set a table that doesn't exist?"

Ian replied, "You asked where the formal dining was, and Dad told you!" The boy was laughing so hard, he could barely get the words out. "You should have seen the look on your face, Ms. Jill! Awesome, Dad!" Ian held his hand up for a high-five from Dave.

As the guys enjoyed their prank, Jill shook her head. "So I get it, you guys are not the formal type. So that begs the question, *where* are we having dinner tonight?" she asked with a good-natured smile.

"We usually just eat at the bar," Ian said helpfully. "I need to get my science junk off it."

"You can do that after dinner," said Dave. He then turned his attention to Jill and explained, "Ian's right. He and I usually eat at the bar, but tonight is special. Tonight we're dining at the kitchen table like civilized human beings!"

"Well, that sounds perfect to me. Kitchen table it is!" she declared. She gave Dave a playful wink and added, "Don't worry—I'll try to behave in the most civilized manner possible!"

They moved back into the kitchen where Jill set the table as Dave finished the dinner preparations. "We're getting close to eating," Dave told Ian. "Why don't you go ahead and take your computer to your room and wash your hands? Be back down here in five."

Jill smiled as Ian saluted his father. "Yes, sir!" he said while picking up his laptop and running up the stairs. "See ya in five!" he called back down to them.

Jill leaned against the center island and said, "In addition to being an expert table-setter, *when* there's actually a table, mind you, I've also been known to toss a killer salad." She looked at Dave wryly as he pulled the salad and dressing out of the refrigerator.

He smiled, handing her the tongs. "It's all yours then," he said.

They worked in silence for a couple of minutes before Dave said, "Thanks for being a good sport about our dining room situation."

"What? No, that was really pretty funny. I shouldn't have just assumed anything. I tend to do that, come in and try to take control of things. I should apologize to you. I hope I didn't embarrass you," Jill said, giving Dave a questioning look.

"No, Jill, I agree, it *was* pretty funny. And Ian was right, the look on your face was priceless!" he exclaimed in delight.

"Okay! All right, the moment's over, you!" Jill said, snapping the salad tongs at him, playfully.

"Right, got it!" Dave grinned over at her and said, "After dinner, I'd like to show you the rest of the house. "It's a pretty cool set up, but I'll warn you up front, it's a big place and there are several rooms without any furniture." He paused for a moment, unsure of what she'd think about that. "I just, well, until I know whether or not Ian's going to want to stay here…" Dave's voice trailed off, and his eyes were on Jill's, needing her to understand.

It was a sobering moment for her. She knew there was the possibility Dave might be moving away. She pushed back the thought and smiled at the man who was working his way into her heart. "Please don't feel like you have to explain it to me, Dave. I understand your situation with Ian."

They heard Ian storming back down the stairs. "I sure hope you've got everything else ready for dinner," Jill teased. "Those sound like the footsteps of a hungry boy!"

Dave laughed, pulling the potatoes out of the oven and sweet peas from the microwave. "That kid is always hungry! He's going to eat me out of house and home!" he grumbled, loud enough for Ian's benefit. Dave then headed to the back patio to retrieve the steaks and corn from the grill. "Ian, get the butter and cheese out for the potatoes," he instructed before going out the back door.

"Peas are my favorite vegetable," Ian informed Jill as he riffled through the fridge. "Not a big fan of salad, but Dad makes me eat a lot of it. He says it will help me grow."

Jill nodded. "Your dad is right. And I'll share something with you, Ian. You know my brother, Mike?" She watched as Ian gave an enthusiastic nod yes. "He wasn't always the giant he is now. In fact, he was small for his age and didn't start getting bigger until he was nearly seventeen years old."

Dave had come in with the grilled food and heard what Jill was saying to Ian. "That's true, Son. I know a lot of guys who shot up several inches later in their teens."

Ian thought about their words for a moment. "I've been researching comedians. There've been a lot of short guys who've done really well, so I guess it doesn't matter if I'm not very tall. Of course, if I decide to pursue a career in the NBA, then it might become an issue." He gave the adults a wide grin and asked, "Did somebody say it was time to eat?"

They filled their plates, then gathered around the table in the octagon-shaped nook. Jill took a moment to study the floor-to-ceiling windows that overlooked an Austin stone patio. She could see there was an area in the backyard that appeared to have been professionally landscaped, but beyond it, there was nothing. *There's probably a sizeable privacy fence back there somewhere*, she thought, remembering her birds-eye-view view of the subdivision from Rock Point Trail.

Dave saw her gazing out the windows, but said nothing. He continued eating in silence, thinking: *I wonder what's going on in that beautiful head of hers?*

"The steak is delicious," Jill said, looking up at Dave. "All of this is really good." She turned to Ian. "I love sweet peas, too! Thank you for inviting me to your home."

"We want you to come over all the time!" Ian exclaimed. "Or we want to be over there, at the ranch. We just want to be with you!"

Dave, touched by his son's heartfelt remark, wasn't sure how to explain Ian's emotional outburst. "Ian, Jill and her family have a lot going on," he said. He then rested his fork and knife on his plate and added, "I'm sorry Jill, but I think I speak for both of us when I tell you there've been times when it's been lonely since we've moved to Texas. Ian really misses his friends, and I'm still trying to get my bearings here, too." He paused, and Jill knew he was thinking about whether they'd end up moving away.

He was smiling at her as he said, "You and your family have made a huge difference in our lives here. Before we met you, we felt like outsiders." He looked over at Ian, and shared, "We don't feel that way anymore."

Jill looked appraisingly at the father and son. "Wow! That's really sweet," she said, smiling warmly. She reached over and patted Ian's hand. "I don't think it was an accident God brought us together up on that hill. Ian, you have so many special gifts. You have an amazing sense of humor, and I cannot wait to see your artwork. You guys are thanking me, but I feel like *I'm* the lucky one to have met both of you."

There was a silence in the room that might have been awkward if it hadn't been for Ian squeezing Jill's hand and pointing to the back window she'd been staring through earlier. "Did my dad tell you that he's thinking about putting a pool in the backyard?" he asked.

Jill burst into laughter, and soon Dave and Ian joined her. "When you live in Texas, it's definitely great to have a swimming pool!" she said enthusiastically. "It gets crazy hot here. You know how to swim, right?" she asked Ian.

"Well… I almost do. I'm not quite there yet," the boy admitted, looking shyly at her.

Jill regarded him fondly. "You're in luck, Ian. If you decide to hang around here, I'll teach you how to swim. We have a huge pool over at the ranch. We even heat it when it gets too cold outside. We'll have you doing laps before you know it."

Ian smiled up at her. "Thanks, Ms. Jill. That would be cool," he said.

After dinner, Dave sent Ian upstairs to shower and get ready for bed while he and Jill cleaned up the kitchen.

"We can just leave all of this in the sink," he told her, motioning to the dirty dishes. "I'll take care of them later."

"No way," she said firmly. "Do you think I'm a stranger to doing dishes?"

Dave shrugged. "I know your family has people who help with this sort of domestic stuff. Plus, you're a guest in our home. I don't want to put you to work."

To his surprise, Jill threw back her head and laughed, mimicking his words, "People who help with this sort of domestic stuff! You've met my grandmother. Do you think for a minute that she let Mike and me skate out on domestic chores?" She didn't wait for Dave's reply. "I know you think I've lived a privileged life, and you're absolutely right. But, after our parents died, our grandparents believed it was important to raise us as normally as possible." She gave Dave a sweet smile. "My brother and I had lots of responsibilities around the house and ranch! We always had chores."

Dave was still smiling at her, not knowing what to say.

He realized Jill wasn't going to take no for an answer as she brushed past him and asked, "So, Mr. Baseball, would you kindly step out of the way so that I may load these dirty dishes into your dishwasher?"

"*Mr. Baseball?*" he asked with a smirk. "Now, the last time you called me that, you were really mad at me!" He drew closer to her and said softly, "Jill, I'd prefer it if you'd just call me Dave. Baseball is my past, and I'm looking forward to my future." He gave her a meaningful look, then motioned toward the dirty dishes. With a devilish grin and a thick, southern drawl, he added, "And for the record my dear, please load away! Far be it from me to prevent you from being one of us *normal folk!*"

"You've got it, *Dave*," Jill said, playfully kicking him lightly in the shin. She shot him a grin of her own. "I never said I wouldn't accept some help. We can load it together."

They were working side by side when Ian came back downstairs. He'd printed his science project report, and the three of them reviewed it together. "You've done a great job on this, Son," Dave told him. "Looks like A-plus material to me. What do you think, Ms. Jill?"

"I think you've nailed it, Ian," she agreed.

The three of them were celebrating with some ice cream when Dave noticed the time. "It's getting late, Ian. We need to get you ready for bed." He looked at Jill and asked if she could stay awhile longer. "I won't be long," he promised.

Their eyes locked for a moment, and she felt her face flush. "Just for a bit, then I'll need to take off." Jill went over to Ian and gave him a quick hug. "Goodnight," she said. "I've had a fun time tonight, and I'm sure we'll see each other again soon."

"Goodnight, Ms. Jill," he said. "I hope so!"

They escorted her to the living room where she took a seat on a large, black leather sofa. "I'll be down soon," Dave assured her with a smile.

"Take your time," Jill said, smiling back at him. "I'll be here when you get back."

CHAPTER 14

Jill sat patiently for a few minutes in the comfortable living area. She liked the high ceilings and the way the room flowed from the kitchen, creating an open design perfect for family gatherings. Unlike the barren formal dining room, the atmosphere here was warm and inviting, filled with tasteful contemporary pieces. She rose and walked over to admire a large oil painting above the mantel. It was a striking abstract with bold colors that complemented Dave's black leather furniture. She continued around the room, studying other paintings, noting the style was similar in each of them. *They must have been done by the same artist*, she thought.

She glanced at her watch and decided she'd text Mike and check in with him, knowing he'd appreciate the gesture. Jill returned to the sofa and punched in a quick message, letting him know she was safe and would be home in a little while. Dave returned as she was pressing the send button.

Noticing the phone in her hand, he asked, "Everything all right?"

Knowing she'd blushed, Jill was grateful for the soft glow of the lamps. She hoped Dave hadn't seen her embarrassment at being caught texting her brother. Then, wanting no secrets between them, she admitted, "I was just texting Mike to let him know when I'd be home."

"Ah, I see," he replied good-naturedly. "That's really thoughtful. I know your brother worries about you."

Jill appreciated him not giving her a hard time about it. "Did you get Ian settled down for the night?" she asked.

"He was already conking out on me while we were reading," he replied, then added, "Right now we're into a book about pirates. We take turns reading a few pages every night."

Jill could see the nightly ritual meant a lot to him. "That's such a special thing to do together," she said.

"And now, it's grown-up time!" proclaimed Dave happily. "Can you stay for a glass of wine? I happen to have a bottle of the good stuff!"

"Sure," Jill said. "That would be lovely."

"I was hoping you'd say that," he said. "Stay put; I'll be back in a flash." She watched as he strolled lightly to the refrigerator and removed the bottle of wine she'd given him earlier. He made quick work of opening the bottle, then pulled two glasses from the cabinet, filling them with the wine. *It really is a pleasure just watching him*, she thought.

Dave returned with a glass in each hand, delivering one to Jill. "Here you go," he said, "and thank you again for the wine, by the way."

Jill smiled and took a small sip. "You're welcome and thank *you* again for the wonderful meal. As I told Ian, it's been fun being here with you guys."

Pleased to hear she was enjoying the evening as much as he was, Dave beamed. "Would you like to see more of the house?"

"Of course," she said, setting her wine on a nearby table and rising to her feet. "Take me on the tour."

"Well, Ian and I spend most of our time in this area," he said, motioning around the room. Jill followed as he led them around the rest of the first floor. Dave's study and bedroom were fully furnished, but the formal areas were empty as was the game room. "I'm thinking about getting a pool table and maybe foosball for the game room," he told her, thinking out loud. "That's it for the ground floor. Upstairs there are four more bedrooms and another living area. There's furniture in Ian's room, of course, and we've got some chairs and a television on the wall in the living room up there. We use that room for playing video games. Ian likes to call it our man cave. Oh, and I've got one of the bedrooms upstairs all set up for when my parents come out to visit." They'd worked their way back to the kitchen. "And that, Ms. Murray, concludes our tour," he said with a smile.

"It's a really great place, Dave. You've made it into a wonderful home for you both," Jill told him sincerely.

"Yeah, thanks," he said warmly. "As I've shared with you, I want Ian to stay with me." He shook his head, trying not to think about what he'd need to do if his son decided to return to Arizona. He grinned at Jill, admitting, "I'm halfway tempted to start digging that pool and bribing him with a dog. I know that'd be wrong, but it might persuade Ian to stay."

Jill smiled at him compassionately, thinking about Mike's suggestion to offer the Wilders one of Simon's pups. "Yes, that *would* be wrong." She shrugged, flashing a bright smile at Dave and said, "It'd be wrong, but it'd probably convince him!" They both laughed at this, then she added kindly, "Ian needs to make his own decision."

"That he does," Dave replied. He took her gently by the arm and said, "Let's go sit and enjoy the wine you brought."

As they walked back into the living area, Dave stopped and flipped a switch on the wall before joining her on the sofa. She chuckled as a roaring fire appeared in the fireplace. "Nice," she commented.

"Well, it may not be as impressive as a wood-burning fire, but it's very low maintenance!" Dave explained with a grin.

"I love it," Jill assured him. "It's perfect."

Dave noticed the way the firelight danced in her eyes. "I'm sure you hear this all the time, but you are so beautiful, Jill." He ran his hand down her long braid, then gave it a playful tug. "I like your hair this way."

She was used to people commenting on her looks, but hearing it from Dave thrilled her. Flattered, she said, "Thank you, Gran braided it for me."

They drank the wine slowly, enjoying the fire and talking quietly. Jill asked him about the paintings in the room and he told her about the artist, a friend of his from school. It reminded her that she hadn't asked to see Ian's artwork.

"Darn! I meant to ask Ian to show me his watercolor paintings," Jill said.

"I've got some of them in my office," he told her. "I'll show you."

She was enjoying their time in front of the fire too much to leave the room. "Great, let's do that when I'm on my way out," she said, looking at her watch. "I should get going, but I've been wondering, what made you decide to move to Texas?"

Dave looked at her in mock-surprise. "What? Who *wouldn't* want to live in Texas? And in the Hill Country, no less?" he asked dramatically. Then he explained, "Seriously, one of my old teammates got married at a place outside of Dripping Springs. I stayed for a few days after the wedding, did some hiking and the wine tour thing, and ate some amazing barbecue." His voice trailed off as he gazed into the fire. "I was struck by the beauty of the Hill Country and when I returned home, I couldn't stop thinking about how it would be to live here. There's just something really special about this area. I flew back to Texas a couple of weeks later and started looking at houses." He looked around the room. "The builder had just put this place on the market. I liked the layout, and the location is great, so I bought it."

Jill leaned back comfortably on the sofa and said with a laugh, "Yes, it's a great location. Did you know it's only fourteen minutes from my house?"

He nodded and smiled at her. "Like I said, the location is great!" He winked, saying, "As it turns out, Ian and I have some awesome neighbors."

Knowing he was referring to the Murrays, Jill grinned. "So since you're no longer playing baseball, what's next for you?"

"I'm in discussions with a buddy of mine in Austin about investing in a couple of businesses together. One is a self-storage company, and the other is a carwash chain," he told her. "In addition to that, I'm thinking about writing a book. It will be about transitioning from a sports career to living in the real world."

"The *real world*," Jill repeated softly. "That's an interesting way to put it!"

Dave shrugged then elaborated, "I know most folks don't have a lot of sympathy for pro athletes at the end of their careers. People think they've rolled in the big bucks and don't have to work anymore. The fact is, I'm one of the lucky ones. I signed a huge contract and was able to play for ten years. There are countless others whose careers are ended by injuries or they get cut and are not picked up again," he explained. "They've devoted their entire lives to their sport. It's all they know. Many of them didn't finish college. Heck, I played with guys who barely made it through high school. Fortunately, there are some organizations to help them now. I don't know," he sighed. "I thought I'd try my hand at writing and see how it goes."

"I look forward to reading your book," Jill said. "I'd also like to hear some of your baseball stories. I know my family would enjoy them, too, especially Jeremy."

Dave smiled broadly. "Thanks, I'd be happy to share some of them with you all," he replied. "I'm nowhere near being the great storyteller Mike is, but I have some good ones. It was a pretty crazy life."

"I bet!" Jill said, noticing how animated he became when he talked about baseball. "I'm sure you miss it."

He shook his head and said, "No, honestly I don't really miss it. Don't get me wrong, it was great while it lasted. But now it's time for the *next* chapter, and as I mentioned earlier, I'm excited about what the future holds." He was looking at Jill intently, and she blushed and looked down.

"I listened to the message you left on my cell phone," she said softly.

She looked up at him and noticed he'd arched one eyebrow inquiringly. "I like when you do that," she told him. "I've always wanted to be able to raise up just one at a time." She giggled, attempting to lift one brow, but both moved up and down.

"Just another one of my many talents," Dave quipped. Then he became serious. "I meant what I said on my message. I hated that Ian and I couldn't get over to your place earlier. I'd really been looking forward to seeing you again. The fact is, Jill, I haven't been able to get you out of my head since the day we met." He watched to see how she would react to his confession and was pleased to see her smiling. "Ian and I were about to jump in the car and head over that day when my ex-wife called." He paused, remembering their conversation.

"Go on," Jill prodded with a slight frown. She didn't hold Missy in very high regard after learning what the woman had done to Dave. "What did she want?"

"She told me I needed to put Ian on a plane to Arizona immediately because they were ready to have him back. I didn't want to have the conversation in front of my kid, so we went back into the house and I finished talking with Missy in my office." He gave Jill a despairing look and continued, "I made it clear that Ian was starting to fit in here and he was making friends. I also told her I was hoping he'd want to stay in Texas with me permanently." At this point, Dave stood and paced back and forth in front of the fireplace. "Well, suffice it to say, my ex was having none of it, reminding me that Ian had called her, begging to go back. I tried to tell her it was before he'd met Jeremy, but she didn't have ears to hear it."

Jill realized how agonizing the situation was for Dave and her heart went out to him when he said, "Honestly, I think the main reason Missy wants Ian back is because it hurts me. I know that sounds mean-spirited, but she can be very selfish."

"I'm sorry, Dave," Jill said sympathetically. "Then what happened?"

"I told her we needed to give it some more time and see what Ian decided to do. It should be his decision, which one of us he chooses to live with. And she informed me in no uncertain terms that she was his mother and, if necessary, she would fight me in court for full custody," he replied.

"Do you share joint custody now?" Jill asked.

Dave nodded thoughtfully and replied, "Yes, and as far as Ian is concerned, we've always been able to work things out. In fact, most of the time when I lived in Arizona, Missy was more than happy for me to take him as much as possible. As I've said, she likes her freedom."

Gazing into the fire, she asked, "So, how did the call end?"

"Well, I've learned that Missy always wants to have her own way. So, I played into that and told her she was probably right, maybe Ian would be better off living with her. Then I asked if she would please give us until the end of the year because it would be easier for him with school."

"That makes a lot of sense," Jill said.

"Thankfully, Missy agreed. I had Ian call and assure her things were going better for him here. While they were talking, I called my attorney to find out my rights as a father," Dave said. "If Ian decides to stay with me, I will fight her in court with every dime I've got."

Jill shook her head. "It's almost as if she's using him as a pawn. That's so wrong!"

"It is wrong, yet I'm believing it's all going to work out. Anyway, that's why we weren't able to be there early yesterday," he explained, eager to stop talking about his ex-wife.

Jill was regarding him thoughtfully. "You poor guy! And I was so horrible to you when you got to the ranch! I still feel bad about how behaved…"

She stared into his eyes and said sincerely, "Dave, I want us to be totally honest with each other, so I'll share something with you. While I do believe it's important for people to keep their word, the reason I blew up on you was because I'd been so eager to see you again."

Seeing this pleased him, she continued, "I'd gotten my hopes up that we'd have some time together and then you were late." Jill gave a self-deprecating shrug. "Maybe I'm a little like your ex! I always want my way, too!" Leaning in closer, she added, "I'm gonna let you in on a secret. I can also be a little bit selfish." He grinned as she held up her forefinger and thumb, showing him an inch worth of space. "Just a little bit," she said with an apologetic smile.

Dave pulled Jill close to him, breathing in her intoxicating scent. "Trust me, you are *nothing* like my ex-wife," he said. "You are kind-hearted, generous, and brave. I've never met anyone like you and frankly, right now I just want to kiss you and see if it's as wonderful as I've imagined it will be."

"Well," she replied softly, "let's see if it is."

Jill handed him her empty wine glass, watching as he set it on the end table. When he turned back to her, she was giving him a sideways grin, giggling as she admitted, "It's funny, but I feel kind of nervous about this kiss. You've just made it into such a big deal and all. It's a lot of pressure! I mean, what if it's not as epic as you've imagined?"

Dave, enchanted with her humor, said, "Jill, there's no way our first kiss could be anything less than epic. There's something between us, something that connects us. I can't put it into words."

"Dave," Jill said impatiently, "Please, shut up and kiss me already!"

She didn't have to ask him twice. Reaching for Jill, Dave gently caressed her face, then tilted her head to such an angle that when their lips met, they meshed together perfectly. The kiss was long and slow, neither of them wanting it to end. When they finally pulled away from each other, the energy between them lingered as they gazed into each other's eyes.

For a time, neither of them spoke, then Dave said simply, "Epic."

Jill nodded in agreement. "Is there a word beyond epic?" she asked, her voice thick with emotion.

"I sure can't think of one!" Dave replied, cozying up beside her. "I'll tell you this—that kiss was even better than I thought it would be."

"I completely concur," she murmured with a sigh as she rested her head on his shoulder. "It's been a perfect evening, but now I really need to go."

As much as Dave hated to see her leave, he knew it was getting late. "I don't want you to, but I understand," he said, rising to his feet. He offered her his hand to help pull her off the sofa. "I can't believe how fast the time flies when I'm with you."

Jill took his hand, and they walked to Dave's office to see Ian's artwork. "He really is a gifted kid," Dave said proudly, pointing out several framed watercolors around the large room.

"These are very good," Jill remarked. "Ian told me he wanted to be an artist like his mom."

Dave leaned casually against his desk, enjoying how she took her time to study his son's work. "He certainly doesn't get his artistic talent from me," he said.

"I'm very impressed with these paintings, Dave. Ian is quite talented. He's a comedian *and* an artist, and he's so young," she said warmly. "I think *gifted* is the perfect word to describe him."

"Well, he's definitely a unique individual, that's for sure!" Dave moved slowly across the room and took Jill's hand. "I think you should know that before you arrived tonight, Ian told me that if I liked you, then I should just go ahead and kiss you," he said, giving her a playful wink. "I'm so glad I took his advice!"

"Me, too," Jill said, beaming at Dave. "Please tell him how much I loved his artwork."

"I will," Dave promised.

"And now, I've *really* got to go," she said.

"I'll walk you out," he told her. "Let's get your jacket."

They walked to her car hand in hand, not wanting the evening to end. "Thanks again for having me over, Dave," she said, stepping into his open arms. When she looked up, he kissed her again, then held her close, their hearts beating together as one.

"Goodbye," he whispered softly in Jill's ear. He opened her car door and waited while she settled in behind the wheel. "I'll call you tomorrow," he said, his voice low and husky.

"I look forward to that," Jill replied as she started her car. "Goodnight, Dave."

"Goodnight, Jill," he said, closing the door and smiling from ear to ear as he watched her drive away.

Fourteen minutes later, Jill was pulling up to Gran's house. Like Dave, she was smiling. *I can't remember when I've had a more enjoyable evening,* she realized, thinking about how much they'd laughed together. *Dave is so sweet. He's really someone special.* She parked in front of the house and closed her eyes for a moment in an attempt to get a handle on her feelings. *Could I be falling in love with this man so quickly?* she wondered.

She was pleased to see Simon running to greet her. "Hey, buddy," she said, bending to give him a good ear scratching. "Did you miss me, boy?"

They walked into the house, and Jill popped her head into the great room. She had a hunch Mike would be waiting up for her. She laughed when she spotted him sitting near the fireplace, an open book in his lap. "Goodnight, big brother," she said in a singsong voice. "You can go to bed now."

Mike looked up at her with a wry smile, "Goodnight, little sister. I hope you had a pleasant evening."

She nodded and replied, "That I did. See ya tomorrow. Come on, Simon, let's call it a day."

As she was climbing into bed, Jill noticed she'd received a text message from Dave. *Thinking about our epic evening. Can't wait to see you again.* She texted him back with a smiley face and one word: DITTO.

CHAPTER 15

The next morning, Jill hugged her nieces and nephew goodbye as Gina readied the children for school. The proud aunt watched from the porch as Mike helped load them up and give his wife a kiss on the cheek. "See you in a bit, babe," he said tenderly, then turned his attention to the backseat. "You rug rats be good and bring me home some A's today!" Jill could hear the kids giggling from the porch.

As he did every school morning, Mike continued waving to his brood until the SUV disappeared down the drive. He was grinning as he jumped back up on the porch beside his sister. "Man, I just love my awesome kiddos," he remarked.

"And you love your awesome wife," Jill added.

"And my awesome wife, that's for sure," he agreed. "Gina really enjoys chauffeuring them back and forth to school. She says their time together in the car is the best part of her day—aside from being with me, of course," he teased.

"Of course!" Jill said, laughingly. "That's a given. Gina is one lucky lady to be married to you."

"You've got that right, Sis," he agreed humbly. "Now, enough talk about me. I want to hear all about your date with Mr. Baseball."

She rolled her eyes. "Please stop calling him that, Mike. And for your information, it wasn't a date. It was just dinner with some friends," she said. "Don't forget, Ian lives there, too."

"Whatever you say," Mike replied, obviously not convinced. "You looked pretty happy when you came in last night, just sayin…"

"I *am* happy, you goose," she told him.

"Well, I hate to spoil your good mood, but I thought you should know that Roger is coming over today," he informed her.

"You're right, that does put a damper on my day. *Why* in the world is Roger coming back here after the stunt he pulled yesterday?" she asked with a frown.

"Come on, Jill, you know Roger cares about you." He saw her knitted brow and quickly corrected himself. "Okay, Roger more than cares for you. He's also been a long-time friend of our family. He called after you left last night and apologized for the way things went down at breakfast. He even spoke with Gran. I think he's sincerely sorry for how he threw Dave under the bus."

"Look, Mike, you know I've gone round and round with Roger, telling him that I'm not interested in being anything more than friends with him. The way I'm feeling right now, I don't even *want* him as a friend. I think what he did to Dave was really rotten and, frankly, I can't stand the way he looks at me these days. It's really creeping me out."

Seeing she was becoming upset, Mike said, "Hey, now don't get all worked up! We're goin' up to the north pond to fish. You probably won't even see the guy. Don't worry, I'll keep him out of your hair."

"You'd better, because he's the last person I want to see right now," she told him.

"Got it," Mike assured her. "And I will talk with him about staring at you with those sad, puppy dog eyes. Honestly, I don't know when he became so fixated on you. I mean he's had a crush on you since we were kids, but since you've moved back, he's taken it to another level."

Jill decided it was time she told Mike about an uncomfortable encounter she'd had with Roger. "I guess I should have told you this before, but Roger cornered me alone in the kitchen once when I first came back. He said he was happy I hadn't gotten married because Stephen wasn't good enough for me." She looked away for a moment, remembering, then continued, "Roger said it was the two of us who belonged together, that we were meant for each other. I laughed it off, hoping he was fooling around. When I started to leave the room, he stepped in front of me, blocking my way and grabbed my arm roughly." Reliving the incident, she touched her arm and frowned. "He told me never to laugh at him again. The look in his eyes was weird, and it really frightened me." She looked up at Mike and finished softly, "I guess Roger realized he was scaring me because he finally let go of my arm and let me pass.

"Since that day, every time he's over here, I keep my distance from him. He keeps trying to get me alone so we can talk, but I have nothing to say to him!"

"Good grief, Jill!" Mike shouted. "Why are you just now telling me all of this? I would have straightened him out then and there! You and I have always talked about everything." He shook his head, disappointed she hadn't confided in him.

"I'm sorry," she apologized. "Maybe I should have told you sooner, but I know you and Roger are very close. I didn't want to come between you. Besides, I'd just moved back and I had other stuff I was trying to work through."

"That's a bunch of bullcrap!" Mike growled. "There's no way Roger's going to make you uncomfortable in your own home. I'm goin' to put a stop to this nonsense today!"

Knowing she'd upset him, Jill decided to change the subject. "Okay, enough of that business!" she exclaimed. "Simon and I are going over to check on Trixie. Wanna tag along?"

Mike took a deep breath, blowing it out slowly in an effort to calm himself. "Sure, let me take our cups into the house and grab my phone. Give me a couple minutes," he said, standing and reaching for her empty coffee mug.

Jill was waiting for him to return when she felt her phone vibrating. Hoping it was Dave, she was disappointed when she saw who was calling. *I thought I deleted that number a long time ago!* she thought.

Mike laughed when he came out of the house and saw the grimace on Jill's face as she debated taking the call. "Let me guess, Roger?" he asked.

She quickly declined the call and looked up at her brother. "No, it was Stephen calling." She shook her head in exasperation. "Men!" she grumbled.

Mike chuckled and said, "Hey, we're not all bad!" He was regarding her with interest. "Haven't heard that guy's name in a while. When was the last time you even spoke to Stephen?"

"When I gave him back his engagement ring," she replied. "I cannot, for the life of me, imagine why he'd be calling after all this time."

"Sister, I've gotta say, your love life is getting to be quite the soap opera!" he joked. Then, taking her by the arm, he grinned and said, "Come on, let's go check on Trixie!"

When they reached the barn, Simon ran ahead to the door where he sat and waited for them.

"Someone's eager to see his wife. We're coming, Simon!" she called. "I'm super excited, too!"

Mike opened the door, and Simon disappeared inside. Jill wasn't far behind him, and she gave a cry of joy as she looked into the horse stall they'd prepared for Trixie to have her pups. "They're here, Mike! The puppies are here! She must have had them last night! Oh my gosh, look at all of them!" Jill could barely contain her excitement as she turned and gave her brother a big hug.

He noticed there were tears of happiness in her eyes. "Congratulations, grandma!" he said affectionately. "Now, let me go, and let's see how many there are."

Simon was very interested in his squirming little pups, busily licking and sniffing each one. Kneeling down beside the dogs, Jill praised the new mother. "Such a good girl. What a sweet momma," she cooed lovingly. "You must be exhausted! Look at all your little ones!"

Mike was counting the tiny bundles of fur as they nursed hungrily. "One, two, three, four, five, six, seven, eight, nine…" He stopped for a moment to readjust a couple of the pups, then continued, "ten, eleven, twelve! An even dozen! Great job, Simon!"

Jill punched her brother lightly in the arm. "I think it's Trixie who did all the work here," she told him. "I was going to have Ned come over and check on her today, but it looks like she took care of things on her own."

"I think you should still have him come out," Mike said. "It wouldn't hurt for him to look over Trixie and the pups." He looked at Simon. "And it may be time to talk with Ned about neutering

Mr. Stud here. What are we going to do with twelve more German shepherds?" He groaned good-naturedly and exclaimed, "It's One Hundred Dogs in One Hundred Days all over again!"

She smiled at him and replied, "For now we're just gonna love them. We'll figure out the rest later. You're probably right about Simon, though. This will be his last litter." Leaning over to nuzzle Simon's face, she added, "He is quite the stud, isn't he?"

After a while, Mike stood and told her he needed to get some work done before Roger arrived.

Jill looked at her watch and noted the time. "I'm going to call Ned; then I've got some things to do, too," she said, taking his offered hand to help her up.

Simon decided to tag along with Jill, following them out as she and Mike left the barn. "Guess Mr. Stud here has had enough of the daddy thing for one morning," she laughed. "Come on, boy, let's go tell Gran the great news."

Gran was tickled pink to learn about the birth of Trixie's puppies. "It's always a thrill to have the little cuties around," she told Jill, giving her a tender embrace. "I'll go over there with you in a bit and see our new arrivals."

"That would be great," Jill said. "I'm going to give Ned a call and have him come by just to check Trixie and the puppies. I'll see you in a bit." She went to her room and called the vet, who assured her he would be over in a couple of hours. *I've got time to get a workout in on the treadmill before he gets here*, she decided, quickly throwing on some yoga pants and a sports tank.

She was heading toward the fitness room when her phone buzzed. Pleased to see it was Dave calling, Jill answered the phone immediately, wishing him a good morning.

"Good morning to you," he replied pleasantly. "I want you to know that I had the sweetest dreams last night."

She smiled and decided to have a little fun with him. "Did you now, Mr. Wilder? Well, I'm so glad you called, because there's something important you need to know about me."

There was a slight hesitation on the other end of the line and then, "Is this part of our pact not to keep secrets from one another?" Dave asked, a hint of concern in his voice.

"Definitely," replied Jill. "Because what I'm about to tell you may change the way you feel about me."

"All right," he said with a sigh. "Let's have it."

She made him wait another couple of beats, building up the suspense. "I'm a grandmother!" Jill said, bubbling over with laughter. "We have twelve new little puppies! Mike and I discovered them this morning when we went to check on Trixie!"

Dave groaned good-naturedly. "Okay, you definitely had me there for a moment! That was pretty funny. You know, I've never dated a grandma before. This will be a first."

She grinned into her phone. "So we're *dating* now?" she teased.

He chuckled softly and said, "Well, I'm sure hoping we will be! That's actually the purpose of this call. I'd like to ask if you'll go out with me. What do you say?"

"Hmm," she said, as if mulling it over. "And, should I agree to go out with you on this *date*, what might we do?"

"You really don't make this easy on a guy, do you, Ms. Murray?" he asked laughingly.

Jill laughed along with him and said, "Of course I'll go out with you! I'm just messing around. Why don't you come over and see the puppies and we can talk about it? I make fantastic PB & J sandwiches. We can go for a hike and eat lunch at one of my favorite spots up on the hill."

"That sounds like it'd be fun. I've got a couple of calls I need to make first. How does eleven-thirty sound?"

"That should work out great," Jill replied.

"Oh, and I like grape on mine," he said.

She was silent for a moment, then giggled when she caught on to what he'd told her. "Well, I'm glad to hear it, Mr. Wilder, because grape is the only kind of jelly that belongs on a PB & J sandwich," she said matter-of-factly. "I'll see you soon!"

Jill decided that since they'd be hiking, she'd forego the treadmill. Instead, she did some yoga, moving through multiple poses, enjoying the feel of her muscles stretching in her neck and limbs. She worked to clear her mind of everything, concentrating only on her body. When she finished, she sat cross-legged on the mat for a few more moments. After a while, she whistled to Simon who'd found a sunny spot in the corner. "Let's go get ready to see Dave," she said, walking to the door.

Jill took a quick shower and dressed for their hike. She'd left the French braid in overnight and noticed a few strands of blonde had come loose, but decided her hair passed inspection. As she applied some makeup, Jill glanced down at her phone noticing the missed call and a voicemail from Stephen. "Dang! What does he want?" she asked Simon, not wanting to take the time to listen to it.

She finished getting ready, then threw herself onto her bed and begrudgingly played the message. *Hey, Jill, it's Stephen. I know you probably don't want to talk to me, but here's the thing…my father is very sick. The doctors haven't given him long to live. I've been spending a lot of time with him and he finally asked me why you broke our engagement. You know he loves you. I told him how I'd let you down. I told him how I'd let you down so many times and that you'd finally had enough.* At this point, she could hear him clear his throat and let out a deep breath; then he picked up where he'd left off. *I admitted you're leaving me was entirely my fault. He encouraged me to get in touch with you and beg your forgiveness, so that's why I'm calling. I need to know you forgive me. Would you please call me back so we can talk? I'd really appreciate it.*

Jill sat for a moment and stared at the phone, then she grabbed some boots, whistled for Simon, and went in search of her grandmother.

She found Gran reading in her sitting room. Jill knocked politely on the half-opened door and waited to be invited inside. Seeing the somber look on her granddaughter's face, the older woman immediately put her book aside and patted the seat of the chair next to hers. "Come here, darling. Now, what's the matter, sweetheart?" she asked. "Is everything all right with the puppies?"

"Oh Gran, I'm not sure what to do about something, and I need your advice. Do you have a moment?"

"I always have time for you," Gran assured her, motioning Jill over. "Tell me, what's going on?"

"Well, of all people, Stephen Conrad called me earlier this morning," Jill replied. "I've had no contact with the man in nearly two years and out of the blue he leaves me this." She placed her phone on speaker and replayed the message.

Gran shook her head. "Do you really need my advice, dear? I think you know what I'm going to say."

"I know what you're going to say, but I just wish Stephen would drop it. It was a long time ago," Jill complained, knowing she was going to have to call him back if she were to ever have peace about the matter.

"To err is human, to forgive, divine," Gran quoted from the ancient poem.

Jill stood and kissed her grandmother on the cheek. "I'm going to go and get it over with. I don't need *this* taking up any more space in my brain!"

"That's my girl," Jill heard Gran say as she left the room.

She went to the great room to make the call, hoping to be finished dealing with Stephen before Dave arrived.

She took a deep breath and hit the return call button, and Stephen answered on the first ring. "Hello, Jill?" he asked.

"Yes, it's me," she replied. "I got your message. I'm sorry to hear about your father's illness. He was always kind to me. Please give him my best."

"I will," he told her. "As I said on my message, my dad always loved you."

"And I love him, too," Jill said. "Tell him I miss our chess games. He was always a worthy opponent." She heard Stephen laugh. "We've been playing a lot together lately," he said. "As I mentioned, I'm trying to spend as much time with him as possible. He's still pretty sharp. Nine times out of ten, he beats me."

She smiled, remembering Stephen's father's quick wit and the gleeful way he'd laugh when he made a great chess move. They'd played frequently while Stephen and his brother watched football on Sunday afternoons.

He took her silence as a good sign. "You and I had a lot of good times, Jill. Do you remember when we went skiing in Tahoe? I almost broke my neck racing you down the mountain. You're such a great skier—and always so competitive!"

Jill had no intention of going down memory lane with him. A quick glance at her watch told her Dave could arrive any minute. "Look, Stephen, I don't want to be rude, but the only reason I called you back is because you'd said you needed to hear me say that I forgave you for what you did. So here it is: I officially forgive you. And again, I'm sorry to hear about your dad. Now, I'm going to have to let you go," Jill told him.

"Wait! Jill, please don't hang up yet," he pleaded. "There's something else I need to say!" Knowing his time was short, Stephen blurted it out, "Jill, I still love you! I never stopped loving you and I want you back."

She'd been standing during their conversation, but his words so stunned her, Jill dropped into the closest chair. Working to wrap her brain around what Stephen had said, she didn't hear Dave come up behind her.

"No, no! You don't love me," she informed Stephen, raising her voice as she spoke. "And if you do, then I'm really sorry for you because I don't love you anymore. That ship has sailed. You broke my heart, and it's taken me a long time to trust men again after what you pulled." She could feel herself getting emotional and was trying not to cry.

"I thought you said you forgave me," Stephen said quietly.

"Yes, I've forgiven you. But as I said, it's over between us. Please don't call me again," she said emphatically.

"I understand, Jill," Stephen said. "But if you come up to Dallas for the *Texans Helping Texans* event, would you give me a call and we could go and see my dad together? I know it would mean so much to him."

Jill rolled her eyes. "I'll think about that, but no promises. I'm hanging up now. Goodbye." She ended the call and stood again, trying to regain her composure. As she turned around, she nearly walked into Dave.

"I'm guessing that was your ex?" He took in her dismayed expression and said, "I'm sorry. I didn't realize you were on the phone.

I saw your grandmother outside when I pulled up and she told me to come on in."

"Please don't apologize, Dave," she said. "Yes, that was Stephen. He told me his father is dying and asked my forgiveness for how he'd treated me when we were together."

Dave waited, knowing there was more based on what he'd heard her saying. He tried to appear casual, but was unable to hide the anxiousness in his voice when he asked, "He still loves you?"

Jill moved closer to Dave and placed herself in his arms. "I guess after all this time, he's finally realized what he lost," she said.

He pulled away, holding her at arm's length, looking into her troubled eyes. "Should I be worried? You're sure you don't have feelings for this guy anymore?" *We said we'd be honest with one another,* he thought. It killed him to ask, but he had to know. "What did you tell him you would think about?"

She felt bad that he'd overheard her conversation. The line of concern on Dave's face made her feel even worse. "Dave, with you I'm an open book," she said solemnly. "As I told Stephen, I no longer love him and, believe me, I'm sure that I don't. What you heard was me telling him that I'd think about visiting his ailing father the next time I'm in Dallas. Stephen knows I'll be in town in the next couple of weeks for the charity work we do through *Texans Helping Texans,*" she explained. "I still chair the annual Christmas Gala committee."

As a wave of relief washed over him, Dave was also moved by her kind heart. It touched him that she'd consider visiting her ex's sick father. "You're a good person, Jill Murray," he said, holding her close to him once more.

She smiled up at him and said, "Well, thanks. I have my moments. I'm sorry you had to hear all of that. I honestly didn't want to return his call at all, but I had some sage advice from a very wise woman."

"Gran?" he asked with a grin.

Jill nodded. "And unfortunately for you, I haven't had time to make our picnic lunch. You wanna give me a hand?"

"Not just yet," he replied, bending to kiss her softly. He then took her hand in his, as they made their way to the kitchen.

CHAPTER 16

Jill wasn't surprised to find Marcie in the kitchen. "You remember Ian's dad, Dave Wilder from yesterday?" she asked. Turning back to Dave, she said, "This woman is not only a marvelous cook, she also does the meal planning here and for all the hands. We're always telling her we think she's a miracle worker!"

Marcie beamed, taking pride in the compliments. Dave moved to shake her hand, telling her how much he and Ian had enjoyed Sunday's brunch. "Thank you, Mr. Wilder. I appreciate that, but I have a lot of help," she said humbly. "You know what they say—it takes a village."

He gave her one of his winsome smiles, and Marcie nearly swooned when he asked her to please call him Dave. "Stop flirting and help me make lunch," Jill scolded playfully. "We're going on a hike and thought it'd be fun to throw a picnic lunch together," she explained to Marcie.

"Well, isn't that nice?" Marcie remarked, still admiring Dave's green eyes. "I'd be happy to help. What were you thinking? I made a nice chicken salad earlier, does that sound good?"

"Your chicken salad is the best, but we were going to make lunch for ourselves," Jill told her with a smile.

Seeing they wanted some privacy, Marcie pulled off her apron and started toward the door. "I'm going to drive down to The Cantina and see how things are going over there. If your grandmother comes in; please tell Mrs. Murray we'll serve her lunch at twelve-thirty per her request." With that, Marcie was gone, leaving Jill and Dave alone in the massive kitchen.

Jill went over to one of the two sub-zero refrigerators lined up against the far wall and peered inside. "Awesome," she said, turning to Dave. "I found the jelly." She was pulling the jar out as she asked him to search for the peanut butter. "I think it's up there in one of those," she instructed, pointing toward a wall of cabinets. "I know for sure where Marcie keeps the bread," she added, opening the door to a spacious, walk-in pantry.

"Wow, I never knew making a peanut butter sandwich could be such a production," Dave said with a smirk. "Maybe we should have taken Marcie up on the chicken salad. It could take all day just to hunt down the peanut butter in this kitchen!"

Jill laughed and asked, "Where's your spirit of adventure?" She watched in amusement as Dave opened a third cabinet and peered inside. Moving over to him, she reached up and pulled a large jar off the shelf. "I prefer this over the smooth stuff," she told him. "I hope that's okay with you."

Dave caught her arm as she brushed across his chest and pulled her close. "Crunchy peanut butter is fine," he said agreeably. "And, in answer to your question, *here's* my spirit of adventure," he added, kissing her deeply.

The two were completely lost in the kiss when the kitchen door swung open and Roger and Mike walked in. Jill abruptly pulled away from Dave and glared at her brother.

Mike looked at her guiltily. "Oh hey, sorry, you guys! I thought you were in the barn with Ned and the puppies," he stammered. *"I'm so sorry!"* he mouthed silently to Jill.

She shook her head, furious with Mike. *He promised to keep Roger out of my hair today and what does he do? He marches the guy right into the kitchen,* she fumed inwardly. *We'll definitely be discussing this later.*

Acting as though she and Dave hadn't been interrupted in the middle of a passionate kiss, Jill set the peanut butter on the counter and spoke to her brother. "Oh, Ned's here? That's great!" She smiled back at Dave and said, "Let's go over, and I'll introduce you to our veterinarian. I think you'll get a kick out of him. We can finish making lunch later."

Dave had a few choice words he wanted to say to Roger, but in an effort to keep the peace, he smiled at Jill and said amiably, "All right then, let's go." He knew it was a little childish, but he made a show of taking Jill's hand in his before the two exited the kitchen using the far door.

Mike, observing the hard stare Roger was giving Dave, felt it was time for the conversation he'd planned on having while the two of them were fishing.

He waited until the door had stopped swinging, then leaned his tall frame against the granite counter. "Roger, I'm gonna cut straight to the chase with you," he said to his friend. "You will *not* be invited back here if you don't stop this crap with my sister."

Roger held up both hands, innocently. He gave a small laugh and said, "I'm sorry, Mike. I don't like that guy. I think he's bad news and definitely not worthy of Jill."

Mike wasn't letting him off the hook so easily. "It doesn't matter if *you* like him or not. It's none of your business. I noticed your reaction when you saw Dave's car out front. You're acting like a jealous idiot," he said sharply.

"Man, that's pretty harsh!" Roger said, defensively. "You know I care about Jill. I only have her best interest at heart." He looked at Mike wistfully. "I know she thinks of me as just a friend now, but I keep hoping that maybe it will evolve into something more between us. I've always believed she and I would end up together."

"Dude!" exclaimed Mike. "*That's* what I'm talking about, *that* right there! I know for a fact that she's told you repeatedly she thinks of you only as a friend."

"If she'd just spend some time with me, I know she'd come around. But Jill won't even give me the time of day," Roger grumbled.

Mike was growing impatient and angry with his childhood friend. *What's wrong with this guy?* he thought. *Why can't I get through to him?* He knew his next words would hurt Roger, but they needed to be said. He spoke in short sentences so there would be no more confusion on the matter.

"You need to listen to me. Get this through your thick skull. Jill does not love you and she never will." Mike paused to let his words sink in. "She told me that if you don't stop with all your nonsense, she won't even be your friend." With this, he pushed himself away from the counter and rose to his full height directly across from Roger. Mike was a formidable presence, his demeanor making it clear to Roger that he was very serious.

"Jill told me you'd frightened her one day in our kitchen. I just found out this information or we would've been having this conversation long before now. I won't have you or *anyone* making my family uncomfortable. I don't care how far back our friendship goes. Tell me you understand what I'm saying to you." Mike waited for a response, his muscular arms crossed over his brawny chest.

Roger eyed him for a brief moment before he reached out and offered to shake hands in a gesture of apology. "I've got it, buddy," he assured Mike. "I still don't care for this David character, but I'll keep my opinion to myself for Jill's sake."

Mike did not move a muscle, ignoring the offered hand. "No, Roger," he corrected him. "You need to do it for *your own* sake."

Realizing Mike had left him hanging, Roger dropped his hand. "Why do I get the impression you're threatening me?" he asked.

Mike shook his head. "I think you're finally getting the picture here, Roger. When it comes to protecting my family, I don't mess around."

"Okay, geez! I've got it. Now, are we going to grab something to eat in here and go fishing, or what?" Roger gave him a big smile, reminding Mike of when they were both young, freckle-faced boys.

It took Mike a moment to loosen up, but he finally relaxed and clapped Roger on the back. "Come on, let's raid the refrigerator like old times," he said.

Jill and Dave continued walking hand in hand to the barn. Neither of them spoke until they were near the door. "I'm sorry about that," she said. "Mike told me Roger would be coming over today to go fishing with him. Apparently, he called while I was at your place last night saying how sorry he was for that stunt he pulled at brunch."

She stopped walking and continued, "I can't even stand looking at Roger. Mike promised he'd keep him away from me," Jill said unhappily.

"I've gotta say, I was surprised to see him, especially after your grandmother asked him to leave yesterday," Dave admitted. "I guess he gets points for being persistent!"

"You're really something. Thanks for being such a good sport about everything. It shows me you can keep your cool," Jill said.

Suddenly uneasy, Dave looked at her and asked, "Are you worried I'm gonna lose my head and punch Roger in the nose?" he asked, concern in his eyes.

Jill wished she hadn't said anything. *Why does there have to be all of this drama?* she thought. *Can't we just have a nice afternoon together?* "No! I didn't mean to imply that at all! Please, let's just drop it." She started walking again, feeling Dave pulling her back to him.

He was looking at her intently. "You never have to be afraid of me, Jill. I won't ever hurt you and, although I'm not a fan of Roger, I understand your family has a history with the guy," Dave said.

"Thanks, I appreciate it. Now, can we please stop talking about stupid Roger Dunn and just go see my adorable grandpups?" she asked, batting her long eyelashes at him beguilingly.

Dave shook his head. "*Now* who's flirting?" he asked with a grin. In two short strides he was at Jill's side, his strong hands circling around her waist, lifting her off the ground, then twirling her in a perfect circle.

Jill squealed with delight, her long, blonde braid soaring through the air. He made her feel young and carefree. "Put me down!" she giggled, wanting Dave to do anything but that. "You're making me dizzy!"

He immediately stopped and held her close. "Sorry, I just got carried away there for a moment. You just looked so cute talking about your grandpups!" he said, laughing. "I've never known anyone who referred to themselves as a grandmother because their dog had puppies. It beats all I've ever heard!" Dave could barely contain himself. "I'm sorry, it just strikes me as being really hilarious!"

Totally enjoying Dave's amusement, Jill stood with a hand on each hip, pretending to be offended. Then, with her face set as straight as she could manage, she looked him in the eyes and asked, "Well, you know how they say that dog owners start looking like their pets?" She didn't wait for his reply. "Well, these puppies are the spitting image of me!"

Not one to be upstaged, Dave volleyed back with, "Then those must be some awfully pretty puppies! Let's go have a look." He took her hand once more, enjoying the easy conversation they shared as they entered the barn.

By the time they'd reached the puppies, Gran and Ned were saying their goodbyes.

"Oh, good, here's Jill now," Gran said, looking at the vet, then turning to Jill and Dave. "Ned was just leaving. Trixie and her pups are all doing fine."

"That's great news! Thank you, Gran, for meeting with Ned." Jill smiled kindly at the man who had cared for hundreds of dogs and cats at the shelter. "Dave Wilder, please meet Dr. Ned Greely. He's the best vet in Texas, and we're lucky to have him."

Ned went to shake Dave's hand. "Wait! I know you! You're a pitcher, right? Played for the Bears if memory serves." The animal doctor was still pumping Dave's hand.

Jill watched as Dave gave the vet a wide, humble smile and said, "I did, yes. But I'm retired now."

"Wow! I cannot believe it! I'm kind of a baseball fanatic. My wife keeps telling me I'm obsessed, but I really enjoy keeping up with it!" Ned gushed. "Hey, I think I've got one of your cards. Love to have you autograph it for me," he said, shooting a quick glance at Jill. "If that's all right with you, that is..."

Jill laughed. "Ned Greely! I had no idea you were so into sports. I don't know how you find time to do all the things you do with your practice, much less follow baseball," she said warmly. "I think Dave's going to come over with me to check out the shelter soon. If you can find his card, I'm sure he'll sign it for you," she said, giving Dave a questioning look.

"Of course, I'd be happy to do that," he assured Ned. Then he pulled the doctor aside as if he needed to consult with him privately. Dave made a production out of surveying each of the puppies lined up and down Trixie's belly. "Doc, Jill here thinks that these dogs might resemble her since they are, as she phrases it, her 'grandpups.'

I'm curious, which one do you think looks the most like her, so I don't commit a major *faux pas* when she asks me?"

Jill had come up beside the two and slugged Dave playfully in the arm, laughing. "Don't mind him, Ned. He may know baseball, but he doesn't know dogs!" she exclaimed.

She noticed Dave was no longer paying attention. He was sitting cross-legged in front of Trixie, admiring the spectacle of the puppies, completely enthralled with their tiny whines and squeaks. Jill placed her hand on his shoulder, then sat beside him, petting the new mother's head lovingly.

"I've never seen newborn puppies," Dave told her in wonder. "This is so darned special. I think I could sit here all day watching them and listening to their funny little noises. I can't wait for Ian to see them!"

Jill's heart swelled with joy that Dave was enjoying this moment so thoroughly. It also touched her that he wanted to share it with his son.

"We'll have Ian come and meet them in the next few days," she promised.

"You said there were twelve?" Dave commented, looking closely at the nursing pups, unable to determine where one lump ended and another began.

"An even dozen. Mike counted them this morning," Jill sighed.

"This is a good-sized litter, and they're full-blooded German shepherds. We have papers on Simon and Trixie. It's hard to believe these cute little creatures will grow into such fine, big dogs. I know we can't keep them all, I just need some time to think about what we'll do with them."

They'd been so enthralled with the puppies; Jill hadn't noticed Gran and Ned had left the barn.

"I'm starving," she announced, rising to her feet. "Do you want to finish making our lunch?"

He checked his watch. "Wow, it's getting late," Dave said. "As hard as it is to leave these little cuties, I'm with you. I'm starving too! Let's go get those PBJs."

With Simon in the lead, Jill took Dave on the same route she'd taken the day she found Ian. The majority of the trail was uphill and somewhat steep in several spots. More leaves had fallen since the last time she'd been there.

Not wanting Dave to trip and fall, she said, "It's a good idea to step high and watch your footing. With all the leaves, it's hard to see the roots and rocks."

"Sounds like good advice," came Dave's voice from behind her. "You're keeping a great pace. This will be a good workout."

Jill continued up the hill. "Thanks," she called back to him. "Mike and I run this sometimes when we're training. We call this Rock Point Trail. Running it will really kick you in the behind."

She could hear Dave's low chuckle. "Is that a challenge, Ms. Murray?"

He could hear the laughter in her response. "No, it wasn't, *Mr. Wilder.* But I have been accused of being competitive from time to time!"

The two finished the climb in silence, focusing on the rugged trail, weaving their way up the hillside. Upon reaching the top, they found Simon lying beside the large flat boulder where Jill planned on stopping for lunch. The dog cocked his head to one side, observing them as if to say, *"What took you guys so long?"*

Jill looked at Dave who'd come up to walk beside her. "Simon is such a show-off! Now *he's* the one who can set a great pace," she said, walking over to scratch the dog's ears. "If it were up to this guy, we'd be running everywhere we went! Isn't that right, Simon?" she asked the shepherd.

Dave slung the pack off his back and set it on the rock, taking in the breathtaking view of the valley below them. He whistled softly between his teeth in appreciation. "This is a perfect spot," he said, turning to Jill. "I'm blown away by it. Thank you for bringing me up here."

"You're welcome," Jill replied. "I love the view from this vantage point! Simon and I come here often." She patted the rock. "There's room for two up here," she said, climbing up on it. "The perfect spot to eat our lunch!"

Dave smiled and joined her. "Best seat in the house!" he proclaimed.

Jill grinned as she pulled out the sandwiches and bottled water they'd brought, handing one of each to Dave. They ate side by side, their legs hanging off the edge of the boulder, enjoying the splendor around them.

Dave broke the silence. "You can see for miles up here!" he said, scanning the valley, then pointing downward. "I think that's my house! Wow! From here it looks so small." He turned to Jill, giving her a serious look. "You'd said we were going to be close to the pond where you and Simon rescued Ian?"

"Right. It's not far from here," she replied. "Tell me you don't want to go there, because if you do, you'll be going alone."

Dave understood her reluctance to return to Snake Hollow. He shook his head. "No, I don't need to see it. I was just thinking Ian sure walked quite a distance," he said.

Jill nodded. "It's a long way. I was shocked to see a child up here alone. Thank God, Simon heard his cries for help," she said, tossing the last of her sandwich down to the dog. She and Dave both laughed as the shepherd stood and snapped the piece of food out of the air in one quick bite.

Dave reached over and put his arm around Jill. "You know, I'll never be able to thank you enough for saving my son," he said.

"Finding Ian is what brought us together," she reminded him. "We might not have met if it hadn't been for Ian's decision to go exploring that day."

He leaned down and gave her a soft kiss. "So something really good came out of something that could have been very bad," he replied.

"My sentiments exactly," Jill murmured into his lips. "And you, my friend, taste like peanut butter."

"As do you," Dave said with a grin.

They looked back over the valley. "Where does your property line end?" he asked.

"It's hard to point out because it's a really far stretch. Wind River Ranch sits on about thirty-five thousand acres." Jill motioned along the surrounding countryside and pointed to a spot beyond the top of another peak of hills. "My great, great grandfather bought the property in the mid-1800s after he'd made his fortune in the oil patch. I'm told his original holdings covered more than 150 square miles," she explained. "Over the years, parts of the property have been parceled off, including the land your home sits on now."

"How interesting! My little chunk of Texas used to be part of your family's property. Just another thing that ties us together," he said, giving her hand an affectionate squeeze. "I actually considered investing in a ranch when I was looking for a place with my real estate agent, but figured it'd be too much work!"

Jill laughed and nodded in agreement. "Having a ranch *is* a lot of work. We had cattle here in the early days. The Arabians came later. It was my grandfather who took things to the next level with the operation we have now," she said. "Last time I checked with Mike, he told me we have thirty-five full-time employees. Of course, that includes the security team, the hands and all the staff. I'm sure you've noticed, we monitor every visitor entering or exiting the ranch. We consider the people who live and work at Wind River family."

He whistled through his teeth again. "Very impressive. So, Mike runs Wind River?"

"Yes, he may act like a clown sometimes, but my brother is actually a very astute businessman. He's always been good with numbers and, more importantly, with people. He learned a lot from our grandfather, and he also has a master's degree in business from Texas A&M," she said proudly.

"How long has your grandfather been gone?" asked Dave.

"Only six years," Jill replied. "We were all so devastated when he died, especially Gran, of course. For Mike and me, it was a huge loss since we'd been pretty much raised by our grandparents."

"I haven't heard you talk much about your parents," Dave said, looking at her compassionately. "Would you tell me about them?"

"Unfortunately, there's not much to tell," she said sadly. "They were on their way back from a ski trip in Colorado. A friend of theirs had gotten his pilot's license. He and his wife invited my parents to fly with them to their place in Aspen for the weekend. The plane went down. There were no survivors."

Her eyes clouded over as she said, "I don't even remember them. I was barely three years old and Mike was only seven. Losing them was a tragedy that will always hang over our family. I miss them every day. I miss what could have been," she shared, emotionally.

Dave hugged her to him. "I'm so sorry, Jill. I don't know how anyone ever recovers from that kind of loss. It seems so unfair," he said.

"Life can be unfair," agreed Jill. "I'm so blessed to have such a strong, wonderful grandmother. She not only lost her son and daughter-in-law, she and Grandpa Jeremy had to become parents again to their grandchildren. I know part of the reason Gran goes all out for every holiday is because she's trying to help make up for the loss of our parents. Of course, Gran makes every day special. She doesn't take life for granted."

"She's a remarkable woman, Jill," Dave remarked. "From what I've seen, she and your grandfather did a fine job raising you and your brother."

"As I've told you, my family means everything to me," she said reflectively, looking back across the valley. Dave was surprised when a moment later, Jill suddenly shifted gears on him and announced, "I don't know about you, but my bottom is getting sore from sitting on this rock! Ready to head back down?"

"Ready!" he replied, jumping down to stand beside Simon. Dave then reached his long, muscular arms up to her.

"You sure your back can take my weight?" she teased.

He gave her a sunny grin. "Oh, I'm pretty sure I can handle you, babe," he answered, catching her deftly in his arms and pulling her close.

"I think I can handle you, too, Dave," she said softly in his ear before he kissed her again.

CHAPTER 17

Gran found Jill and Dave in the kitchen refilling their water bottles and laughing quietly together.

"How was your hike?" she asked them pleasantly.

"It was incredible," answered Dave. "The view from up there is amazing!"

"I took him up to Rock Point," Jill explained to Gran. "It *was* pretty incredible," she agreed, her eyes on Dave.

Seeing Jill's flushed, happy face thrilled the older woman to no end. "I haven't been there in years," she told Dave. "We used to have picnics up there quite often."

"We're just grabbing some more water. May I get you something?" Jill asked.

Gran shook her head and told them she'd been looking for Mike.

"I think he's still fishing. I can call him for you if you'd like," Jill offered.

"No, dear," Gran replied. "I'll call him myself from my room. I need him to come take a look at Little Lucy. Apparently, she's having some problems. I've already called Buck and asked him to come over." She turned to go, then smiled over to Dave. "Good to see you again, dear," she said warmly before leaving the couple alone.

Seeing Dave's questioning expression, Jill explained that Little Lucy was a pregnant mare. "Usually, horses give birth in spring or summer. We're able to manipulate the breeding cycle so that our foals are born earlier in the year. We've been concerned about Little Lucy for a while." She paused and gave an apologetic smile. "Sorry, as you know, I get carried away when I talk about horses!"

He shook his head. "No, please tell me more," Dave encouraged, leaning against the counter. He *was* genuinely interested in what she was telling him, but he also wanted Jill to continue because he found her totally captivating.

Seeing that he was sincere, she continued, "Well, we had Little Lucy checked out by our vet early in her pregnancy and learned she was expecting twins. This is somewhat uncommon in horses, but when it happens, it's best to remove one of the embryos." Dave watched as her expression became troubled. "You see, if twin foals are carried to term, there is the risk of losing them and their mother."

"Wow, it sounds like Ned must be here a lot!" remarked Dave.

"Oh, Ned's specialty isn't horses," she replied. "For the horses, we have Buck. And yes, he's here quite often. I'm sure you'll meet him, too, at some point."

"I'd like that," Dave said, giving her braid a playful tug. He then checked the time. "I've gotta go pretty soon. I need to be home before Ian's bus comes."

Jill gave him a pretty pout. "I understand, but isn't there something we needed to discuss?" she asked, eyebrows raised.

Dave grinned. "Hmm, I can't think of what it might be." He paused for a moment as if struggling to remember, then snapped his fingers. "Oh, yeah, our first official date!" This earned him a playful swat from Jill.

"Do you honestly think I'd forgotten about our date?" he asked, one eyebrow arched high.

She gave him a guilty shrug then laughed and admitted, "Well, I was *hoping* you hadn't!"

He reached over and took Jill's hand, giving her a serious look. "Babe, I've already told you that you're in my head constantly. I know we've only known each other for a short time, but that doesn't stop me from wanting to spend every minute I possibly can with you," Dave confessed. "And I'm sorry if that's too much too soon, but you wanted honesty, so there it is."

She gave a nervous laugh, then looked into his eyes and said, "That's pretty much the way I feel about you, too, Dave." she admitted. "I told myself I needed to hold back my feelings for you because I know you may have to move back to Arizona. The truth is, I can't stop thinking about you either. I've never been so strongly drawn to any man."

Taking her face into his hands, Dave kissed Jill until her toes tingled, making her giggle. "There's that cute little laugh!" he exclaimed, shaking his head with a grin. "I'm not sure what to think when my girl giggles when I kiss her, but I'm taking it as a good sign!"

"I'm giggling because you make me so happy," Jill assured him. "Now, Mr. Wilder, talk to me about this fabulous date!"

Dave wrapped his arm around her waist as they walked to the front door. "Well, I was thinking it would be fun to take you out for dinner and dancing on Friday night. There's a spot in Gruene I've been to a couple of times. How does that sound?"

"It sounds amazing," she replied. "I love to dance!"

He was thrilled she liked the idea so much. "There's just one thing," he added, holding up his index finger.

"What's that?" she asked.

"It's only Monday, and I don't know if I can possibly wait until Friday to see you again," he said earnestly.

Jill realized she couldn't wait that long, either. "Why don't you bring Ian over tomorrow when he gets out of school? We can show him the puppies," she suggested.

"I think I can hold out that long," he teased. "Though it may be tough!"

She laughed. They'd made it to the porch, and she knew it was time to say goodbye. "It was great being with you today, Dave," she said. "I'll see you tomorrow."

"Tomorrow it is," he agreed, leaning down to kiss her goodbye.

———◦《◉》◦———

Friday arrived, and Jill was waiting for Dave in the great room. Mike had taken his family out to dinner so it was just her and Gran.

"It's so quiet around here tonight, isn't it?" Jill asked her grandmother.

"It certainly is," replied Gran. "I'm glad everyone's getting a night out, but I always prefer to have my family home. I like the noise and chaos."

"So do I, Gran," she said. "Wait! I don't want you to be here alone. I'm sure Dave wouldn't mind staying in. The three of us could play cards," Jill suggested, concern in her eyes.

Gran shot her a stern look. "Jill Murray, you will do no such thing! I wasn't hinting that you should stay here! I *want* you to go out and have some fun." Then, looking into the fire, she said dreamily, "Your grandfather used to take me dancing. Oh, that man would lead me all around the floor. He was so tall and handsome and I was so proud to be in his arms."

Jill could picture the couple in her mind's eye. "It sounds so romantic, Gran. I'm really glad Dave likes to dance! I haven't been dancing in...well, it's been so long, I can't even remember!" she exclaimed.

"I'm sure you'll have a wonderful evening, darling," Gran said. "I'm so happy you met Dave." Gran cocked her head at her grand-daughter and added softly, "I've noticed you two have been spending a lot of time together these past few days."

"Yes, we have. As you know, he came over Tuesday with Ian to see the pups, and we've gone on a couple of great hikes. I also took him to tour the winery yesterday."

"It sounds like you're getting to know one another," Gran said.

Jill sighed. "I can't seem to get enough of him. We have so much fun when we're together," she gushed. "I'm so attracted to him! Not just his good looks. I love his sense of humor and his big heart. I love the way he strives to be a great father to Ian, and I love the way he looks at me, like he's so lucky to be with me..." Jill paused, then added softly, "like he loves me."

Gran chuckled and said, "You're easy to love, sweetheart." She reached over and patted Jill's leg affectionately. "And you deserve this happiness. Just follow your heart."

The doorbell rang, and Jill jumped up quickly. "That's Dave now! I'll bring him in here so he can say hello," she said, bounding from the room with Simon on her heels.

Gran smiled knowingly. "I think my sweet girl is in love," she said to herself.

It was the first time Jill had ridden in Dave's car. He opened her door and helped her inside the sleek 718 Boxster. "Nice wheels," she said, admiring the Porsche's fine leather seats and streamlined dashboard.

Dave grinned and leaned down to give her a quick kiss. "Thanks, babe." She watched as he closed her door and walked around to the driver's side. After climbing inside and starting the engine, he turned to Jill and said, "Listen to that engine! It's like she's purring with power!"

Giving him a good-natured smirk, she remarked, "Boys and their toys!"

Dave threw back his head and laughed. "I know, right? I really should just grow up and get a minivan!" he joked.

She laughed along with him. "Somehow, I can't picture you driving a minivan!"

They'd stopped at the gate, and he entered the code she'd given him to open it. While they waited, he looked at her appreciatively and said, "You look stunning tonight!" He glanced down at her emerald-colored boots. "Part of the 200 Club?" he teased.

"I chose these because I like how they match your gorgeous green eyes," she told him matter-of-factly.

"Why, Ms. Murray, are you flirting with me again?" he asked, flattered.

"You know it," Jill replied. "I should tell you that Mike's the one who came up with calling you Mr. Baseball, but I prefer Dazzling Dave," she said, giving him a sly smile. "Between those green eyes and your striking good looks, I bet you have women beating down your door!"

Dave laughed humbly as he drove through the gate and turned onto the road. "Well, I don't know about all that, but thank you for the compliments. And, again, just plain Dave is fine!"

Jill giggled and said, "Got it! But for the record, there's nothing "plain" about you, Dave." She grew suddenly quiet, trying to figure out where he was taking her. She knew most of the restaurants in the area, and none were in the direction they were driving. "Okay, when are you going to tell me where we're having dinner?"

"Oh, you'll see," he said mysteriously. "It's a surprise."

She wiggled in her seat. "I just *adore* surprises!" she said.

She could see Dave's smile illuminated by the lights on the dashboard.

They'd driven a few miles when he pulled off the main road and onto a private drive that wound through a thick forest. Dave reduced his speed, then stopped the car completely to allow several deer to move off the road. He laughed, watching the graceful creatures as they took their time leaping into the woods. "They certainly weren't in any hurry," he said dryly.

"Aren't they precious?" Jill remarked. "They're so much fun to watch."

With the road clear in front of them, Dave resumed driving, and Jill saw they'd reached a large clearing where a huge mansion stood proudly in front of them. She shot Dave a quizzical glance as he pulled into the circular drive and stopped the car. He did not offer any explanation. Jill looked around. There were several buildings on either side of the home, but she saw no other vehicles. Perplexed, she could stand the suspense no longer. "*What* are we doing here? There's no one else around!"

Dave grinned and opened his door. "Tonight we dine under the Texas stars!" he informed her. "Please stay seated; I'm coming around to get you."

Jill laughed and waited for him to open her door. "My lady," he beckoned, helping her from the low bucket seat.

"I have to admit, Dave, my curiosity is piqued," Jill told him. "What in the world are you up to?"

Dave decided it was time to end her suspense. "This is the place I was telling you about. The wedding venue where my friend got married," he said, as if that explained everything.

It took her a moment to respond. "You brought me to a *wedding chapel?*" she asked incredulously.

Seeing her baffled expression, Dave laughed and said, "Sweetie, I rented it for us. And, don't worry! There's no preacher hanging around. We're just here to have dinner!"

He took her hand. "Come on, you're going to love this place," he assured her.

They walked through the front door of the lovely old mansion. A stately, silver-haired gentleman greeted them in the grand, circular foyer. "Good evening, Mr. Wilder, Ms. Murray, and welcome to Whispering Water Inn. My name is Israel; I'll be your host tonight. If you would, please follow me," he said. The tall man then ushered the couple deeper inside the expansive home, through some French doors and outside onto the terrace.

"Your table awaits," proclaimed Israel, indicating a lone table prepared for two under strings of twinkling lights. It did not escape Jill's attention that, in the center of the table, was crystal a vase with a single yellow rose in full, glorious bloom. Touched by the romantic gesture, she turned to Dave and smiled. "It's magical!" she said breathlessly.

"Magical?" Dave asked, pleased.

"Hmmm," she murmured, taking her finger and running it down the length of his solid chest. "Mr. Wilder, I believe you have outdone yourself tonight. I am thoroughly blown away!"

He put his arms around her and said, "I wanted our first official date to be special. Something you'd always remember."

"You rented this entire place just for us?" Her voice was soft, and his heart melted when she gazed into his eyes.

He nodded. "Shall we sit?" he asked, taking her arm.

They enjoyed the meal as a server brought in the various courses. The menu included Caesar salad, grilled salmon, and wild rice followed by a decadent chocolate mousse.

There was a slight chill in the November air, but the patio heaters kept the temperature comfortable. At one point, Dave noticed her trembling and offered her his jacket.

"No, thank you, I'm fine," she said contentedly. "I'm more than fine, I might be on the edge of delirious after that dessert!"

"Yes, that was pretty awesome!" Dave agreed. He nodded to Israel, then leaned closer to her and whispered excitedly, "I have another surprise for you!"

At that moment, the lights above them dimmed, and the lawn beyond the terrace was ablaze with red and green Christmas lights. Jill was completely awestruck. She'd never seen anything like it. "Oh my gosh!" she exclaimed, standing and hurrying over to the edge of the stone patio. "There must be millions of lights out there! Look at how the clear ones outline the banks of the river!"

Dave was a bit overwhelmed himself. He and Ian had come over to the mansion the night before for a preview, wanting everything to be perfect for Jill. Ian had been the one to suggest running lines of clear lights along the banks of the Pedernales River which ran behind the wedding venue. "It's just gonna take things over the top, Dad," he'd said. "You want to really wow Ms. Jill, don't you?"

"More lights," Dave had said to Israel. "We've got to have more lights. I don't care how much it costs! Let's light this place up like the Fourth of July!"

"Yes, sir," Israel told him. "We'll get more lights."

Dave came over and stood beside her, enraptured by the reflection of the lights in her eyes. He wrapped his arms around her and Jill relished in the strength and warmth of his body. "Thank you, Dave. Thank you for all of this," she said, her voice choked with emotion.

He reluctantly pulled away and saw the tears in her eyes. "Oh, no," he said, confused by her tears. "Why are you crying?"

"Because I'm just so moved by what you've done tonight," she answered. "No one's ever done anything this spectacular for me. It just means so much. *You* mean so much to me," she said, burying her face in his chest.

She felt the rumble of Dave's laughter against her forehead. "You, my dear, are without a doubt the most fascinating person I've ever met. One minute you're smiling, the next you're crying. I'm having a tough time keeping up with you," he said, then added, "but I'm so glad you liked the lights. Ian had a hand in helping me take them over the top. He wanted to make sure I impressed you."

Jill laughed and told him, "Dave, you've done more than just impress me!" She motioned to the lights, then back toward their dinner table. "Honestly, I don't see how you could ever top this!"

He shot her a satisfied grin. "Challenge accepted, Jill. I'll do whatever it takes to impress you."

She shook her head. "Dave, what you've done tonight is incredible. But you need to know, I don't need all the bells and whistles to make me happy." She stroked his face tenderly and said softly, "I just need you."

He pulled her close again and finally replied, "I think we need each other." He kept one arm around her waist as they turned to admire the spectacle of the lights a little longer. After a few minutes, he asked, "Are you ready to do some boot-scootin'?"

"I almost hate to leave here, it's just so special," she replied.

"I have a feeling they're ready to lock this place up," Dave said, giving a wave to Israel who was standing on the far side of the patio.

"Got it!" Jill said. "I'm ready to dance the night away!"

Dave chuckled as he offered his arm to escort her out. "I'm right there with you, babe!"

It was late when they arrived at the dance hall, and the joint was in full swing. They could hear the country music blaring from the venue's open windows as they made the trek from the parking lot.

"It looks like this place is really hoppin' tonight," Dave observed.

Jill giggled and said, "It's Friday night! We'll be lucky to find a spot on the dance floor!"

They made their way inside, and Dave went to get them some beers. When he returned, he found a lanky, rugged-looking cowboy leaned in closely to Jill. He shook his head, not surprised to see she'd attracted another man's attention.

"Here you are, babe," Dave said, handing her a long-necked bottle. He gave the cowboy a courteous nod and reclaimed his girl, watching as the disappointed man slowly walked away.

Dave cocked his head and looked at Jill accusingly. "Can't leave you alone for one minute!" he teased.

She laughed, then pulled him close so he could hear her over the loud music. "I understand that you're just joking, but you need to know, you won't ever have to worry about me. I'm a one-man kind of woman," she told him. "Besides, he just came over to tell me he liked my boots!"

Dave rolled his eyes, yet he was smiling good-naturedly. "Yeah, I bet he did! Did you tell him you'd chosen to wear them because they matched your boyfriend's dazzling emerald eyes?" he asked with a wink.

She shook her head and giggled. "No, we didn't get that far!" Her eyes were on the dance floor. "You ready to get out there?"

"Just waiting for you," Dave said, placing his beer on a nearby table next to hers and offering his arm.

They danced the Texas Two-Step for several songs, Jill delighting in Dave's smooth, easy moves. "You're a great dancer," she told him. "It doesn't surprise me. I've noticed you're very light on your feet. I love to watch you move."

"Thanks! I took some aerobic dance classes in the off-season one year. It started out as an alternative to running sprints," he explained. "Both have been proven to increase pitching velocity. My dance instructor was really into country dancing. She's the one who taught me some moves."

Jill grinned and repeated the words he'd said to her earlier, "Yeah, I bet she did!"

Giving her a coy grin, Dave took that moment to twirl her around and catch her back in his arms.

The band finished the upbeat number and started a slower song that brought the couples closer to each other as they moved as one to the gentle rhythm of the music. Jill and Dave were pressed firmly together, enjoying the intimacy of the dance, when she felt someone tapping on her shoulder from behind.

She heard, "May I cut in?" Jill stopped dancing and turned to see Roger, his eyes pleading, his hand extended to her. *Not on your life, buddy*, she thought.

She glanced quickly back at Dave, then said to Roger, "I'm sorry. But we were actually just leaving." She felt Dave take her by the arm, escorting her off the dance floor, leaving Roger standing in the middle of the room amid a sea of swaying couples.

If either Jill or Dave had looked back, they'd have seen the dejected man's angry glower as he watched them leave the dance hall.

CHAPTER 18

Dave drove back to Gran's house where he and Jill recapped their evening. "How late did you tell the sitter you'd be?" she asked.

Dave consulted his watch. "I told her I'd be home by midnight, so we've got just a little more time left," he replied, touched that Jill was concerned about his arrangements for Ian. "She's a senior in high school and was happy to earn some extra money. She told me to stay out as late as I wanted, and she'd just crash on the sofa until I got home if it got to be too late."

Smiling, she asked, "So the babysitter's meter is running? She sounds like an enterprising young woman."

"She is," Dave agreed. He fixed his eyes on Jill, wanting to focus only on his date. "I had a wonderful time with you tonight."

"*Best* first date ever!" Jill said, nodding happily. "I can't wait to tell Gran about all the lights along the river. She loves Christmas so much! She's got crews coming out Monday to start decorating."

"Wait! You guys decorate for Christmas *before* Thanksgiving? Isn't that bad luck or something?" Dave asked.

Jill laughed and gave his leg a slight push. "No, silly, it's not bad luck. It's totally awesome! It's the way we've always done it, so we're used to it. You and Ian are going to love it, too! All of the decorations really put you in the holiday spirit," she assured him. "Oh, and that reminds me, I'm supposed to invite you guys over for Thanksgiving dinner."

"So, is this your official invitation?" Dave asked with a wry smile.

She giggled. "It is. Will you come?"

"I'm going to give you a strong maybe," he replied. "I've got to check with Ian's mother. She's been making noises about having him there for Thanksgiving. If she insists, I'll fly to Arizona with him and then bring him right back."

Jill was disappointed he couldn't give her a solid yes, but she understood his circumstances. "Okay, just let me know whenever you can." There was a moment of silence as the two thought about Dave's situation with his ex-wife. Then, suddenly, she brightened and asked, "Hey, what are you and Ian doing tomorrow morning?"

"No plans that I'm aware of," Dave said. "Whatcha thinkin'?" He liked that she enjoyed staying active and was always planning things for them to do. *We're alike in that regard,* he thought. *We both enjoy keeping busy.*

"I thought it'd be fun for you and me and the kids to go on a trail ride together. We could even pack a picnic lunch. I have another great spot in mind," she said.

She's excited about this idea, he thought. *But, I'm going to have to let her down.* Dave was quiet for a moment, then shook his head. "I'm sorry, but on that invitation, I'm going to have to give you a solid, 100 percent, no. But thank you," he said, politely.

His refusal caught her off guard, and he could see he'd hurt her feelings. Jill's normally animated face looked crestfallen. Dave immediately leaned over and tilted her chin up so they were looking into each other's eyes. "Hey, it's not that I don't want to, it's just that..." He paused and the longer it took him to explain, the more frustrated she became.

"Dave, what is it? Please just tell me!" she snapped impatiently, her eyes anxious.

Chagrined, he let out a long sigh and answered, "Well, I'm surprised it hasn't come up sooner, but the fact of the matter is, I've never ridden a horse in my life."

It took a moment for his response to sink in, but when it did, Jill snorted with laughter. Dave quickly realized that Jill thought he was pulling her leg.

Dave gave her an innocent shrug. "No, Jill. I'm dead serious. Think about it; I've been a pitcher all my life. I've gone out of my way to avoid activities where there's a risk of injury. Heck, you should see the list of things I was prohibited from doing when I was playing professionally. It's a wonder I ever left the house!"

"I'm sorry, Dave," she said, sobering, yet still amused by his admission. "I honestly had no idea. Why didn't you tell me before?"

"Well, you never *asked* before! It is kind of funny if you think about it," Dave said with a smirk. "That it's never come up in conversation. I mean you talk about horses all the time."

"Ugh!" she moaned. "I feel so stupid! I just took for granted you'd ridden before." Jill gave him an apologetic smile and added, "It just goes to show, we still have a lot to learn about each other."

"There's time for that," he said, leaning over to kiss her. "You fascinate me. I want to learn everything there is to know about you. Oh, and in regard to riding, just start me out with Horses 101. I'm a quick study, and so is Ian." He looked at his watch and frowned. "I guess I'd better take off," he told her. "Let me come around and help you out."

Jill was concerned she'd been insensitive about Dave's lack of experience around horses, and as they approached the house, she apologized again. "You surprised me, that's all. I can't wait to have all of us riding together. Horses are just the most amazing creatures," she said.

He laughed and said, "I assure you, my feelings aren't hurt, Jill. I have pretty thick skin." He abruptly stopped walking, held up his hand, and said, "Wait! I thought you'd told me *dog*s are the most amazing creatures." Dave had an amused look on his face as he waited for clarification on the matter.

Jill laughed as Simon suddenly appeared, running over to welcome her back home. "There you are, pal!" she said, scratching his ears. Then, turning her attention back to Dave, she explained, "You see, dogs are more like people to me than horses. But both dogs and horses are pretty special!"

Dave thought she looked so adorable in the moonlight; he had to kiss her again.

"You, Jill are the one who's pretty special," he said sweetly, circling his arm around her waist. "I've had such a good time tonight! Let's go dancing again soon."

"I'd love to," Jill said. "It's definitely been a night to remember. Thank you again for everything."

"It was my pleasure, Ms. Murray," he replied.

She was searching her handbag for her house key when she heard him say, "And, on second thought, if you can wrestle up two sweet-natured horses, Ian and I will be here bright and early for that trail ride."

Jill looked up, keys in hand, and gave him a huge smile. "I'm sure that can be arranged, Mr. Wilder. Now, kiss me goodnight and go home. I'm sure your babysitter's meter is now running on overtime!"

Jill was happy Mike was still up when she popped her head into the great room. "I'd like to think you aren't waiting up for me, but I'm not even going to give you a hard time about it if you are," she said.

In spite of his guilty look, Mike retorted, "A man's got a right to sit in his own living room and read, doesn't he?"

Seeing her bemused expression, he asked, "So, what's up?"

Jill told him Dave and Ian would be coming over in the morning and asked if he and Gina and the kids would like to join them on a trail ride.

"Gina and the girls have plans, but Jeremy and I will go. Sounds good to me," Mike said.

Jill started to leave then turned and said lightly, "Oh, and I just found out that neither of the guys have been on a horse. So, we'll need to spend some time with them before we hit the trail. You can help me choose the best horses for them. Goodnight, Michael," Jill called sweetly to him as she left the room.

She heard her brother's playful groan as she and Simon headed down the hall.

When the Wilders arrived on Saturday morning, Jill and Mike had their horses saddled and ready for the trail ride. They spent time allowing the two to become acquainted with the mild-mannered geldings they'd chosen for them and explained some of the basics before Mike helped the novices into their saddles.

The siblings had decided that Jill would work with Dave while Mike and Jeremy helped Ian. After riding around one of the corrals, it seemed everyone was comfortable enough to get started.

Mike and Jeremy took the lead with Ian and Dave following. Jill brought up the rear with Simon not far behind. The majority of the trail required they ride single file so, as the trail narrowed, horses and riders formed into one line.

Knowing Mike was keeping close tabs on Ian, Jill focused on Dave and his horse Leland. From her vantage point, Jill could see Dave was doing just fine. *For someone who's never been around horses, he has a natural ability*, she thought.

She'd admired his manner with the large animal and had been impressed when Dave smoothly mounted Leland, sitting straight and tall in the saddle. *We'll make a cowboy out of you yet, Dave Wilder*, she thought.

The group rode for the better part of an hour before taking a break for an early lunch. They'd stopped in a clearing with a circle of large stones around a makeshift fire pit, tethering the horses to some nearby trees. "We roast weenies and marshmallows up here sometimes," Jill explained to Dave. "It's a lot of fun for the kids."

"It's fun for everyone," Mike corrected her. "Nothing better than s'mores over an open fire. Ain't that right, Jeremy?"

"Right, Dad," Jeremy agreed. "And the weenie roasting—that's awesome, too!"

"Well, Son, I'm glad you said that because your dear, old dad here just happens to have..." Jill watched as her brother pulled hot dogs, buns and the makings for s'mores from his pack, waving them in the air.

Jeremy squealed with delight as he poked Ian in the ribs and said, "You're gonna love this, man!"

"Mike," Jill protested, "it's ten-thirty in the morning! We can't have s'mores at ten-thirty in the morning!"

"On the contrary, my dear sister," he replied, looking at the boys. "Who thinks it would be all right to eat hot dogs and s'mores at ten-thirty in the morning?"

"We do!" both boys shouted gleefully.

"I'm in!" Dave called out, holding up his hand. "Sounds amazing!"

Jill shook her head and looked over at Simon who was hungrily eyeing the weenies in Mike's hand. "I'm not even going to ask for your vote!" she said ruefully.

Mike had the boys help him gather kindling for the fire and, before long, they had a roaring blaze going.

Seeing Jill was busy pouring some drinking water from her canteen for Simon, Dave came over to sit beside them. "Your brother is really great with kids," he said.

Jill nodded in agreement and said with a grin, "And you're really great with horses! I have to admit, you looked like a real stud riding Leland!"

Dave tipped his ball cap to her. "Why, thank you, ma'am," he said in a sexy, southern drawl. "But I think Leland is the stud. You guys chose the perfect horse for me. I'm having a great time." He looked over at Ian who was attempting to spear a hot dog with a stick Mike had sharpened for him. "He's having the time of his life. I was so proud to see him up there riding that horse." He gazed at Jill adoringly. "You just keep making our lives better and better! Thank you."

Touched by his kind words, Jill looked away for a moment, and Dave was struck again by her beauty as the wind caught her long hair, blowing it softly around her face. Seeing his stare, she rolled her eyes self-consciously and smiled back at him. "Well, I feel like you're making *my* life better, so you're welcome, Mr. Wilder!" she exclaimed, working the stray locks into a neat ponytail then pushing it under her straw hat.

He leaned over, giving her a quick kiss, then announced, "I'm going to find us some sticks. We can't let the boys eat all those hot dogs!"

Jill chuckled as he began his search. "It's not the kids you should worry about," she called after him. "It's Simon. He adores hot dogs!"

Mike came and sat next to her as they watched Dave hunting for roasting sticks. "I'm going to agree with Gran, Jill. Dave's a good egg. I really like him, too," he said.

"Mike, I didn't mention it last night, but Roger was at the dance hall when we were there. He tried to cut in on Dave and me during a slow dance. I told him we were leaving, which we did," Jill said. "It was harmless, but I thought you should know. I have a feeling my refusal wasn't well received."

Her brother considered this information for a moment, then said, "I had a long talk with Roger, Jill. I think he and I are on the same page now." He gave his sister a friendly shove. "You can't blame him for wanting to dance with you. I don't think you should make it into a big deal."

"You're right, then. I won't," she said agreeably, resting her head on his shoulder. They were quiet for a moment before she told him, "I've gotta go to Dallas."

"The charity event?" Mike asked. The siblings stopped talking when Dave returned carrying several long branches.

Noticing their silence, Dave stopped and shuffled his feet, uncertain as to whether or not he should interrupt. "You two need a moment?" he asked.

"No, no, Dave! Please come back and sit down," Jill insisted. "I was just telling Mike that I need to go to Dallas for a couple of days next week. I think I've told you that I still chair the Texans Helping Texans Christmas Gala and I've already missed the first two meetings. It's imperative that I'm at the next one," she explained.

Not liking the idea of Jill traveling alone, Dave looked over to Mike. "Will you be going with her?" he asked.

Mike shook his head. "Ordinarily I would, but we've got a situation with one of our mares…"

Before her brother could finish, Jill interrupted, "Stop it! Both of you!" she demanded. "I'm *not* a child. I lived in Dallas for years without some he-man looking out for me. I've got this. I'm perfectly capable of going by myself."

"Of course you are, Sis," Mike assured her, giving Dave an apologetic shrug. "Didn't mean to imply otherwise."

<hr />

The crews were working hard, diligently removing the many pumpkins and assorted gourds that had adorned the ranch, replacing the fall decorations with all things Christmas. The scope of work made this an enormous task, and Jill knew from experience it would take several days for them to finish the project.

She'd packed for her Dallas trip the night before and was ready to head out, knowing the traffic on I-35 would be heavy until she got north of Georgetown. Stopping in the great room, she watched Gran, who was busy overseeing the decorators. Jill smiled as they positioned the giant tree in its customary spot by the window.

"I'm leaving now," Jill said, reaching over to give her grandmother a hug. "I'll be back soon." Admiring the work that had already been completed, she sighed happily and added, "It already looks amazing in here! Thank you for always making the holidays so special for all of us."

Gran returned her hug. "Please call me when you get to Dallas, dear," she said. "You know I worry about you being on the road alone."

"Of course, please don't worry. I'll be fine and back before you know it," Jill assured her.

She'd spoken with Mike earlier after he'd thoughtfully pulled her car around to the front of the house. "I was hoping maybe Dave would go with you," he'd said.

"Dave's got Ian and his own life to think about, Mike," she'd told him. "Stop being a worrywart. Geez! This is important work we're doing. Without this event, there'd be some families who wouldn't have anything for Christmas."

She shook their conversation from her head, grabbed her overnight bag, and started toward the front door. She almost did a double-take when she saw Dave, arms crossed, leaning casually against the side of her BMW.

He'd never seen Jill dressed for business and his knees nearly buckled as she strode toward him in an exquisitely cut suit that accentuated every angle of her perfect figure. "I couldn't help myself," he told her. "I had to come over and tell you goodbye."

"Oh Dave, you're so sweet, but we said our goodbyes last night, remember?" She gave him a wry smile, secretly pleased he'd come over. "I'm not even going to be gone that long," she reminded him.

Dave reached over and took her bag with a slight frown. "I don't want you to go, Jill," he said, looking into her eyes. "I hardly slept last night thinking about it. I hate that you're going alone." He took her in his arms and murmured in her ear, "I'm sorry I can't come with you."

She melted at his words, torn by the strong desire she felt for him. "Please don't worry about me. I lived by myself in Dallas for years, and I've got tons of friends and business contacts there so I'll hardly be alone," she assured him, softly. "There are plenty of people I can call if I want to go out."

He pulled her back into him, inhaling the sweet smell of her hair. "All right," he said. "I'm sorry. I'm sure everything will be fine. It's just that..."

"It's just that *what*, Dave?" Jill asked, concerned.

"Look, I'm just going to lay my cards on the table. When I was married to Missy, my focus was never on her, it was always on baseball. I wish I could tell you that she broke my heart, but she didn't. I was totally self-absorbed. All I cared about was the game." Dave looked at her, needing Jill to understand. "I punched Parker because he was my best friend, and he betrayed me. But when it came to Missy, I wasn't really surprised by what she did.

"Everything is different for me now. Everything! For the first time in my life, I'm getting my priorities straight. I've never been a jealous man, Jill. But the thought of you going to Dallas and possibly spending time with your ex-fiancé is ripping me apart. Please, tell me you're not going to see him while you're there."

Jill's heart was filled with love for the tall, handsome jock who'd become such a huge part of her life. She put her hand to his lips and looked deeply into his eyes. "Dave, please stop," she said.

He shook his head. "I know it's pathetic," he replied. "Here I am begging you to stay away from Stephen. I know I have no right to ask you to do that."

Jill placed her hands on his broad shoulders and kissed him, hoping the gesture would leave no doubt in his mind. "You're wrong about that, Dave," she said, throwing her hair back over one shoulder. "You have every right. Do you know why?" she asked, her steel-blue eyes penetrating his.

He shook his head, unsure of what she might say. "No, why?" he asked, returning her stare.

"Because, Dave Wilder, as you'll recall, I told you—I'm a one-man kind of woman. And I'm a woman who is totally and completely in love with you."

CHAPTER 19

Jill arrived in Dallas shortly before noon, driving directly to her old employer's television station for the meeting. She was glad she'd chosen to wear a bright red, Prada suit, thinking the festive color would help brighten the atmosphere.

All eyes were on her as she entered the conference room. Towering nearly six feet tall in designer heels, she was a commanding presence. Ordinarily, she didn't wear dark lipstick, but today Jill had applied a shade of vivid red that matched her suit perfectly. She was not a vain person, yet she was aware that her looks attracted attention.

As she walked around the room, greeting people she knew and catching up on their personal lives, the secretary announced the meeting was about to start, and everyone took their seats around the long conference table. Jill listened as each committee member gave their report, taking notes on her laptop. She was impressed with the progress that had already been made for this year's event and expressed her appreciation when it was her turn to address the group. The meeting went on for a couple of hours, and Jill was glad the studio had ordered box lunches for everyone.

Finally, they were adjourned, and everyone slowly filed out of the room. Jill was collecting her things when her old station manager came over and gave her a hug. "Thanks, Jill, for all you and your family do for this event. We couldn't do it without you," he said warmly. "Any chance you'd consider moving back to Big D?" he asked. "I'd happily give you your old job back."

Laughing graciously, she replied, "Thanks, as tempting as that sounds, I'll have to pass. The Hill Country is where I belong."

"Let me know if you change your mind," he said. "There'll always be a place for you here at Channel 9." Jill hugged the older man again and assured him she'd be back in the next couple of weeks. She spent time visiting with some of her former colleagues, then drove to her condo, glad to have left early enough to avoid rush hour traffic.

Within a few minutes, Jill could see the top of West Highland Park Tower, the highrise building where she'd purchased a 1,600-square-foot condo after being accepted into nearby Southern Methodist University. She'd debated selling the property after moving back in with Gran, but hanging onto it had proven to be a sound real estate decision. The condo's upscale address and full-service amenities made it a valuable investment. The residence also served her family well whenever they came to Dallas.

She pulled in under the covered entrance, giving her key to the valet. As she was getting out of her car, Jill heard a familiar voice greeting her. "Why, Ms. Murray, what a pleasure to have you back!"

She recognized Joe Kaiser, who'd worked as a doorman at the property for as long as she could remember. "Joe!" Jill exclaimed. "Oh, my gosh! It's so good to see you!" He was offering her his hand, but she reached down and gave the small, uniformed man a hug. "How are Barbara and all your grandkids?" she asked, then waited while the older man proudly shared some photos.

"Everyone is doing well, thank you! It's great to see you, Ms. Murray," Joe said. "May I help you with your bag?"

Jill shrugged and said, "No, thanks! I'm only here for the night, Joe. I'm traveling light this time."

He escorted her down the sidewalk, stopping to open the door for her with a flourish. Joe then rang the elevator for Jill's floor. "Good to have you home, Ms. Murray," he said with a warm smile, his eyes twinkling with delight at seeing her again. "Yes, ma'am, it's good to have you home."

Still smiling from her encounter with Joe, Jill unlocked the condo door and placed her keys on the entry table. *It's been a good day*, she thought, kicking off her heels and walking toward the wall of windows in the living area. Looking out over the impressive Dallas skyline, Jill thought about Dave's reaction that morning when she'd told him she loved him. *It was probably too early in our relationship,* she worried. *But it sure felt like the right moment. He seemed so concerned about me coming to Dallas alone.*

It troubled her that Dave hadn't told her he loved her in return. *That's just great!* she fretted. *I've come on too strong and probably scared the poor guy to death!*

She'd called Gran, then texted Dave and Mike before her meeting, letting them know she'd arrived safely.

Now, I'm going to find something fun to do tonight, Jill thought. She plopped onto the sofa and made some calls to a few of her sorority sisters who still lived in Dallas, hoping to see if anyone was available for dinner. Unfortunately, she couldn't find any takers on her offer. She was kicking herself for not making arrangements in advance. *Now what am I going to do?* she wondered.

Restless, Jill went into the kitchen and was thrilled to find a bottle of chardonnay in the fridge. An idea sprang into her mind. *How long has it been since I had an evening entirely to myself? I've got a bottle of wine, a Jacuzzi and a good book. Life is good!*

Excited with her plans for a self-indulgent evening, Jill went into the master bedroom closet and found her soft, long robe. She lit some candles in the bathroom and started running water into the deep, jetted tub. Returning to the kitchen, she paused long enough to appreciate the sunset casting beams of color across the sky. *I kind of miss it here,* she thought.

After opening the wine and filling her glass, she headed to tub, turning on the powerful jets and slipping out of her robe. Sinking down into the hot, foaming water, she gave a moan of pleasure. "This is divine!" Jill said out loud, quickly pulling her hair up in a high ponytail.

She'd nearly dozed off when her cell phone buzzed. Her heart skipped a beat when she saw it was Dave and Jill answered eagerly, her fingers leaving sudsy marks on the phone.

"Hey," he said softly. "How's it going there?"

Jill could barely hear him over the roar of the hydro jets. She hit the power button and the bathroom grew silent. "It's going great," she replied happily.

"Where are you? What was all that racket?" he inquired.

Jill was so relaxed by the hot water and wine; she felt a little giddy. "I'm taking a bath. That was the Jacuzzi you heard, but I turned the jets off so we could talk."

Dave had to shake the image of her in the tub out of his mind so he could think straight. Clearing his throat, he said, "So, tell me about your day."

"Well, we had a very productive meeting and planned our next steps," Jill replied. "I think this year might be the best one ever for our event. I hope you and Ian will be able to come to the gala. I'll fill you in on all the details when I get back."

"We'd love to," Dave replied. "I miss you, Jill. I wish I were there with you."

She sighed. "It's no big deal. Remember, I've driven back and forth many times while I was in school. I do think it'd be fun to show you and Ian the sights up here. There's so much to do and see. This is a two-bedroom condo so you guys would have your own room."

"I'll make that happen," Dave promised. "So what's on your agenda for tonight?"

Jill giggled and said, "If you must know, I found my soft robe and fuzzy slippers. If I ever get out of this tub, I'm planning on just staying in and reading a book. I decided I want to get on the road early tomorrow."

Dave was thrilled to hear she wouldn't be going out, yet he didn't tell her so. Afraid of sounding too possessive, he said, "I'm glad you'll be coming back soon."

She was about to respond when her doorbell rang. "Hey, can you hold on a minute?" she asked. "I think someone's here."

Placing the call on hold, Jill stood, quickly grabbing her robe. Knowing the condo tower had state-of-the-art security, and only residents and their guests were permitted in the building, she figured it was one of her neighbors.

Wrapping the robe around her wet body, Jill walked over and peered through the peephole. The man outside her door was running his hands nervously through his hair, pacing back and forth in the hallway. She reluctantly unlocked the door and opened it slightly, leaving the security chain in place.

"Stephen!" she said crossly. "What are you doing here? How did you even *get* up here?"

Jill's ex-fiancé stopped pacing and spoke to her through the sliver of space she'd provided. "A little bird told me you were in town," he replied cheerfully.

"Go home, Stephen," Jill said. "I've said everything I need to say to you." She moved to close her door.

"Jill! Please don't shut me out," he begged. "Joe let me come up. He knows how much we mean to each other. Can I come in for just a minute?"

Jill groaned in frustration. She couldn't fault the doorman for allowing Stephen access. She'd left Dallas so hastily, she'd forgotten to remove her ex from her approved guest list. "You need to go," she told him firmly. "I told you, there's nothing we have to say to one another."

She started to shut the door, irritated that he was being so persistent, when Stephen reminded her, "You told me you'd think about visiting my father when you came back! Can we just do this, please? Just get dressed and come with me to see him. It would mean the world to him!" he pleaded.

It's early, Jill thought, *and I don't have anything else to do tonight. It would be a kind gesture to visit a dying old friend—even if the man is Stephen's father.*

She spoke to him in a tone that was less than friendly, "Okay, I'll go and visit your father because I care about him and we used to be close. But you don't need to tag along. I know where he lives."

She waited a moment for Stephen to respond.

"I think it's better for us to go together," he said sadly. "He's in pretty bad shape and he may not even recognize you."

Jill shook her head, frustrated by the situation. But as always, her compassion won out. "Give me a few minutes to get dressed," she sighed, defeatedly. "I'll meet you downstairs in the lobby."

Jill threw on some jeans and a sweater. Within minutes, she was taking the elevator down to where Stephen was enjoying a lively conversation with Joe. She gave the doorman a polite acknowledgement and forced a smile, making a mental note to update her approved guest list.

"I'm driving my own car," she told Stephen sternly. "Just go on, and I'll meet you at your dad's place."

Stephen nodded but made no move to leave as she'd requested. "I'd feel better knowing you're right behind me," he said, motioning to a sleek black Jaguar parked a few feet away. "That's my Jag there. Is someone bringing your car around?"

Jill saw no need to reply to his question as she saw the valet pulling up to the entrance with her car. "I'm ready, but just so you know, Stephen, I'm not planning on staying long," she informed him. "I'll just say hello, then I'm leaving. And I'm not doing this for you, I'm doing it for your father."

"I understand, Jill," he assured her gratefully.

Once en route, Jill called Dave from her car. He answered immediately. "Jill! What the heck? I've been sitting here worried about you. You put me on hold over twenty minutes ago. What's going on?" She could hear the frustration in his voice.

"I'm so sorry! I meant to call you right back," she apologized. "Stephen showed up at my condo. He begged me to go with him to see his father," she explained. "I'm on my way there now."

"I see," Dave said quietly. "So, you're going with him?"

"I *really* was planning on staying in tonight," she said. The silence on the other end of the line told her she needed to say something more. "I told Stephen I wasn't going to stay long, but it's really on my heart to do this. His dad and I were friends for a long time and, according to Stephen, Mr. Conrad doesn't have long to live."

"I know how good-hearted you are, Jill, and I think it's very kind of you to visit the man," Dave said, reluctantly. "I just hope your ex isn't using his father to get to you. Based on what you've told me, Stephen doesn't sound like a trustworthy guy."

"It will be fine. Please don't be angry with me and please don't worry about me. I told you how I feel about you this morning," she reminded him. "I've got to go. We're here now. I'll call you later."

"Please do," he replied. "I'll be waiting."

Jill followed Stephen's car through the gates of his father's Highland Park estate. As she drove up the long brick drive, she began to wonder if this visit had been such a wise decision after all. Dave was clearly unhappy about it and now, as the massive Tudor home appeared in view, Jill began to feel very melancholy.

I'm here now, let's just get this over with, she thought.

Stephen was walking over to her car, offering his hand to help her out. "Thank you for doing this, Jill," he said, looking up at his father's home. "We sure had some wonderful times here together."

Jill did not respond. Something had been niggling at her since he'd appeared at her door. "How did you know I was in Dallas?" she asked. "Only a few of the people on our committee knew I was going to be here."

She watched Stephen's face, knowing he had an inside source. "Darci told me," he admitted.

Darci! Jill thought about the slim brunette who'd been so accommodating at the meeting earlier. She was suddenly furious. "You had someone on my committee *spying* on me?" she fumed.

Stephen shrugged. "No, Jill! Now, don't get all crazy on me. Darci and I have been kind of going out for a while. You know, since you dumped me." He gave her a wounded expression and looked down, dejectedly.

Jill rolled her eyes, then pointed her finger at him. "I'll go in there, say hello to your father, then I'm gone," she told him in a sharp tone. He watched as she turned and started up the flagstone steps toward the front door.

Stephen quickly followed her, deliberately brushing past Jill to unlock the door. He looked over at her as they heard the lock click and said, "Please let me go in first and tell him you're here."

The elder Conrad had been genuinely pleased to Jill her again. When he'd taken her hand and asked if she would stay for a game of chess, Jill couldn't refuse.

The two enjoyed the match, reminiscing about old times and even talking a little smack to each other as they'd done in the past. Jill could see the man was ill, but his mind and wit were as sharp as ever. Stephen, who'd been sitting nearby, appeared to enjoy listening to their easy banter. When she caught him staring at her, he'd quickly averted his eyes.

The game went on much longer than she expected. Jill was considering taking a dive and letting the older man win, when he made a shrewd move. With a roar of laughter, he cried, "Checkmate!"

Knowing she'd been bested, Jill conceded the win.

She'd left shortly after her defeat, hugging the ailing man gently and assuring him that he'd be in her prayers. Stephen walked with Jill to her car. "I can't thank you enough for coming tonight. I know you'd said it was for my father, but it meant a lot to me, too," he said. Knowing she was anxious to leave, he opened the door and waited until she'd started the car to say, "Maybe I'll see you next time you're in town."

She shook her head. "No, you won't, Stephen. This was it. Please don't call me again. I really mean it."

"Is there someone else, Jill?" he inquired.

"Look, I don't want to be nasty to you, but that's none of your business," she told him firmly. "Goodbye, Stephen. Now, please shut my door so I can go."

Pulling onto the freeway, Jill called Dave. Instead of his usual cheerful greeting, she heard him say, "Well, there you are." Knowing he was concerned about the lateness of the hour, she replied, "Yes, here I am, and I'm sorry it's so late, but I told you I'd call." She had a hard time stifling a yawn as she spoke.

Dave heard her yawning and looked at his watch for the umpteenth time that night. "You sound sleepy, and it also sounds like you're in your car. Please be careful driving."

"I will," she promised. "It's a pretty short drive back to my place from here."

He wasn't sure where "here" was, but decided not to grill her about her evening. "Did you have a good time?" Dave thought of all the other questions he wanted to ask her, like: *Where have you been? Who were you with? Why are you getting home so late?* And, what he wanted to know more than anything else: *Did your ex make a move on you?*

"You know, I did end up having a good time. Stephen's father asked me to play a game of chess, which he eventually beat me in. It was pretty brutal!" Jill replied with a laugh. "But you haven't told me what you did today."

Dave shared the highlights of his day which included working on his book and fooling around with his new pool table. "I'm trying to teach Ian how to shoot pool. He's impatient with it because it's hard for him to reach across the table."

"You probably should have gotten the foosball table," she remarked.

She heard his chuckle. "I just ordered one. It'll be here in a couple of days."

"Sounds like there's going to be lots of fun things to do at your house," Jill mused.

"Nothing's as much fun as it is when you're here, babe," he said.

"Well, I'll be there before you know it. My plan is to leave here first thing in the morning to get ahead of this crazy Dallas traffic. I should be home around mid-morning."

"I'm desperate to see you again, Jill," Dave said huskily, thinking about kissing her soft lips. "Let me know when you get home, and I'll come over. If that's all right, of course."

Jill couldn't wait to be wrapped in his arms again. "I have a better idea. Why don't I come straight to your place? You can show me your new pool table," she suggested. "Maybe I'll show you a couple of my trick shots."

She heard him groan in amusement before he asked, "Please tell me you're not a pool shark, too? Is there *anything* you're not good at, Ms. Murray?"

"Stop it! I'm not good at everything, just the things I enjoy. I'm sure you're much better at pool than I am," she told him with a humble laugh.

"Oh, I guess we'll just see about that now, won't we?" Dave replied, confidently. "Sweet dreams, babe!"

CHAPTER 20

As she was preparing to leave the condo the next morning, Jill sent a hurried email to the management company to remove Stephen from her approved guest list. She planned on returning soon and didn't want any more surprises from her ex.

With the Dallas skyline in her rearview mirror before the sunrise, Jill made great time, driving smoothly back home, eager to see Dave again. Making a quick pit stop in Austin for gas, she called to let him know she would be there soon.

"I'll be ready, Jill," he said warmly, sending a current of excitement through her.

Jill blinked in surprise as Dave threw open his front door. He wore a five o'clock shadow, which added a rugged, sexy dimension to his already handsome features. She found herself at a loss for words. "Hey there," she stammered.

"Hey, yourself. Come here." He pulled her inside the house and kissed her deeply, leaving her breathless. "I told you I was desperate to see you, Jill. Whatever spell you've got over me, please don't break it," he murmured as he nuzzled her neck.

"Oh, Dave," she said laughingly. "I've only been gone one day! Get a grip already!"

"Oh, I assure you, I've got a grip, Ms. Murray," he said, pressing his body firmly against hers. "And that's the problem. I don't ever want to let go!"

Jill went into a fit of giggles as he tickled her mercilessly for a moment. "Stop it, you fiend!" she cried, still laughing. When Dave immediately ended the torture, she smiled and reached out to gently stroke his cheek. "Hmm, what's going on here? Has someone lost their razor?" she teased.

Dave released her and ran his hand over his stubbly face. "You don't like it?" he asked with a crooked smile. "I'm considering growing a beard."

She shook her head, smiling. "It's a little scratchy, but I'll get used to it. I've missed this face," she said, reaching up and wrapping her arms around his neck. She stood on her toes and rubbed her soft cheek against the beginnings of Dave's bristly beard.

He caught her hand. "We really need to talk. There's something I need to say, but I didn't want to do it over the phone," he explained, leading Jill into the living room.

She picked up on the serious note in his voice and her brow furrowed with concern as they sat down on the sofa.

"What is it?" she asked.

He studied Jill, taking in her worried expression. Looking away for a moment, he hesitated, wanting his words to be perfect. Slowly, he began to tell her how he felt. "When you told me you loved me yesterday, I was floored. I don't know why it surprised me as much as it did, but hearing you say it made everything real."

She started to apologize for telling him too soon, but Dave held up his hand. "No! Please let me finish," he insisted. "There's no denying there's something very powerful between us. I felt it the moment I met you." His voice was choked with emotion as he continued, "I don't know what's going to happen with Ian. If he chooses to go live with his mother..." Dave thought for a moment before saying more determinedly, "Then, you and I will cross that bridge when we come to it!"

He stood, pulling Jill off the sofa, holding her at arm's length so they were face-to-face. "After you drove away, it was all I could do not to jump in my car and follow you all the way to Dallas. I wanted to look into those incredibly blue eyes of yours and tell you that I love you, too, Jill Murray. I'm completely beguiled by you." He leaned down and kissed her as he'd never kissed her before. When Dave finally released her, he said, "With you in my life, I'm the luckiest man on earth."

Jill felt tears of joy swell up in her eyes, and Dave noticed they became an even more brilliant blue than normal. *How is that even possible?* he wondered.

They were silent for a few moments, then Jill sat back down on the sofa, giving his arm a tug so he'd join her. "Wow," she said. "Pretty heavy-duty stuff, eh?" She was grinning, her cheeks rosy from his rough face.

Dave nodded, stroking his stubble thoughtfully. "Yes, very," he agreed. "Now that we've got all that settled, what's next?" he asked, fixing her with a serious look.

"What's next?" she asked, reaching over to kiss him. "Next, Mr. Wilder, you take me to that new pool table of yours and let me show you how it's done!"

Amused and excited by her confidence, he gave her a wolfish grin. "Okay, let's see what you've got, babe."

"So, maybe we put a little wager on our game?" she suggested playfully.

"Sure, whatever you want. I've got all afternoon," he replied cockily as they walked toward the game room. "And, just know, I don't plan on losing."

Jill looked over, giving him a sphinx-like smile and a deep, throaty chuckle. "Neither do I, Dave," she assured him, pulling him close to her once more. "Neither do I."

Time passed, and the couple spent the ensuing days before Thanksgiving getting to know one another better. "I feel like I've known you all my life, Jill," Dave told her one afternoon while they were having lunch in a quaint little eatery in Wimberley. Their table had a marvelous view of Cypress Creek, but they only had eyes for each other. "I never knew what it was like to truly love a woman. It's an amazing feeling."

Jill agreed, "I know you're my soul mate, Dave. Being in love with you is like nothing I've ever experienced before."

They'd finished lunch and were walking hand in hand around some of the many shops on the square. "I have no idea what to get you for Christmas," Dave said. "Some hints would be nice." He gave her a hopeful look.

"What? We haven't even celebrated Thanksgiving, and you're talking about Christmas presents?" she teased. "I thought you had strong feelings about celebrating Christmas *before* Thanksgiving. What was it you said?" she asked, trying to arch one eyebrow and failing. "Oh yeah, I remember! You said it was *bad luck!*"

He stopped walking and pulled her to him. "First of all, you need to leave the eyebrow arching to me," he insisted. "You're terrible at it, and when you try to do it, it reminds me of Groucho Marx." He moved both brows up and down several times, imitating her earlier attempt, which cracked them both up. "Secondly, providing the man you love with some gift ideas is *not* in the same league with decorating for Christmas the day after Halloween. I'm just sayin'…"

Jill nearly doubled over giggling and, when Dave heard her adorable snort, he was so amused, he had to sit down on a nearby bench. He patted the spot next to him.

"I can't believe you said I look like Groucho Marx!" Jill exclaimed, playfully punching him in the shoulder.

Dave shot her a devilish grin. "Hey, stop! That's my pitching arm!"

She leaned back comfortably on the bench beside him. "It's hard to think that tomorrow is Thanksgiving! I'm so glad you and Ian will be with us this year," she said.

"Lucky for us, his mother decided she'd rather go to Barbados than have him come to visit," Dave replied. "That gives me another reason to be thankful. Of course, I'm most thankful that you're in my life."

Jill leaned over and kissed him chastely. "Ditto," she said. "Do you still want to swing by and see the shelter on the way home?" she asked.

"Absolutely!" he told her. "I've been looking forward to it."

It was less than a thirty-minute drive from Wimberley to the animal shelter. Dave was at the wheel, and Jill was enjoying the pleasant hum of the sports car's powerful engine. "I like that they call this town The Gateway to the Hill Country," Dave said as he read the words painted on a nearby water tower.

"Dripping Springs is a great little town. Did you know that you can actually still see the original springs?" Jill asked. "They're right off Mercer Street, in that direction." She nodded her head west. "The shelter is just ahead. You can stay on this road. It's up a ways on the right. Just past it is another place I'd like to show you sometime. It's called The Springs Inn. They serve the best chicken fried steak in Texas, and they have a cool little shop with a lot of eclectic things. It'd be a fun spot for us to check out together."

"I'm in!" said Dave, looking around while he drove. "There's a lot more to do in Dripping Springs than I realized, although I have seen the original springs. They were part of my reconnaissance before moving here. I did a lot of touristy stuff like that."

"*Reconnaissance?* Sounds like a serious mission!" Jill shot him an accusatory grin. "And how many of the vodka distilleries did you visit while you were collecting all of this important data?" she asked.

"Let's just say my research was quite thorough," he replied with a chuckle.

Jill pointed ahead. "The shelter's coming up. Looks like we've got several visitors today. That's always a good sign. It'd be great to see more of our dogs and cats find good homes before the holidays."

They found a spot to park and walked together into the shelter where a spunky, young woman with bright pink hair greeted them. "Jill!" she exclaimed, rushing around the reception desk to exchange a quick hug. "Long time, no see!" She turned, looking Dave up and down appreciatively. "And who do we have here?" she asked, batting her blue, mascara-coated lashes at him.

Jill laughed. "Down, girl!" she said, moving a little closer to Dave. "Dave Wilder, meet Shelly White. Shelly runs the shelter," Jill explained. "She's also a good friend of mine."

Dave held out his hand. "Nice to meet you, Shelly," he said politely.

"Likewise, I'm sure," Shelly answered. Then, when Dave had looked away for a moment, she mouthed to Jill, *"Oh my gosh, he's so hot!"* She ran her hand through her pink spikes and asked if Dave would like a shelter tour.

Giving Shelly a roll of her eyes, Jill quickly responded for Dave by saying, "No thanks, I've got this! I saw Ned's truck out front. Is he in his office?"

"He was outside a few minutes ago. You might check there first," replied Shelly.

Jill was already walking to a nearby door. "Come on, let's go this way first," she called to Dave. "Thanks, Shell."

As they stepped outside, Jill began telling Dave about the operation and pointing out the highlights of the facility. "All these kennels to the right are connected to ones inside so the dogs can go in and out as they choose. The ones on the left are larger, as you can see. They're used for bigger dogs on days like today when it's nice enough for them to enjoy the sunshine. This way, when families come to visit, they have more space to interact with the dogs." She pointed to a greenbelt in the distance. "Now, over there we have a wonderful park where potential new owners can play with the dogs and really get to know them before they decide whether to adopt." She looked at Dave. "We want to make sure every adoption is the right match of pet to people," she explained.

The sheer size of the shelter impressed Dave, not to mention how meticulously it was maintained. He smiled as Jill stopped to greet every dog they passed, most of them by name. They heard a shout and turned to see Ned waving to them at the door they'd used earlier. Jill laughed and said, "You get a lot of exercise working here! Can't wait to show you inside. Let's go talk with Ned."

Once they were inside, Jill let Ned take over the tour, showing Dave the interior kennels, surgery and recovery rooms and two small offices. "Down this hallway is a kitchen and we also have a bathing/grooming area," the vet explained. "And this is what we call Kitty Corner. It's where all of our cats and kittens are housed," he said, opening the door to yet another wing of the shelter.

Dave gave a low whistle. "This place is much larger than I expected it to be," he said. He put his arm around Jill, who was busy baby talking to a purring calico.

"It's one of the finest facilities I've ever been in," Ned told him. "The Murrays spared no expense when they had this shelter built," he said, beaming at Jill. "It's a pleasure working here." He paused, then looked at Dave a little shyly. "I've got your baseball card in my office. Would you mind signing it for me?"

Dave smiled and clapped him on the shoulder. "Sure! I'd be happy to do that. Lead the way," he replied.

<hr />

Thanksgiving at Gran's house was everything Dave imagined it would be and more. He and Ian arrived mid-morning as Jill had requested. He'd asked Jill what he could contribute to the meal and she'd laughed. "Just get here around ten-thirty. I've signed us up to make the fruit salad and jalapeno corn." She explained that it was a tradition that everyone was involved in preparing a dish at Thanksgiving. "Mike smokes an enormous brisket, and Gina and the girls usually bake brownies. I think Jeremy is doing the green bean casserole with a little help from Gran."

"Oh, and Gran is in charge of the turkey and dressing, which is always delicious."

Jill giggled, nearly out of breath and Dave could tell she was remembering past holidays as she shared, "All of us work together in the kitchen. It just about drives Marcie nuts! Of course, she still makes a ton of other stuff."

He listened as Jill rattled off about fifteen more dishes. "It sounds like I'll to need to take advantage of your fitness room after that meal!" he exclaimed.

She laughed, gently squeezing his hand and said, "Well, that will make two of us!"

When they'd gathered for the meal in the dining room, Gran asked everyone to stand and join hands. "It's a Murray family tradition at Thanksgiving to take turns sharing what we're most thankful for." She nodded to Mike, who got them started. After he'd spoken, each person said a few words. When it came time for Dave to talk, he found himself getting choked up. He felt part of something very intimate. *The love in this room is almost tangible,* he thought.

"I'm thankful for Jill, and for every person gathered around this table. Ian and I are full of gratitude that we've been welcomed into this incredible family. I'm blessed beyond words." He looked at Jill lovingly. "Blessed, beyond words," he repeated.

A few days later, Jill and Dave were taking a break on the boulder at Rock Point. The trees were nearly bare now, and there was a cold breeze blowing. "I'm glad I wore my cap," Jill said, pulling the blue beanie further down over her ears.

"I'm glad I have a beard!" Dave said, smiling. "Jill, I've been wanting to ask you, have you and Mike always lived with Gran? I mean, even when your parents were alive?"

She shook her head. "No, our parents have—*had* their own home. It's located on the other side of that ridge." She motioned with her hand. "The house is still there, and we've got several more horse stables around it. I seldom go there, but I'll show you sometime if you'd like to see it." She looked at him curiously. "Why do you ask?"

"No reason," Dave replied. "I was just wondering."

Jill was still studying at him. "You think it's unusual that I live with Gran and Mike and his family?" she cocked her head to one side, interested in his answer.

Dave decided to tell her what had been on his mind for some time. "If you must know, I've been thinking about us. About our future together," he replied.

She smiled and took his hand in hers. "I like the sound of that. Our future together," she repeated dreamily. Then she sat up straight. "I think I see where you're going with this..."

Dave tucked Jill's head under his chin as he stroked her back and said, "Well, I sure hope you do. I love you, and I want to spend the rest of my life with you." He thought for a moment then held her in front of him so that she could see his arched brow. "This is not my official proposal, mind you. I'm just planning my strategy."

"Ah, I see," Jill said. "Your *reconnaissance?*"

"Hey, hold on! That's *my* word!" he teased, relishing in the thought of spending every day with her.

Dave had no way of knowing, but Jill was thinking the same thing when she suddenly began laughing uncontrollably. "Oh my gosh! It just hit me! You're not sure if I'll ever move out of my grandmother's house and you're wondering if you and Ian are going to have to move in there, too!" Jill hooted and snorted, so caught up in amusement; she nearly rolled off the boulder.

Dave watched as she thoroughly enjoyed the moment. He knew it was at his expense, but he didn't mind. He was thinking, *that's exactly what I've been worried about...*

He waited until she'd regained control, then smiling, said, "If you've finished laughing, Ms. Murray, I'd like to continue." He watched as she pulled herself back together. "Here's the thing. I can't imagine you being happy living with Ian and me at our place." Dave shrugged and finally came out with what was on his heart. "I know you're accustomed to a much grander lifestyle than I can provide."

"Hey," she replied, nuzzling her face into his warm neck. "It's like you said, 'We'll cross that bridge when we get to it. We have a lot of options.'" They were so close, she could feel the rhythmic beat of his heart. "So, you think you'd like to marry me, eh?"

His kiss answered her question, telling Jill everything she needed to know.

<hr/>

It had grown cold, and Dave couldn't believe how quickly time was passing. He and Jill had been wrapping gifts for Ian, stacking them under the Christmas tree.

"I still don't know what to get you, Jill!" Dave groaned. "You've got to help me out with some hints!" *What do I buy for someone who has everything?* he wondered.

Jill giggled and motioned to the mountain of presents he'd already bought. "It doesn't look like you need any help in the gift-giving department," she said.

"Finding gifts for Ian is a piece of cake," he told her. "*You*, however, are proving to be quite the challenge."

"Please, you don't need to get me a single thing, Mr. Wilder. Everything I want is right here," she said, poking him playfully in the chest.

"I hate that I have to leave in the morning," Dave said, curling a lock of Jill's hair idly around his fingers. "I'm going to miss you like crazy."

Jill responded by giving him a swift kiss. "I'm going to miss you, too." She was glad he and Ian were going to Arizona for the first part of the school break. They'd return to Texas a few days before Christmas.

She moved to the sofa while Dave poured some wine. When he returned, he set their glasses down and sprawled out on the sofa beside her. "I'm exhausted," Dave complained good-naturedly. "All this Christmas cheer is wearing me out!"

Jill shook her head and moved to massage his shoulders. "It's a lot of work, isn't it, babe?" she asked. "Between the gala, the shopping and trying to coordinate our schedules, I don't know if I'm coming or going!"

"That feels incredible," he replied, giving a moan of pleasure as he felt her strong fingers working his tight muscles. He started thinking about how incredible Jill had looked the night they'd attended the gala in Dallas a few days before. "I keep thinking about you in that green gown. You looked like you should have been on a runway and I was so proud to have you on my arm."

She smiled, remembering the event. "It was a spectacular evening. You looked so debonair in your tux. I was the envy of every woman in the room," she sighed. "And most importantly, the gala was a huge success!"

"It was amazing," Dave agreed. "I can see now why you do it. So many people benefit from your efforts. Next year I want to play a larger role. What you're doing makes a real difference in a lot of people's lives."

"Next year we'll do it together," she promised, thrilled he wanted to be involved in something so important to her. "I love you, Dave Wilder," she whispered in his ear. "You make me so happy!"

⸻ ⬧ ⸻

With the colder temperatures, Mike and Jill were enjoying their morning coffee in the great room. They were surprised when Gina sauntered in and joined them. "Is this a private party or can anyone attend?" she joked, reclining comfortably next to Mike by the large Christmas tree.

They quietly watched the splendor of the twinkle lights illuminating Gran's multi-colored heirloom ornaments.

Jill sighed. "This is the best Christmas tree in the world. Seeing all these beautiful decorations reminds me of all the wonderful holidays we've shared in this room. I think I could sit here for hours just staring at it."

Mike chuckled and said, "I know what you mean. And I'll agree, it's a magnificent tree. But Jill, who are you kidding? You can't sit still for ten minutes, much less an hour!"

Jill laughed, knowing his remark was true. "It was just an expression, Michael," she scolded.

"When do Dave and Ian fly to Arizona?" Gina asked.

"They left this morning," Jill replied. "I'm already missing them."

"I think it's great that Dave's ex-wife was so accommodating about Ian," Gina said kindly. "She could have insisted on having him there on Christmas Day."

Jill nodded and agreed, saying, "You're right, I should count my blessings. Apparently, she and her husband have a ski trip planned later in the month, so this ended up working out better for them and certainly better for us."

<hr>

Dave had been gone a couple of days, and Jill felt the hours dragging by. *What did I do before him?* she wondered. *I feel so lost when he's not here!*

She was in the barn playing with Simon's pups, their adorable antics helping to take her mind off Dave. The spirited little German shepherds were nearly eight weeks old, and Jill was laughing as they pounced and played with one another. Totally enchanted with the puppies, she didn't bother to check to see who the caller was when her phone buzzed. Certain it was Dave, she answered with a cheerful giggle.

"Hey, sweetie, if you hear me squealing, it's because I'm being mauled by a dozen crazy pups!" she laughed into the phone.

"Jill?" came a man's voice on the other end of the line.

She removed two of the dogs from her lap and stood. She heard him say her name again. "Jill? It's Stephen. I, I hope it's not a bad time," he stammered.

"Stephen! *Why* are you calling me?" she asked irritably.

"I really need to talk to you, Jill. It's my father, he's gone," said Stephen. "He passed yesterday."

She could hear the sorrow in his voice, and her heart broke for him. "I'm so sorry, Stephen. He was a good man," she told him, unsure of what else to say.

She could hear him weeping softly. "I could really use a friend right now, Jill. I want to be with someone who loved him, too. I didn't know anyone else to call. I'm on my way down to see you. I'm hoping we can have dinner together."

"Oh, Stephen," she said, uncertain about what to do. "I don't think that's such a good idea. I know you're hurting, but I don't think we should see one another. We've talked about this before."

"Please! I had to get out of Dallas for a couple of days and get my head around all of this," he pleaded. "It's just dinner."

Jill shook her head no, but heard herself agreeing to meet him at The Springs Inn. "It's the place just past the animal shelter."

"I remember where it is. I'll be there at seven," he said. "I'll get a table for us. Oh, and Jill, thank you."

"I'll see you there, Stephen," Jill replied, ending the call. *Why can't I ever just say no?* she asked herself.

<hr />

"Hey, where you headin' hotshot?" Mike asked as his sister stopped by the great room where he was busy working on a puzzle with his family.

Gran, who was reading in the corner, glanced up from her book, giving Jill a questioning look.

Jill hadn't told anyone she'd agreed to meet Stephen. She knew how her family felt about the man and hadn't wanted to worry Dave with it. *I'll tell him when he returns,* she rationed.

Pulling on her coat, Jill looked around the room at the people she loved. "I'm meeting Stephen for dinner. His father passed away, and he really needs someone to talk to."

Mike immediately stood and excused himself from the game table. "Let me walk you out, Sis." His voice was calm, but Jill could see the spark of anger in his eyes.

He waited until they were beyond earshot of the others. "What are you *thinking?*" he demanded. "Stephen Conrad is bad news. Let me get this straight. He lets you down, breaks your heart, and now you're going to meet him?" Not waiting for her reply, he continued, "I think you shouldn't give this loser the time of day, much less have dinner with him!"

Jill slowly nodded and said, "He did Mike, but I've forgiven him for all of that. It's in the past. Right now, he needs a friend. He told me he didn't have anyone else to call." She looked up into his eyes. "I feel like it's the right thing to do. He just wants someone to talk to." She could see her brother didn't understand. "Look, we're meeting for dinner at The Springs Inn. I'll be home right after that."

Seeing that her mind was made up, Mike shook his head in frustration. "I think this is a mistake," he said as he opened her car door. "But I know you well enough to know I'm not going to talk you out of it!"

"No, you're not," she replied firmly. "I'll see you later. Love you!"

"You know I love you, too," he said, closing the door, watching as her tail-lights disappeared down the drive.

Later, Mike was glad he'd told Jill he loved her. Those were the last words he remembered saying to his sister before she disappeared.

CHAPTER 21

It was after midnight when the rumble of his cell phone woke Mike from a deep sleep. *I must have dozed off!* he realized, noting the time and shaking his head to clear the cobwebs. "Hey Dave," he croaked into the phone, rubbing his eyes to become more alert.

"Hi, Mike. Man, I'm really sorry to be calling you this late, but I've been trying to get in touch with Jill. She told me she'd call me around nine and I've not heard from her."

He could hear the concern in Dave's voice. Alarms began ringing in his head. Because he'd fallen asleep; Mike wasn't sure if his sister had come home. If she'd come in, she hadn't woken him. He decided to buy some time. "Hmm, that doesn't sound like her. Jill's such a stickler about following through on what she tells people," he replied. "Maybe she wasn't feeling well and went to bed," Mike mused. "Tell you what, I'll go check on her and text you back."

"Thanks, I'd really appreciate it," Dave said.

Mike started down the hall toward Jill's room, then began to think more clearly. He turned around and went to the front of the house and his fears were confirmed. Simon was lying in the entry, waiting for his mistress to return. When the shepherd saw him, the dog stood and whimpered.

Petting his sister's best friend reassuringly, he said softly, "Hey, buddy. So, she's not home yet and you're worried. Well, that makes two of us." Mike auto-dialed Jill's number, groaning when the call went straight to voicemail.

"Damn it, Jill! Where are you?" Simon was at his side as Mike stepped outside to see if Jill's car was parked out front. He then walked to the back parking bay, and peered into the window of the garage she used. As he suspected, her BMW was not inside.

Mike's mind was reeling. *Surely she couldn't still be talking with that loser Stephen Conrad? It's been hours. I had a bad feeling about her meeting that guy. I should've tried harder to talk her out of going!*

Mike could see his breath in the cold night air as he exhaled deeply, debating what to do next. *I'll drive over to The Springs Inn,* he decided, knowing the restaurant would have long-since closed. *If Stephen's staying at the inn, they might still be talking. And if I don't find her there, I'll call the cops.*

He and Simon were moving quickly back into the house when Mike received a text from Dave. *Worried. What's going on with Jill?*

Mike was conflicted about how to respond because loyalty to his family always came first. He didn't know if Jill had told Dave she was meeting her ex-fiancé for dinner and didn't feel it was his place to tell him.

"Great!" Mike grumbled. He was pulling a jacket out of the entry hall closet when Gran came up behind him and asked, "What's great, Michael?"

Slowly closing the closet door, Mike took a deep breath in an effort to calm himself. "Um, hi, Gran. I hope I didn't wake you." *This thing with Jill may be nothing,* he thought. *No sense in having Gran worried.*

"Going somewhere?" Gran stood tall, arms crossed in front of her chest. Her eyes bore right through him.

Mike busied himself with zipping up his jacket. He couldn't look his grandmother in the eye. "I'm just going to drive over to Dripping Springs to see if Jill is still over there talking with that jerk Stephen. I'll be right back." He went to kiss her on her cheek.

Mike could see the ripple of concern that swept across Gran's face as she took in what he'd told her. "And you're sure Jill's not here?" she asked.

He nodded and replied, "Yes, I'm sure. She's probably still sitting over there letting that guy bleed his heart out to her. You know how Jill is!" Mike started heading toward the front door.

"Wait! Have you tried calling her? You know she doesn't like when you invade her privacy. She has a right to talk to Stephen without you storming over there. Jill might get mad if you intrude," she warned.

"Gran, look, I've been trying to call her, and my calls go to her voicemail. Now I've got Dave calling and texting me. Jill's not responding to him, either. I don't want to upset you, but I'm going over to The Springs Inn where Jill told me she was meeting Stephen. If she's not there, I'm calling the police."

"Go on then, Mike. Take Simon with you," urged Gran. "Please let me know what the situation is as soon as you can."

"Love you, Gran," Mike said, giving her a quick kiss on her cheek.

"I love you, too," she replied. "Be careful."

Hoping he'd find his sister and she'd respond to Dave, Mike had ignored her boyfriend's many text messages. When his phone rang, he knew it was time to tell Dave the truth. "Here we go!" Mike said, shooting Simon a worried look as he answered the call.

"Hey, Dave. Look, I know you're concerned about Jill. I can tell you she met a friend for dinner in Dripping Springs and hasn't come home yet." Working to keep his tone light, he added, "I'm sure it's no big deal, but she's not answering my calls either. Thought I'd drive over and make sure she didn't have car trouble or something."

Mike heard a heavy sigh on the other end of the line. "At the risk of sounding like the jealous boyfriend, who is this *friend* she was meeting?" asked Dave.

It was Mike's turn to sigh. "She met Stephen Conrad. The guy's father passed away, and he came here wanting to cry on Jill's shoulder."

"I see," said Dave. "I've got to admit; I sometimes wish your sister didn't have such a compassionate heart. I'm sure Jill will tell me about it when we talk. So, where are you now?"

Mike relaxed, relieved that Dave was being so cool about Jill meeting her ex for dinner. *If it were me, I know I wouldn't be such a good sport about it*, he thought.

"I'm not far from The Springs Inn. That's where Jill told me she was going," Mike said. "I'll keep you on the phone with me if you'd like while I check things out."

"That'd be great," Dave replied. "I'm not going to be able to sleep until I know she's okay."

"Sure," Mike said agreeably. "Nice to have a little company besides Simon. We're just about to pass the shelter... *What the heck?*"

Dave heard the alarm in Mike's voice. "What is it? What's going on?" he demanded, hating that he was so far away.

"Hold on. I'm turning around. Jill's car is parked at the shelter, and the driver's side door is wide open. I've gotta let you go!"

Dave heard the line go silent. He stood and began pacing the floor of his hotel room, feeling utterly helpless. *Something is majorly wrong,* he thought. *I need to get back to Texas. I need to know what's going on with Jill!*

Mike pulled into the lot next to Jill's car, leaving his truck door open so Simon could jump out after him. They ran as one to the BMW, Mike roaring in frustration when he spotted Jill's handbag on the passenger's seat. A wave of fear washed over him as he rapidly surveyed the area. "Simon, go find Jill!" he commanded loudly, pointing to the front door of the shelter which stood slightly ajar.

The dog immediately obeyed, darting into the shelter without a backward glance. Mike grabbed Jill's purse, slammed the driver's side door shut and took off after the shepherd.

Once inside the building, Mike called out Jill's name, his eyes quickly darting around the reception area as he moved toward the sound of Simon's urgent barking. He found the dog in the surgical room, aggressively sniffing around a kennel where several puppies were lined up, whining against the side of their enclosure.

Mike bent to examine a large, empty cardboard box sitting nearby. His mind was working, trying to put the pieces together. The soiled box appeared to have been used to house the puppies. *Likely, someone abandoned them at the shelter. Had Jill stopped to bring them in out of the cold? Where was she now?* he wondered again.

Mike stood and quickly pulled Jill's phone out of her bag. He saw several missed calls from himself and Dave. Beside himself with worry, his hands were shaking as he called 911.

Only a few moments had passed, but Mike knew he needed to phone home. While he waited for the police to arrive, he called Gina. When she answered, he said, "Honey, I need you to please stay calm and listen to me. I'm at the shelter. Jill's car is here, but I don't know where she is. I've called the police. Gran is awake and, of course, she's worried. I need you to go sit with her. Tell her I'll call you when I know more."

Awakened from a sound sleep, Gina struggled to comprehend what her husband was saying. Hearing the anxiety in Mike's voice, she knew how important it was to be strong for his grandmother. "I will, hon'," she assured him. "Please call us as soon as you can. I love you."

"Thanks, babe. I love you, too. Oh, and Gina, would you please say a prayer that Jill's all right?" he asked, his voice cracking at the end of the request.

"Of course," she replied. "Be safe."

His next call was to Dave, who answered immediately. "Mike! What the hell is going on?"

"No news. Jill's car is here, but she's nowhere in sight. I just called 911. In fact, the police are here now. I'll keep you posted."

Mike rushed over to the squad car, not recognizing the man who got out. He tried to keep the rising panic out of his voice, but his words came out in a rush. "I'm Mike Murray," he told the officer. "I'm the one who called. My sister Jill is missing. I was passing by and saw her car parked here. The driver's side door was open, and her purse was inside."

"Lyle Newcomb," the officer said, accepting Mike's offered handshake. "Kind of late to be out for a drive, isn't it, Mr. Murray?"

Unimpressed with the man's weak handshake, Mike fumed, "What kind of question is *that*? I wasn't out for a *drive*. I was trying to locate my sister! She met her ex-fiancé at The Springs Inn for dinner and should have been home hours ago!"

"And what time was this?" Officer Newcomb asked, jotting something on a notepad.

Mike gave an exasperated growl. "Look, Officer, I've been here maybe ten minutes," he said, looking at his watch. "It appears that

Jill was here at some point tonight. Those are hers." He motioned to the ring of keys still dangling from the shelter door.

"I see," said the officer. "So you've been inside?" he asked, without looking up from his notes.

"*Of course* I went inside! She could be in danger! We're wasting time here!" Scowling angrily, Mike pulled his phone out. "Look, Roger Dunn is a friend of mine. I'm calling him now. I should have just done that to begin with!"

The officer held up his hand. "Roger's out of town. He took a few days off. I think he told me he was going to Mexico to sit on the beach."

Mike shook his head in frustration and punched in Roger's number in spite of what he'd just been told. After several rings, he ended the call before it went to voicemail.

Officer Newcomb shrugged as if to say, *I told you so*, then closed his notebook. "I understand your concern, Mr. Murray. Let's go inside and take a look around," he suggested. "This may all be some kind of misunderstanding."

"This is no misunderstanding! Something's seriously wrong here. I can feel it in my gut," Mike replied, remembering he had Jill's phone in his pocket. "You go on inside, Officer. I need to make a quick call."

Mike walked over to his truck, Simon not far behind him. "Get on in, buddy," he said, allowing the dog to hop into the cab. He began quickly scrolling through Jill's call history, stopping when he came upon the number he was seeking.

Hitting redial, he muttered, "I've gotcha, loser!" His short-lived sense of relief faded when the call went into voicemail. Furious, Mike pounded the steering wheel several times. "I'll find you, Conrad! And when I do…"

Officer Newcomb was walking toward Mike's truck when he saw the big man's fit of rage. He slowed his pace and quietly approached the driver's side door. "I didn't find anything inside," he remarked.

Mike hadn't heard the man approaching. Startled, he nearly jumped out of his seat.

"Sorry, didn't mean to frighten you. Everything okay out here?" the officer asked, eyeing Mike warily.

"No! Everything is *not okay*!" He got out of the truck and stood across from the officer, towering over the shorter man. "I just used my sister's phone to call the guy she met for dinner and it went straight to his voicemail. I'll bet you money he's involved in this!" he thundered.

Hoping to calm the distraught man down, Lyle said, "I understand this is tough. I called my chief when I was inside, and he's on his way. He knows your family and believes we need to get the sheriff's department involved in this, too."

What Newcomb didn't mention was that because he was fairly new to the area, his superior had taken the time to explain how wealthy the Murray family was. He thought about what the chief had said...*with the kind of money these people have, we could be looking at a possible kidnapping.*

Mike heaved out a sigh and said quietly, "That's good, Officer Newcomb, thank you."

"I feel like we got started off on the wrong foot. Please call me Lyle," Newcomb replied, not looking at Mike, but around the parking lot. "What about these security cameras? Maybe they caught something that will shed some light on things."

For the first time since they'd met, Mike felt a glimmer of hope. "That's a great idea!" *Where's my head?* he asked himself. *I should have thought of the cameras.* He began frantically scrolling through Jill's phone contacts again, remembering his sister had told him the shelter director was a real techie. *Shelly can help us play back the footage!* he hoped.

He was relieved when she answered. "Shelly! It's Mike Murray. I'm at the shelter with the police. Jill is missing. Her car is here, and it looks like she went inside. I need you to come over right away and help us download what the cameras caught earlier."

"What? Jill is *missing?*" stammered Shelly, as she fought to become more fully awake. *Jill is missing!* It took a moment for the information to sink in. When it did, she said, "I'm on my way! Give me ten minutes."

Mike had just ended the call with Shelly when a second police vehicle pulled into the lot. "Here's Chief Sullivan now," said Lyle.

Robert Sullivan had been on the police force for nearly forty years. A tall, wiry man, he'd dedicated his life to protecting and serving the citizens of Dripping Springs. When Lyle called and said he was with Mike Murray, the chief had wasted no time getting to the shelter. He hurriedly parked and approached the two men, giving a nod to Lyle and offering his hand to Mike.

"Robert Sullivan," he said as they shook hands. "Your dad and I used to run around together when we were kids. Still hard for me to believe he's gone, even after all these years." He paused for a moment and studied Mike's face, seeing his friend Mathew Murray in the younger man's ruggedly handsome features. "I swear, you're the spitting image of him." He shook his head as if to clear it and was suddenly all business. "Now, tell me what's going on here."

Mike nodded and thanked him for coming so quickly. He filled Chief Sullivan in on everything he knew, including Jill's history with Stephen Conrad. "This guy was rotten to my sister, and yet, she agreed to meet him to console him on the loss of his father." Mike was still angry with himself for letting her go. "I'll never forgive myself if he hurts her."

The three men looked up as Shelly's Volkswagen Beetle came flying into the parking lot a few moments later. The young woman had thrown a purple parka over red flannel Christmas pajamas. She was out of the car in a flash and rushed over to the men. "What are you guys doing out here?" she asked. "Let's check out this video footage!"

They gathered in her small office, fast-forwarding through the last few hours of images from the surveillance cameras. At one point, they could clearly see Jill coming through the front door with a large cardboard box in her arms. "That's the box that I saw in the surgical room!" Mike stated. "Shelly, can we see the recordings from that camera around this same time?"

She nodded, her fingers moving deftly across the keyboard. They watched as Jill entered the surgical room, carefully placing the box on the floor. She then walked over and removed some blankets off a shelf and used them to line a corner of a large enclosure in the room. "Jill's got such a soft heart for animals," Shelly said. She began to get choked up as she saw her friend open the flaps of the box and slowly lift out three long-legged puppies one by one. Jill was placing the third dog inside the enclosure when the box tipped over and a fourth puppy appeared and began running playfully around the room. They could see Jill was laughing as she chased the feisty run-away, finally cornering it and scooping it up in her arms. She petted the animal before tenderly adding it to the kennel with the others.

"Someone must have left the box of pups out front," Shelly said. "It happens all the time." They continued to watch as Jill latched the kennel and left the room.

"Shelly, show us the footage from the parking lot," Mike requested.

"Doin' that now," she replied, one step ahead of him, her fingers racing over the keys. "This was around eight-thirty last night." They watched the monitor as Jill's car pulled into the parking lot. The exterior footage was not as sharp as what they'd seen from inside. "This footage is grainier because it's so dark outside," Shelly explained. "It looks like when Jill got here, the box was on its side. I bet those puppies had gotten out."

Sure enough, they watched as Jill walked over and inspected the box then turned and looked around. She stepped out of the camera's range for a couple of minutes, but then reappeared with a puppy tucked under each arm. She placed them in the box and used the welcome mat to hold the flaps in place so the pups couldn't escape. "Smart move, there," Shelly commented. "Now what's she doing?" she wondered out loud as they watched Jill walk to her car.

"She's probably getting her keys to the shelter," Mike speculated. "She keeps them on a separate ring." He watched as his sister emerged from her car, poked some keys into her pocket and headed out of the camera's view again.

All eyes remained locked on Shelly's monitor as Jill came back into view with two more puppies in hand. Placing them in the box with the others, she then used her foot to secure the lid while unlocking the shelter door. After that, she picked up the box and went inside.

"This coincides with the footage we saw earlier as far as the timeline," noted Chief Sullivan.

"Let's keep watching the feed from this camera," Mike said. "We know she came back out, because the door was open when I got here and her keys were still in the lock."

"I don't like the way she left her car door open," Lyle observed. "It seems like she would have closed it."

"You'd think so," Mike said. "But I can tell you this, when it comes to taking care of animals, my sister has a one-track mind."

They continued watching the footage from the parking lot. Finally, the door to the shelter opened and Jill stepped out and started to lock it. Suddenly, another dog appeared in the frame and started jumping up on the back of her legs. Jill turned and they could see she was laughing as she pushed the door back open. She leaned down to pick up the small animal, but just as she was about to grab it; the dog ran off.

"That must be the puppies' mother," Mike said, giving an agonized groan as they watched Jill run after it.

The silence grew thick in Shelly's office as the group watched the monitor for another thirty minutes waiting for Jill to return. Chief Sullivan, who'd been leaning over the desk, stood and looked over at Mike, "You said Jill was meeting this guy at The Springs Inn?"

Mike's head was beginning to throb and his stomach felt sick. "That's right."

"Lyle, you stay here with Ms. White and continue watching the security videos." He looked at his watch. "Sheriff Needham should be here any moment. Mike, let's you and I take a drive over to The Springs Inn."

CHAPTER 22

Mike gave the police chief a physical description of Stephen Conrad as they made the short drive to The Springs Inn. "Of course, I haven't seen him in a couple of years so his appearance could be completely different," he said. "But when I knew him, he worked out, kept himself up. He had an air about him. Always wore custom-made suits and expensive shoes. Had that 'money look'... know what I mean?"

An interesting description coming from a member of one of the wealthiest families in Texas, the lawman thought as he nodded. His eyes were surveying the inn's dimly lit parking lot.

There was a scattering of cars, but Mike had no clue if any of them belonged to Stephen. "As I told you, my sister hadn't spoken to this guy since she broke their engagement off a couple of years ago. Then, last month, he calls her out of the blue and asks if she'll go with him to visit his dying father. Because she's such a sweetheart, Jill went to see the man, but she made it clear to her ex it was only because she cared for his dad. As far as Stephen was concerned, she never wanted to see him again, and she told him as much before she left Dallas."

"It sounds to me like Jill is a very caring person," remarked the chief, checking his watch. "It's nearly three. Doesn't look like there's anything going on here. Shirley Winters owns this place. I'll call and ask about her dinner crowd last night and the overnight guests. There are only ten suites, so if Stephen Conrad is here, I'm sure she'll know."

"Thanks, I'd appreciate that," Mike replied. He then called Gina and gave her an update. "Please tell Gran not to worry. Let her know that Robert Sullivan is involved now. He's the Chief of Police and said he and my dad had been friends. I'm sure she'll remember him."

"I'll tell her," Gina said, looking over at Gran and giving her an encouraging smile. "We love you. Keep us posted."

Dave had just gotten off the phone with Mike who'd updated him on Chief Sullivan's conversation with the owner of The Springs Inn. The woman remembered Jill and a tall, dark-haired man having dinner in the restaurant the night before. The man had paid for their meal in cash. He was not a registered guest, and they'd left around eight-fifteen, she thought. Mike told Dave that he and the police chief were on their way back to the shelter.

Dave stopped pacing and stared out the hotel window. *This waiting is driving me crazy!* he thought, wondering if he should have jumped in his rental car and headed back to Texas after he'd first spoken with Mike. *It's at least a fifteen-hour drive, and I've had no sleep. A flight will be faster and safer.*

Grabbing his travel bag, Dave headed to the airport where he returned the car and purchased a ticket for the next flight to Austin. *Once we find Jill, she and I will come back together and get Ian*, he thought. *When we find her...*

When Mike and the chief arrived back at the shelter, they found Shelly and Lyle still seated, reviewing the video footage. Simon trotted over to them as they entered the office, his eyes hopeful. "Sorry, buddy, no news yet," Mike said, scratching the dog's ears.

Lyle stood and told them, "We've watched some of the footage twice, and I believe we've seen everything there is to see. Whatever happened to Ms. Murray, it occurred outside of the range of the security cameras. I went ahead and searched the perimeter of the building and checked out the vacant lot next door. I didn't find anything, but with it being dark and all..."

They all looked up as they heard the front door to the shelter open and a voice calling out, "Robert, you in here?"

"Yes, we're back here, Lance," the chief replied loudly, moving to greet his friend and colleague.

Mike, Shelly, and Lyle looked up as the two entered Shelly's office together. "Everyone, this is Lance Needham with the Hayes

County Sheriff's Department. Our agencies work together when we need to," Chief Sullivan explained.

After the introductions had been made, the sheriff took notes and asked questions as the group told him what they knew. Once they were finished, the chief stepped over and put his hand on Mike's shoulder. "I'm about to call Detective Bruce Lampart from our special investigations department. Since this is the last place we know Jill was, I'd like to set up a temporary team here. They're going to need access to those surveillance tapes," he said, looking at Shelly.

"Of course," she said, bobbing her pink head up and down. There were tears in her eyes as she stood and left the room, telling the men she was going to put on some coffee.

Not wanting anyone to overhear his conversation, the chief stepped out of the room to call the detective in private. He wasn't aware that Mike, not wanting to be left out of anything involving his sister, was standing close to the door, quietly listening to every word. He had the top of the door frame in a vice-like grip as he heard Sullivan say, "And we need to locate a man from Dallas named Stephen Conrad. He's Ms. Murray's former fiancé and, to our knowledge, the last person to have seen her last night."

Mike walked over to the window, tears prickling in his eyes. As he looked out at the parking lot, he said to Simon, "As soon as it gets to be light out there, you and I are doing a perimeter search of our own."

Gran and Gina were sitting in the great room, waiting for news. The tea Gina had made them had long since grown cold. "I think Jill enjoys Christmas as much as I do," the older woman said, staring blankly at the beautifully decorated tree. "As a child, she would beg me to put up the tree as soon as there was a slight chill in the air. I've always let her think it was my idea to begin decorating for Christmas so early in the season," she said with a sigh. "But it was for Jill. She takes so much joy in all of it."

Gina gave her a loving pat and said, "You know, I used to think it was odd that this family decorated for Christmas before Thanksgiving. Now, it just seems normal."

Lost in thought, Gran nodded.

Seeing her normally strong grandmother-in-law in such distress was heartbreaking for Gina. She noticed, as the sun began to rise, the light on the woman's worried face made her look every one of her eighty years. "They'll find her, Gran," Gina said softly. "I know they will."

Detective Lampart and his team arrived at the shelter just before dawn and had gathered to watch the video footage with Shelly.

At the first sign of daylight, Mike whistled for Simon and headed outside with Chief Sullivan and several other officers.

Sullivan addressed the group, telling them to spread out and assigning them different areas to search. He glanced quickly over at Mike, who was working with the German shepherd.

"Simon, go find Jill!" Mike commanded, pointing him in the direction they'd seen Jill go on the video footage.

Simon perked his ears, put his nose to the ground and started off, moving in the direction Mike had indicated. Mike was aware that Sheriff Needham had stayed with him as he followed closely behind the dog, his eyes trained on the ground. When they reached the end of the pavement, Mike looked up and saw that one of the officers had placed police tape around the parking lot. Simon continued his tracking, moving underneath the tape while the men stepped over it. The lot adjacent to the shelter was covered in high, dead grass and weeds. They'd gone a few yards when Simon stopped abruptly and began barking. Mike quickly caught up to where the dog was furiously sniffing and pawing at the ground.

"What is it? What did you find, boy?" He was squatting down beside the shepherd when a glint of silver caught his eye. Lying in the thick weeds, he saw Jill's silver cuff bracelet. The unique piece of jewelry had a large turquoise stone centered on the front. "This belonged to our mother," he told the sheriff, holding the bracelet up. "My sister seldom takes it off."

As soon as he landed in Austin, Dave called Mike for an update. "The detectives identified signs of a struggle in the vacant lot next to the shelter," he told him. "They think Jill was abducted in that field while she was searching for a stray dog. They've called in a couple more guys who are combing the lot and also analyzing some tire tracks they found."

"Do you think it's Stephen? Do you think he followed her after she left the restaurant?" Dave asked as he grabbed his bag out of the overhead and waited impatiently in line to deboard the plane.

"I can't imagine who else it could be," Mike replied. "One of the detectives is over at the place where he and Jill had dinner. He's hoping to question their waitress from last night and also review the footage from their surveillance cameras in the parking lot. We still don't know what kind of car Stephen is driving and the guy's not answering his phone."

"I can't believe this is really happening," Dave said miserably as he made his way up the jetway. "I've gotta get my car, then I'll be there as quick as I can." Oblivious to the stares from other travelers, he took off in a full sprint toward the exit.

Mike was standing in the parking lot, talking with Chief Sullivan when he saw Gina pull up with Gran. He excused himself from their conversation and hurried over to them. "I had a feeling you'd come," he said, helping his grandmother from the vehicle.

"I just can't stay in that house any longer, not knowing what's going on here," she replied. She gave her grandson a hug. "Oh, Mike, what if she's hurt? I'm the one who encouraged her to forgive that man! This is partly my fault."

"Gran, please don't say that," Mike said gently. "None of this is your fault. We don't even know for sure if it was Stephen who took her. The detectives haven't ruled out kidnapping. Right now, it's an open investigation."

Mike looked over at his wife, who was weeping silently behind his grandmother. He knew he needed to encourage them. "Gina, sweetheart, come over here, get in this hug," he called to her. Once she'd joined their circle, he said, "Look, we've got a great team here working to find Jill and we *are* going to find her. I think Jill, deliberately left her bracelet in that field to leave a clue for us. We all know what a strong, brave woman she is. She's going to be all right. We have to believe that, and we have to be strong for each other."

As Dave merged onto the freeway, he thought about the last time he'd made a frantic drive from Austin back to the Hill Country. It was the day he'd been rushing back home for Ian. The day Jill had saved his son's life. *Now, her own life may be in jeopardy*, he thought, choking back his building despair. Operating on fear and adrenaline, he raced down the interstate as fast as he could safely drive.

Mike introduced Gran and Gina to some of the law enforcement people inside the shelter. When Gran spoke with Chief Sullivan, she gave a small smile. "Of course I remember you, Robert. You were a fixture at the ranch when you and Matthew were boys," she said. "We appreciate all of your help today."

Mike had lost count of how many times he'd checked his watch and how many cups of coffee he'd had. He retrieved Jill's handbag from his truck and watched as the investigators dumped its contents on the front reception desk. He wasn't optimistic they'd find anything helpful in the purse, but Mike appreciated their thoroughness. He'd already given them his sister's cell phone, so they could study her call history.

Ned had arrived for work and Mike listened as Shelly told him about everything that was going on. The veterinarian sat in stunned disbelief, waiting until she'd finished before speaking. Giving Mike a sympathetic pat on the back, he said, "I'm so sorry! I wish you all would have called me sooner." He then went over to talk with Gran and Gina.

Everyone looked up when Dave arrived at the shelter, moving swiftly through the front door, anxious to hear any news. Once inside, he went directly to Gran who rose to her feet to embrace him. "I'm so sorry this happened, Gran Jen!" he said to her in an anguished voice. "I'm sorry I wasn't here. I just keep thinking that if I'd been in town, Jill wouldn't have gone to meet Stephen."

"Dave," Gran assured him kindly, "my granddaughter has a mind of her own. I'm sure you know that by now."

They all turned when the door opened again, and Detective Lampart stepped back inside. "I have some news," he told the crowd. "I spoke with the server who waited on Jill and Stephen Conrad last night. She told me that, for the most part, their conversation was quiet. But right before they left, the man seemed agitated and, in her words, angry. She said Jill looked upset and that she'd barely touched her meal. She couldn't hear what they were talking about, but she did say that Jill got up and left the restaurant before he did." The detective paused and let the information sink in. "There's more," he said. "We watched the video footage from the parking lot. The waitress identified the man who had dinner with Jill as he was getting out of a black Jaguar. We have the license plate number. We suspect this man is Stephen Conrad. But before we put out an APB on this guy, I need someone to come back with me to The Springs Inn and identify him on the tape."

"Let's go," Mike said, already moving toward the door. "I'd know what that loser looks like enough to confirm whether it's him or not."

"I'm coming with you," Dave said, following Mike.

Back at The Springs Inn, Mike fixed his eyes on the computer screen, watching the surveillance footage of the parking lot. He studied the recording as a black Jaguar parked and a familiar-looking man stepped out of the car. *He looks just like he did the last time I saw him,* Mike thought. "That's Stephen Conrad. There's no question about it," he told the detectives.

They returned to the shelter and delivered the news that an APB had been ordered. "We've issued it for the entire state, and we'll also notify border patrol. Mr. Conrad won't get far if he's driving," said Detective Lampart.

"Now what do we do?" asked Mike.

"We'll check with the forensics team to see if the tire tracks in the lot next door could have been made by a Jaguar. We don't have a whole lot more to go on right now, Mike," answered the detective.

Chief Sullivan said, "I've got several officers out in the area, knocking on doors to see if anyone saw or heard anything that can help us." He looked over at Gran, then back to Mike. "Why don't you and your family go home and get some rest?" he suggested. "It's been a long night."

Gina knew Mike was not about to leave. "I'll take Gran home, babe," she said. "I need to get back and check on the kids anyway. I'm sure Marcie is ready for me to take them off her hands."

Gran stood, and Mike walked her and Gina out to their car. "I will call you when we have some news," he told them. "I love you both."

When Mike returned to the shelter, he saw several people preparing to leave. "What's going on?" he asked Sheriff Needham, feeling like they were abandoning the fort.

"We've done everything there is to do from this location, Mike. I'm heading to my office and I believe Chief Sullivan's people are about to do the same. We can get more done there. Don't worry. Finding your sister is our number one priority," he said.

Sullivan walked over to where Mike and Dave were standing. "Lance is right, there's nothing more we can do here. I'll be in touch with you the moment anything new develops." He watched as the last of the law enforcement officers filed out the door, then shook hands with Mike, Dave, and Ned. He then turned to Shelly and said, "Thank you for your help with the surveillance footage."

Realizing Mike was distressed they were leaving, Robert put his hand on the younger man's shoulder. "I wish we had something more to go on," he shared, shaking his head. "I just don't see a motive here with this Conrad guy. I mean, after all this time, why would he abduct your sister?"

Dave was watching the police chief closely. He'd been thinking along the same lines as Sullivan. *Stephen Conrad could have abducted Jill when she'd been in Dallas. Why drive all the way to the Hill Country to take her?* he wondered. "Mike, think about Wind River. Is there anyone working for your family who might have taken Jill for money?"

Mike considered this and shook his head doubtfully. "Most of our employees have been at the ranch for years. I just don't think so," he replied.

Dave waited a moment before raising the question that had been nagging at him since he'd arrived at the shelter. "Man, I hate to ask you this, but what about Roger?" he asked evenly. "Roger's familiar with the shelter. He'd know to stay out of the reach of the security cameras."

Mike gave Dave a hard look, then slammed his fist down onto the reception desk angrily.

"No! It's *not* Roger! I tried to call him for help last night, but Lyle told me he's not even in the country! Apparently, he's gone off to Mexico."

At his words, Chief Sullivan froze. "Mike, are you guys referring to Roger Dunn?"

Mike nodded. "The guy's had the hots for my sister for as long as I can remember."

Robert appeared shaken as he said quietly, "Roger's not in Mexico. His trip was canceled." He looked at Mike, carefully choosing his next words. "I've known Roger for years. Recruited him onto the force. He's like a son to me…"

Mike loomed large in front of the chief, his fists were balled, his face distorted in anger. "So, do you know where he is?" he snarled.

Sullivan held one hand up and said slowly, "Now, just calm down, Mike. I saw him last night. We had dinner together at The Rusty Peacock."

"Don't tell me to calm down!" Mike roared. "Roger would have driven right by the shelter on his way back home! Did you guys leave the restaurant around eight-thirty?" Seeing the chief's nod, Mike looked over at Dave and shouted, "Let's move! We're going to Dunn's place!"

Dave was already heading out.

"Hold up, Mike! I'll go with you!" Chief Sullivan shouted. "Let me call for some backup to…"

Mike didn't let him finish. "Sorry, Robert. Whoever finds him first, gets him!" he replied as he dashed out of the shelter after Dave with Simon close behind.

As the two men left, the chief contacted the station. "Get a unit over to Officer Dunn's house, now! He may be involved in Jill

Murray's disappearance. We need to get there before her brother does!"

They left Dave's car parked beside Jill's and got into Mike's truck, driving in silence for the first few minutes. There was a palpable urgency in the air as they flew down the country roads. "How far is his place?" Dave asked.

"We're getting close," Mike replied gruffly. "In a million years, I wouldn't have believed he'd do this to us! I trusted him."

Dave glanced over at the speedometer. "Mike, we'll find her," he assured him. "But, please slow down. It's not going to help Jill if we end up in a ditch."

Mike glanced over at Dave, and reluctantly reduced his speed as they swerved along the winding road.

"I'm planning on marrying her. I was going to ask Gran Jen for her permission, but I'd like to know if you're okay with it, too," Dave said. "I understand how close all of you are."

Mike's eyes did not leave the road. He was a man on a mission. "Dave, I think that's great. I know my sister loves you. She told me you guys have been talking about a future together."

Mike's words hardly surprised him. "Is there *anything* you two don't talk about?" Dave asked. "I love Jill so much, I can't imagine my life without her."

"Jill is a remarkable person," Mike said. Dave could see the tears in his eyes. "I don't know what any of us would do without her."

Lost in thought, both men were startled when Mike's phone rang through the truck's Bluetooth.

Dave blinked at the information displayed on the screen. The caller was Roger Dunn. A recent photo of the man appeared next to his phone number.

Mike quickly accepted the call. "Roger!" he shouted. "Do you have my sister?"

They waited a couple of moments for a reply. Much to their surprise, the voice they heard was not Roger's.

"Mike?" It was Jill.

CHAPTER 23

"Jill! Where are you? Are you all right?" cried Mike, his voice cracking with emotion. He looked over at Dave, who was leaning forward, straining to hear her reply.

Jill's voice was quiet, her words coming in fragments. "Ph-phone losing ch-charge," she stammered. "De-deer in ro-road, ra-ravine…" They heard her cough weakly, then, "De-vil's Ba-Ba…"

Struggling to keep his voice calm, Mike asked, "Jill, are you saying you're near the Devil's Backbone?"

They heard another weak cough. "Yes. I th-think so…ra-ravine… down…"

"Jill, it's Dave. We're coming to get you. Stay on the line with us, babe."

Mike had already turned the truck around. "Jill, honey, we're on our way. Can you tell me anything else to help us find you?"

There was silence on the end of the line for what seemed like an eternity. Finally, Jill stuttered, "We dr-drove I th-think through Fi-Fischer toward Wi-Wimberley Junction. It wa-was da-da-dark. De-deer in rrr-oad."

"Okay, that's great information, Jill, that's good," Dave encouraged. He was worried about the way Jill was slurring her words, repeating things she'd just said. "Mike knows where you are. We're coming. Please hold on, babe." Dave looked at Jill's brother, hoping that he *did* know where to go.

"Jill, we're coming up to Wimberley Junction, and I'm about to turn onto FR 32," Mike said. "Is there anything else you can tell us about where you are? Is Roger with you? Can you put him on the phone?"

They waited, but Mike's questions were met with silence. Cursing softly, he reached into his back pocket and pulled out his wallet, tossing it over to Dave. "I stuck Robert Sullivan's card in there. Find it and use your phone to call his direct number," Mike instructed. "Hand me the phone once you've got him on the line!"

He was still listening for a response from Jill. "Sis? Honey, are you still there?" he prodded gently.

"R-Roger's h-here," came Jill's small voice. "Ba-but, I th-think he's…"

Mike could hear her weeping softly. He felt like weeping himself. Instead, he said comfortingly, "Jill, don't cry, sweetheart. Everything's going to be all right. We're almost…" Mike didn't finish his sentence. He could see they'd lost their connection.

"No!" Mike shouted, giving the dashboard a furious thunk of his hand. He couldn't believe they'd lost the call.

"Mike," said Dave, handing him his phone, "It's Chief Sullivan."

Dave half-listened to their conversation as the truck continued along FR 32. He was keeping his eyes fixed on the sides of the road.

"Jill just called using Roger's phone," Mike was saying. "So we know she's with him, but it sounds like she's hurt. From what I could gather, there was an accident. She said she's in a ravine somewhere near the Devil's Backbone. We're heading west on 32 now, but she could be anywhere off 3424, 484, or…hell, I don't know! The phone died, so that's all we've got."

Chief Sullivan assured Mike he would dispatch every unit at his disposal and also contact Sheriff Needham with the update. "We'll get a chopper in the air along the ridge," he said. "If Jill's in a ravine, and she's hurt, we'll need to airlift her out."

Mike and Dave exchanged worried glances, knowing they were on borrowed time.

They drove along the twisting road high in the hills. From time to time, Dave would catch a glimpse of the valley far below through gaps in the trees. His stomach muscles tightened when he saw the rugged, rocky terrain along the hillsides. *Where is she? How badly is she hurt?* he wondered.

They'd been traveling at a reduced speed, both of them carefully surveying the sides of the road, looking for any signs of an accident. Several vehicles passed them, some of the drivers honking impatiently. Mike paid them no regard as they went by.

"Mike, up ahead there, look!" Dave said, pointing and suddenly excited. They were approaching a sharp curve in the road with a cautionary sign warning drivers to drop their speed down to fifteen miles per hour.

Mike eyes went to where Dave was pointing. On the side of the road was a large dead buck. The animal had clearly been struck and killed by a vehicle.

"Should I call Sullivan?" asked Dave anxiously.

Mike shook his head. "Not yet," he said as he pulled over onto the gravelly shoulder and turned on his hazard lights. "There are deer everywhere up here, and they're always getting hit. Let's go check it out." He was already getting out of the truck.

The two men ran to the deer and inspected the area a few yards past the dead animal. Their eyes roamed the wooded area along the roadside. "There are no skid marks," Mike observed, shaking his head. "And I don't see any indication that anyone's gone over on either side. We need to keep looking."

They rushed to the truck and pulled back onto the road, slowly turning the sharp corner. They'd only driven a short distance when Dave shouted, "Stop here! Pull over!"

Mike hadn't placed the truck in park before Dave jumped out with Simon right behind him. Hastily turning on his flashers, Mike began pounding in 9-1-1 on his phone as he raced after them. They were running at full speed toward another hairpin curve. As he ran, Mike's eyes caught a downed, crumpled caution sign and the telltale signs that a driver had missed the turn. He only had to wait a split second for the call to connect. "It's Mike Murray! I think we've found my sister! I'm on FR 32 about three miles west of Wimberley Junction. My truck's parked on the side of the road, flashers on. We need help here fast!" He poked the phone into his pocket and disappeared over the embankment after Dave and Simon.

⸻ ◈ ⸻

It was dark when Jill regained consciousness for the first time, shortly after Roger's truck had plowed over the embankment. The truck's airbags had deployed when they'd hit the large, metal caution sign and clipped the end of a concrete barricade. Jill had no recollection of the their harrowing tumble down the hillside. She couldn't remember the vehicle rolling over several times before it had come to a stop.

Dazed and disoriented, Jill tried to work herself free of the airbag, squirming forcefully to right her body into a taller sitting position. Her head was pounding. *Every part of my body is aching*, she thought, trying to get her bearings. She looked around and realized she was in Roger's truck. *Roger!* she thought. Jill looked at the man slumped over in the seat next to her. They were immersed in darkness except for the dim glow of the dashboard lights. Seeing that he wasn't moving, Jill let out a whimper. She'd never felt so helpless, so tired. *I just need to rest*, she thought, closing her eyes against the image of Roger and the cold, dark night.

She awoke again a few hours later. As before, it took some time to regain control of her mind. *The airbag must have knocked me out*, she realized. Jill sat for another few moments, trying to concentrate. *I can't just sit here! I need a plan.* She unlatched her seatbelt and moved closer to Roger to see if she could find a pulse, freezing immediately when she heard a loud creaking noise and felt the truck shifting slightly. *Oh my gosh!* she panicked. *Where are we?*

Jill slowly moved forward in her seat and peered through the cracked windshield, over the hood of the truck. In the beam of the headlights, she could make out illuminated tall branches. *We must be caught on the trees!* she thought. From the position she was in now, she could see that the driver's side of the truck was severely smashed. She knew if Roger were alive, he was in very bad shape.

Why, Roger? Look what you've done! Jill despaired. The events of the past few hours were coming back to her now in bits and pieces. She remembered leaving Stephen at the restaurant then driving past the shelter. Seeing a box next to the front door, she'd gone to investigate and found the abandoned puppies. She thought she'd gotten all the strays gathered and secured inside the shelter when another dog jumped on her. She recalled chasing after it through the field. Then Jill remembered how everything had taken a horrible turn. She shuddered thinking about the shock she'd felt when someone had grabbed her roughly from behind, pulling her arms behind her back and handcuffing her wrists together. She'd kicked and flailed to no avail.

She hadn't known who her attacker was until Roger forced her into his truck. The gleam of triumph in his eyes at finally getting her alone was terrifying. "If you don't stop kicking, I'll cuff your ankles together, too," he said. "We just need to talk, Jill, that's all." He held up his hands as if surrendering. "Can we just do that, please?"

She knew if he bound her ankles, she'd have no chance of escaping. Defeated, she said, "All right, Roger."

Roger smiled and said, "See? I'm not so bad." He'd driven her around for hours, begging Jill to give him a chance, telling her they were meant to be together.

She'd listened to him rant and rave, saying the most ridiculous things about how he was going to take care of her forever. She remembered when she'd stopped feeling angry and began fearing for her life. In that moment she realized how mentally unbalanced he was.

Jill decided to play into his delusions in the hope of getting away from him. "Roger, you're right," she'd told him sweetly. "You and I belong together. Why don't you take me back to my car now and we can forget all of this happened? We can just start over." Jill had smiled at him sincerely.

"And you'll tell Mike and your family that *I'm* the one you love?" Roger had asked, looking at Jill plaintively.

"Of course," she'd lied. "Now, will you please take these silly cuffs off of me? They're digging into my wrists and it's starting to hurt. You know my brother will be really mad if he sees I've got bruises."

Roger had looked at her warily. "If I take off the cuffs, do you promise to behave and stop running away from me?" he'd asked.

"I'm not going to run away, Roger. Come on, you can trust me. Just take them off and then we can go tell my family we're in love and we're going to be together." Jill had kept her voice flirty and was thrilled when Roger pulled over and released her hands from the cuffs.

He'd put his hand on her knee and rubbed it affectionately. "I've always loved you, Jill," he'd said. "Thank you for finally admitting that you love me, too." He gave her an adoring look before pulling back on the road.

Jill's flesh crawled at the man's touch. It was all she could do to let him keep his hand on her leg. She'd started to look up at Roger when her eyes caught a large buck standing in the middle of the road in front of them.

"Roger! Look out!" she'd shouted.

With no time to hit the brakes, he swerved and hit the deer with the right side bumper, mortally wounding it.

"You killed it!" Jill had screamed. "You didn't even *try* to stop! What's wrong with you!" She'd grown tired of playing around with the deranged man. Since her hands had been freed, she'd reached over and punched him in the jaw with her fist, then moved to open her door, attempting to jump out. Before she could grab the door handle, Roger was on her, pulling her back to him with an angry yell. The truck quickly swerved out of control as they'd approached the dangerous curve, the vehicle mowing over the caution sign, clipping the barricade, and careening down the hillside.

Now here we are, she thought, wondering exactly where they were. She recalled Roger driving them through the small town of Fischer, and they'd been heading along FR 32 atop the ridge referred to as the Devil's Backbone. Jill knew the ridge separated the Blanco and Guadalupe River basins, but she had no clue as to which side they'd gone down.

I've got to get out of this truck, she thought. *I need to find help!*

She suddenly remembered seeing Roger store his phone in the truck's center console.

Moving cautiously, Jill clicked open the compartment and removed the phone. Her stomach flip-flopped when she heard another loud creak and felt the truck lurch further sideways, forcing her against the car door. She knew the vehicle wasn't going to be anchored in the trees much longer. *I have to get out, but how far up are we? Am I jumping to my death?* She thought about Dave and her family. *I love them all so much. Please God; she prayed, let me see them again!* The truck made another loud, metal groan, and she knew it was time. Placing the phone in her pocket, and slowly opening the door, she said one last prayer before taking a deep breath and jumping out into the darkness.

<hr />

Dave was picking his way carefully down the steep incline, moving as quickly as he could. It was a challenging descent. There was no trail on the rocky terrain. Loose, small pebbles and shale made finding his footing difficult. At one point, he nearly lost his balance and gone tumbling downhill. Grateful for the occasional mesquite tree or wild grass along the way, he grabbed at the vegetation, using it to help stabilize his descent. Dave took a moment to see how Mike was doing and was surprised to see him rapidly closing the distance between them. Simon was further below, nearing the white truck.

After another few minutes, the ground leveled out. Dave straightened and dashed across the plateau where the truck hung precariously in the trees. He was surveying the vehicle, trying to determine how to climb up to it, when Mike ran up beside him. They heard the wail of sirens in the distance.

"I'm trying to figure out the best way to get up there," Dave said.

Mike was studying the position of the truck in the trees. He could see it was tilted down lower on the passenger's side. He shook his head, saying, "We *can't* go up there. Put any additional weight on that thing; it's gonna come down." He continued analyzing the situation. "I'm already worried about how much longer those trees can hold it up there." He pointed to the bowed branches of the oak trees. "It's just a matter of time. Those branches could break any minute." Mike paused, thinking out loud, "The passenger's door is open."

"I see that," said Dave, bouncing anxiously on the balls of his feet. "Do you think maybe Jill got out of the truck?" Before Mike could respond, Dave looked past him and asked, "Hey, where's Simon?"

Mike shouted for the dog, "Simon!" he bellowed. "Simon!"

A series of excited barks rose from the valley below. Dave didn't have to think twice. He took off like a shot across the plateau, sprinting toward the barking dog.

He began the final, steep descent, continuing to move as rapidly as possible. Thorns from the scrub bushes cut into his hands, and he lost his footing several times as loose gravel rolled under his tennis shoes, yet Dave kept moving downward. The closer he got to Simon, the faster he was able to move as the ground began to level out near the base of the hillside.

Finally, he saw her. Jill was lying on her back near the river, her left leg twisted at a crazy angle. Simon was licking her face, and Dave was close enough now to see she wasn't responding.

Suddenly, Dave heard loud, cracking sounds from above and the unmistakable creak of metal. He was running at breakneck speed, moving so quickly his feet barely touched the ground. He didn't look back when Mike shouted his name or flinch when he heard the final, resounding snap of the trees above him as they surrendered Roger's truck to the valley below.

Dave reached Jill and stopped to quickly gather her into his arms. He didn't look up. There was no time. He could hear the ear-splitting sound of the heavy vehicle as it tore down the hillside, splintering trees and scattering rocks in its path. "I've got you, my love," he whispered in Jill's ear as he ran for all he was worth, narrowly escaping the battered pickup as it finally came to rest on the white, limestone banks of the Blanco River.

CHAPTER 24

Christmas morning found Jill nestled under a thick sea of soft blankets. She'd missed seeing the last few sunrises, her body needing more rest since the accident. She could hear the rattling of pots and pans down the hall and knew breakfast was being prepared for her. Smiling, she pulled her arm from beneath the covers to admire the sparkling ring on her left hand.

A few moments later, the bedroom door opened quietly. "Good morning, Mrs. Wilder," greeted Dave cheerfully as he walked in, carrying a tray. Simon followed closely behind him. Seeing Jill's preoccupation with her wedding ring, Dave chuckled. "When are you going to stop looking at that thing?" He'd arched one brow, aware of the effect the gesture had on her.

She giggled and rested her head back on the pillow. "It's almost as dazzling as you, Mr. Wilder," Jill replied. "Almost…" She was grinning up at him. "Thanks for taking care of Simon." They both looked over at the German shepherd who'd curled up on the floor near the foot of the bed.

"He's such a good boy," Dave said, laughing as the dog's ears pointed up. "I think he knows when we're talking about him."

"Of course he does! Because Simon is the smartest dog in the world!" she exclaimed. "I'm excited to see which of his pups Ian will choose. They're all so adorable, it's going to be a tough decision!"

"Oh, I think Ian's made up his mind. He's had his eye on the runt of the litter," Dave replied. "He's been calling him Bruno."

"That's a great name," Jill said. "And Mike's going to surprise Jeremy and let him pick a puppy for Christmas later today. That will leave ten awesome dogs we'll be able to donate to the Veteran's Service Dog Program for training."

"That's such a worthwhile organization Ned found," Dave said as he brought the breakfast tray over and set it on the nightstand. "Now, let's get you propped up," he suggested as he began carefully arranging the pillows behind Jill's back. He fought to keep the smile on his face as he noted the many cuts and bruises on her face. He knew her body was also covered with them, painful reminders of the night he'd nearly lost her.

He could feel her watching him. "The bruises will fade, Dave," she said quietly.

"That's not what I was thinking," he replied. "If you must know, I was actually thinking that even with all this," he said, waving his hand over her, "you are still the most stunning woman I've ever seen."

Jill caught his arm as he moved across her. "I need a Christmas kiss, husband," she demanded with a smile.

"Merry Christmas, babe," he said, bending to gently kiss her. Noticing her wince as she moved to meet his lips, Dave quickly pulled away. "Jill, honey, are you sure you're up to going to your grandmother's this morning?"

She rolled her eyes. "It's just a broken leg, Dave. I'm not missing Christmas morning at Gran's just because of a stupid broken leg," she told him.

Mindful of her cast, Dave sat on the end of the bed. "I figured you'd say that," he replied, chuckling at her stubborn pout. "I just thought I'd check. Actually, I'm glad you want to go because that's where I'm going to give you your Christmas present," he said with a mysterious smile.

Jill's own smile quickly vanished, and her expression became troubled. Dave took her hand. "What is it, babe? Are you hurting? Should I get you something for the pain?"

She shook her head no, and he saw tears welling up in her eyes. "No, I don't need anything. I just feel so terrible that I don't have many gifts for you. With everything that happened, I didn't..."

"Hush, sweetie," he said softly, holding up his hand to show her his wedding band. "You've given me a gift that transcends all others, the gift of your love. When you agreed to be my wife I wanted to shout my happiness from the rooftops. I still can't believe we're married!"

Her smile returned as she held her other hand out to him. "I know, it's so amazing. I love you so much, Dave."

"You sure you don't regret tying the knot so quickly?" he asked. "I had envisioned a much more romantic proposal and a huge Texas wedding." He looked at her wistfully. "You deserved to have all of that, Jill. I'm sorry if I rushed things. The night you disappeared, I was devastated beyond words. I vowed to marry you as soon as I found you and I plan on spending every day of my life trying to make you as happy as you make me."

"Your proposal was perfect," Jill replied, remembering when she woke up in the hospital. Dave's worried face was the first thing she'd seen. "I love that you asked Gran *and* Mike for their permission for my hand in marriage—very chivalrous!"

"And *I'm* glad they both said yes," he said with a smile, running his finger across the top of the large, Old European cut diamond she wore. "I'd already picked out your ring!"

Looking into her eyes, he asked, "Jill, do you remember the morning when you told me you loved me for the first time? I was so mad at myself for not telling you that I loved you, too. It was a missed opportunity. From the moment I met you, something clicked in my heart. I suppose you could call it love at first sight." He paused for a moment, remembering. "When Mike told me you were missing; I got back to Texas as quickly as I possibly could. I proposed to you in that hospital room because you are my soul mate and I needed to make you mine."

Her heart swelled. "And you, Dave, are mine. We belong to one another," she said, her blue eyes sparkling in the morning sunshine.

He caught a note of sadness in her voice. "So, why is there a slight frown on my wife's beautiful face?" he asked, concerned.

"I'm sorry," she sighed. "I was thinking about Roger. Thinking about how he really believed that he and I were meant to be together." Jill shook her head. "I feel so sorry for him."

The mention of the man's name sent a surge of anger through Dave. *I can't believe she actually feels sorry for Roger after he nearly killed her!* he thought, marveling at Jill's compassionate heart. "Honey, I *don't* want to talk about him. I hope that when he gets out of the coma, *if* he ever gets out of the coma, they'll lock him up and throw away the key." Dave was eyeing the red welts around Jill's wrists and he looked away in anguish, remembering the last few days…

———◦《◊》◦———

The day after the accident, Dave and Mike had been with Jill in her hospital room as she told Chief Sullivan what she could remember about the night Roger abducted her.

Jill had left The Springs Inn after arguing with Stephen at dinner. "I'd gone there to comfort him," she said. "At least, our conversation started off that way. Then I figured out the real reason he'd come was to tell me he wanted me back. He said he was willing to do whatever it took for us to start over. I was furious. I told him repeatedly not to ever contact me again, that he and I were history. We argued, and I left the restaurant." She'd looked at Dave apologetically. "You were right. He used his father's death to play on my heartstrings. I was such a fool to think he'd changed."

"A tiger doesn't change its stripes," said Mike. "And you're no fool, Sis. Just a little too soft-hearted sometimes." He smiled lovingly at her and continued, "When we suspected Stephen, the police put out an APB on him. Too bad they didn't find him before we realized it was Roger. It'd served that guy right for all the crap he's pulled." Mike shot a glance over to Chief Sullivan. "I'd also like to point out that if it hadn't been for Conrad, my sister wouldn't have driven by the shelter and seen the puppies. As far as I'm concerned, he's guilty, too."

"Be that as it may, we were able to cancel the APB before we located Mr. Conrad," Sullivan said. "He never knew he was wanted for questioning."

"Good riddance to bad rubbish," Mike said with disdain.

"I understand how you feel about the guy," replied Sullivan. He then turned back to Jill and said, "Now let's get this report finished so you can get some rest. Do you think Roger Dunn was stalking you?" he asked. It still pained him that Roger had been behind Jill's abduction. The crime had shocked the department and the entire community.

She thought for a moment, then answered, "No, I don't think so. He did a lot of talking while we were in the truck. He said it was no accident that he happened to be driving by the shelter and saw my car. It was fate. Fate had told him to cancel his Mexico trip and stay in town. Fate had allowed him to finally be with me. He told me that when he saw me running after the stray dog, he knew it was his chance, the opportunity to fulfill our destiny. The more he talked, the more I was convinced he was nuts."

"Roger had been trying to get Jill alone for a long time," Mike explained. "I had a serious talk with him about how he'd been hassling her. I thought he'd finally backed off."

"I didn't hear him come up behind me," Jill said, her mind back in the vacant lot. "I was intent on getting a dog into the shelter. It was really cold that night. Roger pulled my arms behind my back and handcuffed me. I tried to fight back by kicking him," she told them. "He was just so much stronger than me." Tears were in her eyes as she relived the experience. "I managed to work my bracelet off, hoping someone would find it." She looked down at her bare wrist mournfully.

"That was a clever thing to do, and don't worry, Simon found your bracelet. It's at the house," Mike assured her.

"Well, that's some great news!" Jill's face brightened as she smiled at her brother then back to Robert. "Anyway, Chief Sullivan, I was able to convince Roger to remove the handcuffs by playing into his delusions and telling him that I loved him. It was shortly after that, he killed this poor deer, and I just lost it! I started hitting him and tried to open the door and get out." Jill shook her head. "Roger was trying to stop me when he lost control of the truck..." She hesitated, the horrific sound the vehicle made as it crashed into the concrete barricade echoing in her mind. "Thankfully, I don't remember going over the embankment." She gave the chief a weak smile. "Once I'd regained consciousness, I realized I was still in the truck. I'm not sure how long I sat there, trying to get my bearings and come up with a plan. I knew we were suspended because whenever I made even the slightest move, the truck would rock to one side."

"So, that's when you jumped out of the vehicle?" Sullivan asked.

"Yes. I knew my time was short. I'm sure that's when this happened," she said, nodding toward her full leg cast. "It was a further drop down than I thought it'd be and then, I guess I rolled downhill for a spell. But thankfully, I don't remember that either." Jill had been looking at the police chief as she spoke. She didn't dare look at Dave or Mike for fear she would cry. The memories were still very fresh; the pain in her words almost tangible.

"That's about it, except that I grabbed Roger's phone before I jumped out. I must have come to long enough in the ravine to call Mike." She finally stole a quick glance at her brother and said proudly, "And, that's when he, Dave and Simon came and rescued me. End of story."

Shortly after Jill recounted her harrowing experience, Chief Sullivan reached for his Stetson hat, readying to leave. Before going, he took her hand and said warmly, "Jill, I hope you'll call me Robert in the future. I shared with Mike that your dad and I were close friends when we were growing up. He was a good man, and I see his strength of character in both of you." He paused a moment, and she could see the sorrow in his eyes. "I also told your brother that Roger Dunn was like a son to me. Words cannot express how shocked and sorry I am for what he did to you."

"Thank you for saying that," Jill replied. "I'll get past this. I've already forgiven Roger for what he did. I hope when he wakes up, he'll get the help he needs."

Mike had some things he wanted to say about that but decided to keep his mouth shut, knowing Jill had been through enough already. "Robert, I'll walk out with you. I think these two would like to be alone," he said, reaching over to give his sister a tender pat. "Love you, Sis. I'll come back later."

Once they were alone, Jill reached for Dave's hand. She could see the adoration in his eyes as he gave her hand a gentle squeeze. "I almost lost you," he said, the enormity of the ordeal she'd suffered still cutting through him like a knife. "I need to make sure no other men out there ever have any doubt *who* you belong to." He got down on one knee beside her hospital bed. "Jill Murray, I love you with all my heart. Will you marry me?"

———————◉———————

Jill had been released from the hospital the following day. On her first night at Gran's, Dave stayed with her, sleeping on a cot next to her bed. Before she'd gone to sleep, he let her know he'd made arrangements to fly Ian back to Texas the following day. "I'll need to go pick him up. He and I have a couple of quick errands to do in Austin, but then I'll get right back to you," he said, hating to leave her side.

"I'm excited to see Ian," Jill replied. "And don't worry, I'll be fine. Everyone's been taking such good care of me, especially my handsome fiancé."

Dave gave her a warm smile, then took her hand in his. "Jill, I meant what I said about marrying you right away," he said seriously. "I don't want to wait."

Her eyes were twinkling in delight as she nodded and said, "Well, I don't want to wait either! We can get married here at Gran's as soon as you get back with Ian. Is that soon enough for you?" she suggested with a coy smile.

He grinned from ear to ear and said, "*That* would make me incredibly happy. *You* make me happy! Just think, babe, by this time tomorrow, you'll be my wife!"

———————◉———————

They'd exchanged their vows in front of the Christmas tree in Gran's great room the following evening with Jill leaning on Dave for support.

"I'm going to take you somewhere amazing for our honeymoon as soon as we get you out of that cast," he promised.

She giggled. "I'll hold you to that. Maybe we can go skiing!" she teased.

He kissed her again and laughed. "No, we *won't* be skiing, Mrs. Wilder. If we did, *I'd* be the one wearing a cast!"

"I was just kidding, babe," she said. "Wherever we go, I'm sure it will be perfect because we'll be together."

"Always," Dave agreed.

Dave was watching Jill now as she poked at the food he'd made for her. "Wife, you'd better eat your breakfast. I slaved over a hot stove for hours making those eggs," he scolded with a smile.

She sighed and took a small bite. "Thanks for bringing me breakfast in bed." Then, with a mischievous grin, she added, "I suppose it's good *one* of us knows how to cook!"

"Don't forget, you make a mean PB & J!" he reminded her.

They were laughing when Ian knocked lightly, then poked his head around the bedroom door.

"Can we open presents now?" he asked, his voice hopeful.

"Good morning and Merry Christmas, Son!" Dave exclaimed happily. He walked over to Ian, lifting him into the air, causing the boy to erupt into a fit of giggles. Then, giving Jill a conspiratorial wink, he asked, "Hmm, I don't know about any presents, do you, sweetie?"

She rolled her eyes at Dave. "Merry Christmas, Ian! I think I noticed quite a few gifts under the tree with your name on them. Let's go check it out!" she said excitedly, moving to get up.

"Oh, boy!" Ian squealed. "I can't wait to see what I got!"

Laughing at his son's enthusiasm, Dave said, "Go on into the living room and wait for us. Take Simon with you. I think I saw a couple of things for him, too. We'll be there in a couple of minutes."

Jill reached over and petted her dog who'd come to sit by the bedside. "Simon, you go with Ian," she instructed in a warm, sweet tone.

"Come on, Simon! Come on, boy!" Ian called, and the two were out of the room in a flash. "We'd better get in there fast," Dave chuckled, coming over to help Jill out of bed. "I don't know how much longer he can hold out!"

"There's nothing better than Christmas morning!" Jill exclaimed, reaching for her robe.

Dave kissed her softly, then gave her a devilish grin. "Oh, I can think of one thing, Mrs. Wilder," he said.

The Wilders arrived at Gran's later that morning, gathering with the rest of the family in the great room.

"Our crazy kids were jumping in our bed at five this morning, wanting to see what Santa had brought them," Mike told Dave. "If only it were so easy to get them up on school days!"

Dave chuckled at his brother-in-law's comment as he helped Jill get situated on a loveseat, propping her leg up on a footstool. He noticed the room was in a state of disarray from the gifts Santa had delivered to Mike and Gina's children. In addition to several unwrapped toys, wrapping paper, bows, and ribbons were everywhere. "Well, it looks like Santa was good to everyone," he laughed.

"Jeremy, why don't you and Ian pass out the presents?" Gran suggested.

The boys happily complied, and within a few moments, they each had a pile of gifts in front of them. Dave was stunned. "What? I can't believe this! These can't possibly all be for me!" He was double-checking the tags to make sure the kids hadn't given him someone else's gifts.

"Look, Dad!" Ian squealed excitedly. "Look at all of mine!"

Gran chuckled. "Santa was good to *everyone*," she said to her new grandson-in-law. "You and Ian are part of our family now, and we love you both." Looking at Jill, her eyes grew misty. "If not for you, my granddaughter might not be here with us now. Thank you again for saving her life." Seeing Dave's humble nod, the elderly woman realized she'd placed a heavy note on what should be a joyous occasion. Giving everyone a warm smile, she exclaimed, "Now, let's open all these presents!"

They made their way through the many gaily wrapped boxes and bags, each person taking a turn opening a gift, then holding it up for the others to admire. They took their time, laughing and sharing stories, reveling in being together.

After the last gift had been unwrapped, Mike and Dave started clearing the trash while the children began carting away some of their loot.

"We're going to be having lunch in thirty minutes," Gran told the boys, who were eager to play one of Jeremy's new video games.

"Yes, ma'am," Jeremy said.

"Yes, ma'am," echoed Ian.

They thanked Gran and hugged her before running side by side out of the room. The twins were playing quietly in the corner with an elaborate dollhouse Santa had brought them.

Jill looked at the people around her. "I need to share something with all of you about what happened a few days ago," she said. "After the accident, I knew I had to jump out of the truck." Tears were flowing freely from Jill's eyes as Dave moved closer to her for support.

"Hush," he said softly. "It's okay, babe, let's not talk about it."

"I'm all right, sweetie. It's important to me that I share this with everyone." Seeing Dave's understanding nod, she continued, "I knew I might not survive the fall. I had no idea how high up we were..." She shook her head. "It wasn't that I was afraid of jumping." Jill paused, remembering. "I was terrified that I may never see all of you again. I prayed to God that I would be with you again. He answered my prayer." She turned and smiled at Dave, then added softly, "He answered all of them."

There wasn't a dry eye in the room except for the twins' who were happily giggling as they played. The sound of their joyful laughter helped to lift everyone's spirits again.

"We're all very blessed," Gran said. "Merry Christmas, family." She looked over at Dave. "Wasn't there one more gift you had for Jill?"

"What? Another gift?" Jill asked, still dabbing at her eyes.

"Well, let's just say, it's an *idea* for a gift that your grandmother and I have been discussing. If you like the idea, then we'll do it!" said Dave, wearing his mysterious grin once more.

"Just tell her already!" Mike chimed in excitedly.

"Yes! Tell me! You know how I *love* surprises!" she exclaimed in anticipation.

"Yes, and I know how much you love living here at Wind River," Dave said. "What would you think about you, Ian and me moving into your parents' house? I know a great architect who could help us make some updates."

Jill looked at Gran, a huge smile on her face. "This was your idea?"

Gran chuckled and replied, "Actually, it was Michael's, but I think it's wonderful!"

"It *is* wonderful!" Jill declared exuberantly. "I love it! We could design our own workout room and a pool for Ian and…"

"Don't forget a room for that crazy boot collection of yours!" Mike contributed, chuckling merrily.

"Yes! And a room for my crazy boot collection!" Jill enthused. "And a room for all of my husband's baseball memorabilia and the pool table and…"

Dave was laughing, thoroughly enjoying listening to the list of things she wanted to do to the house. He was nodding in agreement with everything Jill said, thrilled that she loved the idea as much as he had.

Suddenly a thought occurred to Jill and she abruptly stopped rattling off possible changes they could make at her parents' home.

"Oh, my gosh, Dave! I'm so sorry! What about your beautiful house?"

"You mean, *our* beautiful house?" he asked, arching one eyebrow. "Well, we'll live there while we're doing the remodeling. From the sound of that list, it's going to take a while to get everything finished," he said with a grin. "Once we're settled, I'd like to move my parents down to Texas. They can live in the Lone Star Springs place, if that's okay with you."

"That's a brilliant plan!" Jill agreed enthusiastically. "We'll talk with them about it tomorrow when they're here. I can't wait to meet them!"

Dave smiled happily at his bride and said, "They're going to love you, Jill!"

She leaned over and gave him a quick kiss. "And I love *you*, Dave," she replied. Jill then looked around the room at the people she held most dear. "I love *all* of you! This has been the most wonderful Christmas *ever!*"

That night, as Dave held her in his arms, Jill asked him what the best part of their first Christmas together had been. He stroked her hair lovingly. "That's easy," he said without hesitation. "Since I met you, the best part of every day is when we're together. With you in my life, every day feels as special as Christmas morning."

"Oh, Dave, I feel the same way about you! I'm so happy I could burst!" she told him. "Merry Christmas, my love and thank you for my awesome surprise today!"

"You're welcome," he replied. They spent the next hour talking about the renovations they'd be doing at their future home on Wind River Ranch.

"It's going to be *epic!*" Jill said sleepily.

"Epic," Dave repeated softly, knowing she'd fallen asleep.

Watching as the moonlight played on his love's precious face, Dave's heart was full. *I couldn't be any happier*, he realized, wondering how to describe his complete contentment. He was remembering their first kiss and the question Jill had asked him afterward. There was a smile on his face as he, too, drifted off, wondering...*is there a word beyond epic?*

Also By Monica E. Simmons

I Have a Complex, But I'm Managing It (Volume I & II)

30 - Love

Match Point

ABOUT THE AUTHOR

Monica Simmons is a native Texan who grew up not far from the beautiful Hill Country. In addition to writing, she enjoys traveling, hiking, and spending time with family and friends. The outdoor enthusiast is also a full-time marketing director for an advertising firm near Dallas. She has two grown sons and is married to her long-time love, James Simmons.